A BITE OF THE APPLE

Sarah hardly heard Lord Farringdon's apologies, for she could be sure that the most notorious rake in all of London did not mean them.

"Forgive me, Lady Sarah," he said as he released her from his embrace. "I had not the least intention of, of . . . I mean, I do not think of you as just . . ."

"Another flirt," Sarah said, desperately trying to keep her tone cool as she reminded herself that this was what he did and said to every woman, and that he saw her as just another weak female to be lured into doing what he desired. She was happy at least that she had kept her knees from buckling and from casting herself with total abandon against his broad chest and winding her arms around his neck as she longed to do. She had even managed a flippant reply to conceal how much his kiss had shaken her.

The trouble was, she had not quelled entirely the warm breathlessness that threatened to overwhelm her, nor the quivering in the pit of her stomach. And if this was what the first taste of temptation did to her, what would become of her with the next . . . ?

The Reluctant Heiress

Evelyn Richardson

A SIGNET BOOK

SIGNET
Published by the Penguin Group
Penguin Books USA Inc., 375 Hudson Street,
New York, New York 10014, U.S.A.
Penguin Books Ltd, 27 Wrights Lane,
London W8 5TZ, England
Penguin Books Australia Ltd, Ringwood,
Victoria, Australia
Penguin Books Canada Ltd, 10 Alcorn Avenue,
Toronto, Ontario, Canada M4V 3B2
Penguin Books (N.Z.) Ltd, 182–190 Wairau Road,
Auckland 10, New Zealand

Penguin Books Ltd, Registered Offices:
Harmondsworth, Middlesex, England

First published by Signet, an imprint of Dutton Signet,
a division of Penguin Books USA Inc.

First Printing, May, 1996
10 9 8 7 6 5 4 3 2 1

Printed in the United States of America

To Ora Anderson
with admiration.

Chapter One

"And to my granddaughter, Lady Sarah Melford, I do hereby will and bequeath my entire estate so that she may remain free to conduct her life in whatever manner she chooses without regard to pecuniary necessities," the lawyer intoned solemnly, not daring to look up from the sheaf of papers in front of him. There was a deathly silence following this pronouncement, until at last Mr. Trevelyan glanced up at the little group gathered before him in the richly paneled library at Cranleigh. It was just as he had warned her it would be when Lady Willoughby had first broached the subject of her will with him. The recipient of all this good fortune, Lady Sarah Melford, sat stunned, her eyes dark with misery, her face wan and pale, too preoccupied with the loss of her grandmother to care about anything else while the room's other occupants also remained speechless, though for entirely different reasons.

The already florid countenance of Harold, Lord Melford, Marquess of Cranleigh, had turned, if possible, an even deeper shade of red at this latest and final outrage on the part of Lady Willoughby. His grandmother had never had appropriate respect for propriety and tradition when she was alive, and now it appeared that the outrageous old woman continued to flaunt the conventions even from beyond the grave. Why, nothing could be more absurd, or improper for that matter, than to leave an immense fortune to a young woman who had just turned twenty-one. Moreover, the young woman to whom she had bequeathed these vast sums was already independent enough as it was—most unbecomingly so to Harold's way of thinking. The last thing his sister needed added to an already wayward character was further encouragement.

Lord Melford pursed his fleshy lips in an effort to contain his rising aggravation. The ingratitude of it was staggering. After all, it had been he, Lord Melford, who had offered the old woman a home after she had been widowed. To be sure, she had contributed to the repairs on the west wing and extensive modernization of the rest of Cranleigh, but that was only natural given his provision of bed and board. Nevertheless, Harold supposed he might have expected such a queer start. Lady Willoughby, for all her wealth, had never had any breeding—certainly nothing that compared to the Melfords. Daughter of a mere baronet who had amassed one fortune in mining coal and put that toward amassing another in shipping, Lady Willoughby very nearly ran the risk of smelling of the shop and had been, in Harold's opinion, very fortunate in her marriage to Lord Willoughby. Her husband had been an impoverished member of the cadet branch of minor nobility, but despite these setbacks, he had been the descendant of an ancient and once powerful family. The fact that Lady Willoughby had saved her husband and his family from ruin and that her daughter's immense dowry had done very nearly the same for the equally impoverished Melfords was beside the point. However, despite her long association with illustrious families possessed of impeccable bearing, Lady Willoughby had retained to the last a certain irreverence that a kind person might label eccentric, but Lord Melford could only call ill-bred. What was worse, she had encouraged a similar attitude in her granddaughter. Lord Melford shuddered at the thought.

A conscientious man, the Marquess of Cranleigh blamed himself in part for his younger sister's unbecoming strong-mindedness and her lack of suitable respect for the proprieties. If he had had more time, he would have remained at Cranleigh after the death of his parents, insuring that she was educated in a manner befitting a young woman of gentle birth. As it happened though, his budding political career had kept him in London, consigning his sister to the supervision of her grandmother and to the local vicar, both of whom exhibited dangerous tendencies toward free thinking and radicalism.

Harold shook his head in disgust and glanced over at his wife. At least he had brought a woman of exquisite sensibility and social grace to Cranleigh as its mistress, and it was to be hoped that in time her presence would exert a beneficial effect on her sister-in-law. Rosalind, Lady Melford, possessed all of the qualities that one would wish in the Marchioness of Cranleigh. Daughter of the Melfords' closest neighbor, Lord Tredington, she had been considered the toast of Kent from the moment she had returned from the select boarding school in Bath where she had been sent to acquire the finishing touches to an already devastating allure.

Her reputation had not suffered in the least as she progressed to the more sophisticated society of the metropolis, where she at once had been hailed an incomparable, a role that she filled to perfection. In fact, Rosalind was so assured of her own charm and beauty that it never even occurred to her anyone else might not be equally convinced of it. This serene confidence in her powers only made them all the more potent to the hapless males who crossed her path. Unfortunately for Rosalind, and through no fault of her own, she had been blessed with a ruinously expensive family.

Rosalind's father had already gambled away one fortune even before his daughter's first Season and was starting in on the next, which he had acquired by exerting his not inconsiderable attractions on a wealthy but infirm widow, who had quickly succumbed to her infirmities. Fortunately for his children, Lord Tredington had soon followed in his wife's footsteps and had died before he could run through her entire fortune. However, his only son, Richard, exhibited, if possible, even more ruinous tendencies than his parent along with much of the legendary Tredington charm. Rosalind herself had inherited extravagant propensities, although hers found their outlet at expensive modistes and milliners rather than at the gaming table.

Anyone at all acquainted with the Tredington genealogy knew that alliance with any member of the family was sure to mean an inevitable and severe drain on one's finances. Thus, while Rosalind was constantly surrounded by hordes of admirers possessing considerable rank and fashion, none of them seemed inclined to come up to scratch. Any man with half a brain in his head could see that marrying Rosalind meant supporting Richard, and that prospect made even the most besotted suitor sit up and think.

Such was the state of affairs when Lord Melford had appeared on the scene. Inured by long association to the ways of the Tredingtons and confident of coming one day into the vast fortune of his grandmother, the Marquess of Cranleigh had moved forward where others had hesitated and thus captured a prize that otherwise would have been far beyond his grasp.

However, the prize did not come without a sacrifice, which was to settle all of Richard's debts and to keep the marchioness fashionably attired and supplied with ample pin money. It was a hefty price to pay, but it had been worth it, Harold thought as he gazed proudly at his wife.

Rosalind Melford, Marchioness of Cranleigh, was undeniably a beauty of note, and she captured attention and admiration wherever she was, whether it was the gloomy library at Cranleigh or the brilliantly lit ballrooms of London. Fashionably dark, she possessed the rosebud lips and retroussé nose currently demanded of a diamond of the first water. The flawless complexion was enhanced by glossy brown curls, dark brown eyes, and a bewitching dimple at the corner of her mouth. Her figure was exquisite, tantalizingly rounded in all the right places, and every movement she made was one of grace and elegance. Her chief feature was her eyes, dark and sparkling, fringed with long curling lashes and set under delicately arched brows. They were eyes that a man could lose himself in. And it was these eyes that she now fixed so intently on the lawyer that he broke off in mid-sentence, transfixed for a moment by the sheer loveliness of the owner. Quickly recollecting himself, Mr. Trevelyan coughed awkwardly and proceeded with the reading of the will.

Though outwardly calm and wearing a serious expression appropriate to the moment, Rosalind was seething within. The old witch, she fumed silently. How could she do such a thing! Sarah had no need for this inheritance. Why the plain black gown she wore that had been hurriedly fashioned for the occasion was the first new article of clothing she had ordered since Rosalind had known her. Whatever did someone who spent her time galloping about the countryside in a most unbecoming fashion and closeting herself in the library with books and journals need with a fortune worth a king's ransom? It was all so monstrously unfair when she, Rosalind, would have used it to such good effect—ridding Cranleigh of its worn and faded carpets and drapes, its dingy, outmoded furnishings, and refurbishing both it and its mistress in the height of à la modality and good taste. Rosalind's discontented gaze slid from the dull library draperies to light contemptuously on her sister-in-law. All the fashionable clothes in the world would do nothing for Sarah, drab little thing that she was. If they were not careful, she would spend it all on books or give it all away to the poor or do something equally ridiculous.

Rosalind's eyes narrowed slightly. The only thing that had made the dull and pompous Harold at all acceptable as a husband—she was conveniently forgetting that no one else of any social standing had applied for the position—was the fortune he was destined to inherit. To be sure, Rosalind was determined to make the Marquess of Cranleigh a name well known in the highest political circles and transform his various establishments into magnets that attracted the most exclusive and influential members of the *ton*. But none of this could be done without incurring a great deal of expense. Rosalind had managed to spend a fair amount of his money already, and she was not about to let all the rest of it slip through her fingers to lie dormant in the possession of Sarah—not without a fight anyway.

The object of all this good fortune sat as if turned to stone, too numbed by misery and loss to care about anything except the loneliness that had haunted her since her grandmother's death.

Lady Willoughby, so sharp and quick, so interested in everything going on around her, had been possessed of such an abundance of energy and vitality that it had never occurred to her granddaughter that she might die. She had shared so many things with Sarah and had been so much more tolerant and progressive in her outlook than Harold that Sarah had never really thought of her as old, and this had made the loss all that much more unexpected.

Sarah barely remembered her mother, who had died when she was four, and she had seen so little of her father that six years later when he followed her mother to the grave she was barely aware of his absence. All of his love and energy had been focused on his heir. Harold had been the Marquess of Cranleigh's chief interest in life. By marrying into a fortune, Harold's father had procured the wherewithal to save Cranleigh from the creditors, even to improve it, but it had been up to Harold to restore the Melford name to its former glory. Nothing had been denied Harold—attention, horses, education—and he had grown up to share his father's unshakeable belief that the future Marquess of Cranleigh was the center of the universe.

For a long time Sarah, in awe of her godlike elder brother,

had shared this opinion, but as she had grown older and read and observed more widely, she had begun to see that Harold was, at best, no more than ordinary and, at worst, a self-important prig possessed of a limited understanding. Fortunately her father and Harold after him had had no interest in looking after a young girl, and they had engaged a most sensible nurse to keep an eye on Sarah. When she was older, there had been a governess who was not only most capable but highly intelligent. Miss Helen Trimble had been born to an eminent clergyman who had spent most of his meager earnings on the care of the poor and the instruction of his children. Helen, one girl amidst four bright, eager brothers, had received an education that was far more thorough than that of most young men her age. She in turn had passed as much of it along to her young charge as she could.

Left largely to her own devices, Sarah had spent most of her time in the library at Cranleigh, eagerly absorbing all that she could. By the time Harold had deemed it prudent to dispense with Miss Trimble's services, she was far better educated than her brother and quite able to run rings around him in any discussion—a situation that Harold was at great pains to avoid.

The arrival of Lady Willoughby at Cranleigh after the death of Lord Willoughby had served to further Sarah's education, for Sarah, well vested in the classics and the literature of the previous ages, was unaware of contemporary thought, a state of affairs her grandmother was quick to detect. Lady Willoughby liked nothing better than to peruse the morning's papers, reading through the news and parliamentary discussions of the previous days and then drawing her own conclusions as to the true state of affairs. She was delighted to discover in her granddaughter a quick mind and a keen intelligence that grasped all the intricacies of the political and social questions of the day. After some time spent in these discussions, Sarah was able to offer her own opinions, and the two would spend hours wrapped up in stimulating and speculative conversations.

One day the vicar, the Reverend Mr. Thaddeus Witson, called on the ladies and interrupted a particularly brisk dialogue. He had been so intrigued by it all that he had soon become a regular participant, who could be counted upon to furnish them with supplementary reading material.

Their days had sped by delightfully, and Sarah had never

been so happy. With Harold spending a good deal of his time in London, advancing his career and his wife's social aspirations, Sarah and her grandmother had enjoyed a quiet reclusive life free from meddling neighbors. This situation had worked extremely well for everyone involved: Harold and Rosalind could virtually ignore Sarah and Lady Willoughby as they pursued their own goals while leaving the running of Cranleigh, with a good deal of pecuniary assistance from Lady Willoughby, to Sarah and her grandmother. At one point the marquess, not entirely unmindful of his responsibilities as a brother, had suggested that Sarah ought to have a Season, but this idea was greeted with such disfavor by Sarah herself and given so little encouragement by his wife that he had quickly abandoned the plan, and all had continued to proceed smoothly, until now that was.

Mr. Trevelyan cleared his throat again tentatively. Lady Willoughby had warned him how it would be. "I only wish I were going to be there to see their expressions, what with Harold so eager to get his greedy hands on my money and his wife with half of it spent already in her mind on the latest fripperies." Lady Willoughby had chuckled merrily. It was all very well for her to laugh, Mr. Trevelyan thought sourly. She was not faced by a large, angry man and his equally infuriated wife.

Mr. Trevelyan thanked his lucky stars that his business was in London, a city large enough in which to escape the effects of the marquess's irritation. Still, it had been worth it to know that Lady Willoughby's granddaughter would be taken care of. His former client had seen to that. "You make sure that everything is all right and tight so that neither Harold nor his precious Rosalind can lay their hands on what is rightfully Sarah's," she had instructed him. Mr. Trevelyan had assured her that he would do his utmost to look out after the interests of her granddaughter. A quiet little thing weighed down by her loss and no match for her beautiful sister-in-law or her overbearing brother, Lady Sarah Melford looked as though she would need his assistance.

Mr. Trevelyan gathered his papers, stood up, and prepared to depart, then turned to Sarah. "I am always at your disposal, Lady Sarah. Should you wish to consult me, please send me notice and I shall come immediately."

"Thank you so much." The voice was soft and subdued, but

the green eyes looking up at him were full of a lively intelligence. She was not such a dab of a thing after all, the lawyer thought as he made the briefest of bows to the marquess and his wife. Lady Sarah Melford might be overwhelmed for the time being, but that brief glance had shown him that she was well aware of her situation. In that moment, Mr. Trevelyan had received the very definite impression that behind her quiet demeanor lay a good deal of strength. Well, she would need it, he mused later as he climbed into his carriage. Both her brother and her sister-in-law looked to be as spoiled and self-centered as they could be, and neither one of them would take kindly to the loss of a fortune.

Chapter Two

Sarah, worn out by the rigors of the day, excused herself and hurried off to the peace and quiet of her bedchamber, leaving the marquess and his lady to vent their frustration on one another. The marchioness was first, turning to her husband, who was pacing furiously. A frown of annoyance wrinkling her smooth white forehead, she inquired sharply, "How could you have let this happen, Harold?"

The marquess stopped dead in his tracks. *"I?"* Her husband exploded. "How could *I* have known that the old . . ." He controlled himself with an effort. "How could I have possibly dreamt that someone would do something so preposterous, so, so . . . highly improper?"

Rosalind raised delicate brows. "Why, naturally I had assumed that as a man of affairs you had seen that all was suitably arranged."

"I assumed that it was. Besides, what could I do to avert such a disaster, a disaster I could not possibly have foreseen? Should I have demanded to see the will? You know how impossible that would have been. You know what she was like—a more clutch-fisted, closemouthed . . ."

"But you are a man, Harold; men are supposed to know about such things. As head of the family you should have seen to it," his wife continued firmly but more calmly. Really, sometimes Harold was such a child. Rosalind, now that she had gotten over the initial shock, remained outwardly cool and collected. No matter how much she was seething inside, she knew it did no good to become angry. If she was to get Harold to secure the fortune for them, she must remain unruffled and think it all through. Besides, frowning pulled at one's face so that it was bound to become wrinkled. At the moment she could quite cheerfully have murdered her spouse for failing to make certain that the one thing that had made him acceptable as a husband for Rosalind Tredington was the fortune he stood to inherit. There must be some way out of this disaster. Rosalind's brain worked furiously.

"But, Rosalind," her injured husband protested, "you know how Lady Willoughby was; she was an independent old Tartar. How was I to question her about such things?"

"If you had asserted your authority in the proper way, this never would have happened, but you were afraid of her." Rosalind shrugged gracefully and raised a slim white hand to her aching forehead.

The accuracy of this statement was undeniable. Harold flushed a brilliant red and bit his lip before replying, "Well, we shall have to make the best of it. There is nothing to be done. Knowing Lady Willoughby, I am certain she was most thorough in seeing to the provisions in her will."

"No, Harold," Rosalind contradicted him resolutely, "you will see to it that we are not made to suffer from such outrageous eccentricity on your grandmother's part, even if she is dead."

"But how will I do that?"

His wife draped herself in a more picturesque fashion across the back of the settee and gazed out the window at the vast expanse of neatly clipped lawn. "I am sure you will think of something," she murmured languidly.

Harold resumed his pacing, his brow knitted in agonized concentration. The Marquess of Cranleigh was not a clever man. He had succeeded as much as he had in his own little world mostly because he was the Marquess of Cranleigh and somewhat because he could be counted upon to carry out the tedious little details of schemes dreamed up by minds considerably brighter than his own. He was a loyal and dogged follower, slavishly devoted to the twin principles of pride and respectability—a quality that his wife and the leaders of his party exploited to the utmost. This was the most damnable and exasperating of situations, he fumed to himself as he followed the border of the carpet, executing a sharp turn as it made a corner. And the worst of it was that he could see no possible way out of it. Knowing Lady Willoughby, he was certain that she had tied it all up to a nicety and there was no possibility of altering it.

Rosalind stole a glance at her husband, sighing gently. Harold was a fool, but he was her fool, and she was not about to allow him to give up a fortune without a fight. Summoning a smile to her lips, she regarded him with proper wifely fondness and laid a hand on his arm as he passed her. "Yes." She nodded. "I can see that you are thinking the same thing I am thinking." She nodded again approvingly.

"Am I?" Occasionally, just occasionally, Harold had the uncomfortable feeling that his beautiful wife was a good deal brighter than he was. Of course she was as lovely as any woman he had ever seen, and such a witty and flirtatious conversationalist that the cleverest men in his particular set enjoyed talking to her. He was proud of that; however, the suspicion that she might possibly grasp more than he did of what was going on made him most uneasy. It was only the brief, uncomfortable thought of the moment, quickly dismissed as he looked down into the dark eyes so full of admiration and at the bewitching dimple that appeared as she smiled encouragingly at him.

"Yes," she continued. "It really is time Sarah was respectably married and, since she refuses to have a Season"—here Rosalind conveniently forgot her own notable lack of enthusiasm for having Sarah as a charge upon her in London—"it should be someone from here in the country."

"Richard," Harold breathed as a sly look crept into his eyes.

Rosalind mentally congratulated herself. Once again she had proven herself capable of leading the most obtuse of all men to a conclusion. "How clever of you, my love, the perfect solution!" A self-satisfied smile hovered on the beautifully sculpted lips. "I leave it to you to show him where his duty lies. After all, he and Sarah have been companions for so long he could hardly *not* offer for her. If he did not, it would appear after all this time as though he had been trifling with her affections." And, she thought, it would be a good deal easier to push her recalcitrant brother into marriage with an heiress he knew than it had been during her previously unsuccessful attempts to throw her sporting, mad sibling in the way of those who graced fashionable ballrooms.

Having once more done her utmost to extricate her husband from his own blind stupidity—he should have seen the need to be more conciliatory to the old bat while she was alive—Rosalind moved on to the next problem. "It really is too bad of Lady Willoughby to leave us before the Season is quite ended." Rosalind pursed her lips in annoyance. "Black is my least becoming color, and I had quite planned a soiree and a musicale or two before we left town." The sigh and look that accompanied this pronouncement were worthy of an early Christian martyr. "I daresay we shall just have to make the best of it by offering some sort of entertainment down here."

Harold looked up in some alarm. Pompous and overbearing he might be in his own little part of the world, but he was not confident enough of his position in the *ton* even to think of straying from the path of strictest propriety. But his wife was not about to be deprived of all the delights of London as well as her usual crowd of handsome admirers. "Nothing extravagant, mind you," she cautioned. "It would be just a small party of a few select people. After all, we simply must do something for the Duke of Coltishall, who has done so much to introduce you to all the important members of the party. He will bring his charming daughter, and we simply cannot leave her without any young bucks to dance attendance on her. I believe that the Chevalier d'Evron is a great favorite, and I know we could count on Lord Farringdon to do the pretty. After all, Alistair is a good friend of Richard's as well," Rosalind continued smoothly, adding the names of her two most dashing admirers to the guest list.

"Well . . ." Her husband still hesitated.

"And I believe we could even persuade Lord Edgecumbe. He was most devoted to me this Season." Rosalind threw in her trump card with a triumphant smile. Her husband had been trying unsuccessfully for years to attract the notice of this powerful politician; it had taken one dazzling smile from Rosalind and a few minutes of conversation with him at the Duchess of Coltishall's rout to captivate him entirely. A brilliant man, Lord Edgecumbe had been forced by pecuniary circumstances to marry a dull but wealthy woman who was far more interested in her dogs and her horses than she was in her clever husband whom she encouraged to stay in London, preferring that a man so notably lacking in the skills requisite a country gentleman not embarrass her with his ineptitude on the hunting field. Scorned in his own home for his lack of wealth and athletic prowess, Lord Edgecumbe had been easily susceptible to the charms of a sympathetic female, especially one as lovely as the Marchioness of Cranleigh.

Though not attracted to him in the least, for physically he was a most unprepossessing specimen, Rosalind had instantly recognized Lord Edgecumbe's power and influence in political circles and immediately cultivated his acquaintance, adding him to her burgeoning circle of admirers. Her efforts had been swiftly rewarded as men who had hitherto ignored her husband stopped in to discuss the latest news from Parliament with him, and invitations soon flowed in from some of the *ton*'s most noted political hostesses.

Harold beamed. "An excellent scheme, my dear. We may perhaps also convince his wife to visit. She detests London, but Cranleigh is sure to please her. I hear that she is enormously wealthy. Certainly she comes from one of the most ancient families in Buckinghamshire, and her brother, Lord Ware, is not without influence in Parliament." Harold rubbed his hands together in gleeful anticipation. "Yes, I feel that she could also be a powerful ally. I am sure you will captivate her as you have done her husband."

Rosalind had not the least notion of wasting her time or her considerable charm on a mere female, especially some rustic who had not the slightest influence in the fashionable world, but she did not want to say anything that could threaten her plans for filling the house with her own particular flirts. The more people she invited, the less obvious would be the presences of the Chevalier d'Evron and Alistair, Lord Farringdon, Earl of Burnleigh. Just the thought of Lord Farringdon's athletic figure and the chevalier's mesmerizing dark eyes caused her pulse to quicken.

"I shall do my best, my lord, but from what Lord Edgecumbe tells me, she is a rather quiet woman, unaccustomed to going about much. Perhaps she would feel more comfortable with Sarah." There, let her sister-in-law earn her keep. After all, someone as bookish as Lady Sarah Melford had no use for gentlemen anyway, and as long as Rosalind was forced to endure the irritating presence of someone who had no use for the vast fortune she had just inherited, that person might as well be useful.

"Good idea." Harold nodded. "It will keep her from moping about the house."

"I shall tell her this instant so that she may be of some help," his wife replied, rising gracefully, "and then I shall send out notes to the proper people." Glad to have the prospective gaiety to occupy her mind, Rosalind glided off in search of her sister-in-law.

Chapter Three

The person in question was indeed *moping,* as her brother would call it. Sitting alone in her bedchamber, Sarah gazed unseeingly out her window across the vast expanse of lawn to the dark woods of the park beyond. What was she to do now? Her only friend in the world was gone, and it was all too clear that she was not particularly welcome in what had been her home. To be sure, she was not unaccustomed to loneliness, having spent so many years with no one but her governess to show any interest in her, but having enjoyed the companionship and stimulating company of her grandmother, she now found it harder to bear than it had been before Lady Willoughby had come to live at Cranleigh.

Sarah shook her head. There was no use repining. She knew that eventually her own active mind and her natural interest in everything around her would reassert themselves and she would soon find herself almost as busy and occupied as she had been before. It was not like her to sit idle like this, but the shock of it all had taken her by surprise.

There was a tap on the door, and her sister-in-law entered. "My goodness, Sarah," Rosalind began brightly, "you cannot sit here forever looking so Friday-faced." Seeing the sparkle of annoyance in the green eyes, she hastened to soften this apparent criticism. After all, it would never do to alienate Sarah just when she needed her. "I know how much Lady Willoughby meant to you, but she was by no means young, you know." Rosalind did her best to adopt an expression of sympathetic commiseration before launching into her immediate concerns.

You do not understand in the least and care even less, Sarah thought; however, she was not about to share a moment of her own private sorrow with her frivolous sister-in-law. "Yes, I suppose you are in the right of it." She sighed, putting away all thoughts of Lady Willoughby, concentrating instead on her visitor. What did her sister-in-law want? Fully occupied with her own pleasures, Rosalind rarely had time even to notice Sarah, much less consider her well-being. There must be something that she hoped to gain by seeking Sarah out like this.

Sarah studied the beautiful face in front of her for clues as to the meaning of the visit, but beyond a certain watchful expression in the lustrous dark eyes and a slight raising of the delicately arched brows, there was not the least hint as to what her sister-in-law was thinking.

Rosalind observed Sarah with equal curiosity; however, beyond their mutual wary approach to one another, the similarities ended. The Marchioness of Cranleigh was the picture of fashionable beauty from her dress, which although black figured silk was trimmed in such a way as to reveal its Bond Street origins, to her elegant coiffure. She was a work of art right down to the tiniest detail. Gracefully disheveled dark curls clustered around a face that already had artists clamoring to paint it. She was the example of feminine loveliness to which every woman in the *ton* aspired.

Sarah, on the other hand, though neatly enough attired in a plain high-waisted gown of black bombazine with her gold hair wound in simple coils around her head, possessed none of her sister-in-law's *éclat*—quite the opposite, in fact. If one were to think about it, one might almost conclude that she exerted as much effort to remain unobtrusive as Rosalind did in seeking to capture the admiration of the male sex and the envy of the female. However, if the casual observer stopped to consider, he would see that Lady Sarah Melford, though less obviously beautiful than the Marchioness of Cranleigh, possessed a certain attraction all her own—a cool elegance conferred by classic features, a small straight nose, finely sculpted lips, and deep green eyes that revealed a lively intelligence. Her customary expression was one of thoughtfulness rather than flirtatiousness, and she was thus often ignored when surrounded by the more vivacious countenances of other females bent on attracting masculine attention. But anyone who paused a moment to contemplate her face would immediately be intrigued by its character and, upon closer examination, would be attracted by the personality so obviously present in its owner and so obviously lacking in the bland, undiscriminating expressions of those around her.

It was Rosalind who broke the silence. "Sarah, I know this is difficult, but it is not at all ladylike to be so self-indulgent at a time like this. There is so much to be done, people coming to offer their condolences and . . ." The marchioness paused as she sought a delicate way to phrase the next sentence. "Besides, I shall need your help." Sarah looked up in some surprise. Yes, that was the best way, Rosalind decided, one had to appeal to her for assistance. Sarah was ever eager to do good works, and the marchioness had never failed to win what she wanted when she adopted a helpless and cajoling tone.

She sighed and collapsed gracefully into a chair. "Your brother feels he must remain here at Cranleigh for some time, but you know how important it is to be in London where his career is concerned. People are so fickle; the minute one is not around, one is forgotten."

And you should know that better than anyone, Sarah muttered to herself as she recalled the acquaintances that Rosalind had cultivated assiduously, even in such an out-of-the-way place as Kent, and then dropped when they were no longer of any use to her.

"Therefore, if he cannot be in London, we must bring London to us," her sister-in-law concluded brightly. Then, anticipating objections, she quickly added, "Of course, being in mourning, we shall keep it the most quiet of affairs, just a few close friends here for the country air."

For a moment Sarah's air of gravity deserted her. Her lips twitched and a humorous glint dispelled the somber expression in her eyes. The vision of Rosalind, who considered it rusticating to be driven through Hyde Park at anything but the height of the fashionable hour, enjoying country air almost overset her. However, she ruthlessly suppressed the derisive chuckle that threatened to burst out, and nodded encouragingly.

Sarah could never like her vain and selfish sister-in-law, but on the other hand, one could not help but be fascinated by the very boldness of her machinations, nor could one underestimate her determination. She had learned that lesson from watching Rosalind Tredington make herself Marchioness of Cranleigh.

Sarah would never forget the day that Rosalind, hustled off at a tender age to a seminary in Bath by a father too wrapped up in his own amusements to care for a daughter, had come home. It had been a great shock to the entire neighborhood when the elegant creature had emerged from the traveling carriage.

That particular day Sarah had been over at Tredington Hall, where she and Richard had set up a series of jumps and were engaged in challenging one another to ever more daring feats of horsemanship. She had barely recognized the young lady, dressed in the height of fashion, who alighted so daintily and greeted the assembled retainers with cool graciousness.

Sarah had looked in vain for the awkward, whining creature who had never been able to keep up in any of the games they had devised. Even though Rosalind was the eldest of the three of them, she had not been able to run as fast, jump as high, or climb as well as Richard and Sarah, and she was so frightened of horses that riding was out of the question. Sarah, Richard, and the other children in the surrounding countryside had always scoffed at her as a poor, timid creature. Now Rosalind was about to have her revenge.

Every man for miles around, from the squire to the stable boys was now besotted with her, and they fell over themselves to offer her assistance of any sort. If her carriage pulled up in the village, there was a crowd around it, clambering to hold the horses, help her down, or carry her packages. Even the squire's two sons, Tom and George, both thoroughgoing misogynists who had always avoided Rosalind at all costs, gave up their wild rides across the countryside attending this mill or that hunt in favor of lounging around her drawing room.

Sarah had not been able to believe it. Yes, Rosalind had grown; the skinny body had developed curves, and she now laughed flirtatiously, batting long, dark lashes and making a great show of dimples and tiny white teeth when she smiled, but she was still the same old Rosalind—self-centered and slightly vain, interested in nothing but fashion and herself. However, no one but Sarah seemed to realize this, and suddenly the whining useless girl everyone had tried to avoid had become a most fascinating creature, sought out by one and all—women as well as men—for wherever the men were, all the women wished to be, and the men were all paying court to Rosalind.

Suddenly, Sarah found herself feeling very much alone. With Rosalind returned, Tredington Hall became the hub of neighborhood activity. The Tredingtons had always been a wild and fun-loving crowd, up for anything, and Rosalind wheedled her father into giving one party after another, from Venetian breakfasts to masquerades, even a medieval tournament with Rosalind presiding as the dispenser of prizes. For respectability's sake, Rosalind was always accompanied by a colorless, silent spinster, Aunt Honoria, actually a remote cousin plucked up from drudgery as governess to provide proper companionship for her beautiful young relative.

At all these festivities Sarah found herself watching her former acquaintances make utter fools of themselves. Being lively, inquisitive, and adventurous herself, Sarah had always spent more time with Richard Tredington and his friends, preferring their company to that of their sisters, who did nothing but chatter endlessly of fashions and sigh over young men who were far more likely to spend time with a horse than with a girl. Now all of this was changed. Her companions who formerly rode all over the countryside in search of one lark after another were content to dance attendance at Tredington Park, doing nothing except admiring Rosalind and listening to her chatter.

Disgusted though she was by this behavior, Sarah could not help being curious, and she had hung on the edge of these conversations in order to hear what Rosalind was saying that was so fascinating. Perhaps she had learned something after all at her select seminary. But Sarah was doomed to disappointment. After several hours of listening, she discovered that the conversation contained a good deal of gurgling laughter and revolved around only one subject—Rosalind Tredington.

Completely baffled by this sudden transformation in her childhood companions, from lively young people to complete simpletons, Sarah had complained to her grandmother. Lady Willoughby had laid a comforting arm around her granddaughter's shoulders and replied ruefully, "It is all rather silly, my dear, I know, but this is the way of the world. When men, young or old, see a beautiful woman, they behave like perfect idiots."

"But . . . but she is not even very nice," Sarah had wailed tearfully, for Rosalind, quick to recognize that Sarah could not be won over by her coquettish airs had not been slow to hint, ever so delicately of course, that Lady Sarah Melford was rather eccentric in her tastes and therefore not someone whose companionship or opinion was of any importance. The others, slavishly following the lead of their goddess, and without second thoughts, had abandoned Sarah to her own devices.

"I know." Lady Willoughby had sighed sympathetically. "She does not have to be nice, but believe me, you would not truly wish to be friends with the sort of people who seek out her company. In time you will discover those who enjoy discussing more important things in life than the trivialities that dominate her conversation."

Her granddaughter had derived some consolation from this, for she considered her grandmother to be the wisest, most knowledgeable person in her world, but as time wore on, she began to give up hope that this state of affairs would ever come to an end.

Apparently, people in London were no more discerning than those in Kent, for reports of Rosalind's resounding success in taking the *ton* by storm had made their way back shortly after she had left for her first Season. It was not that Sarah aspired in the least to a place in the fashionable world, but it did seem unfair that someone as vapid as Rosalind should so quickly be hailed as an incomparable. There was some consolation, however—and Sarah was disgusted at herself for even thinking such petty thoughts—which was that all of Rosalind's brilliant admirers had remained precisely that. No one had asked her to become his wife.

With some difficulty Sarah had stifled a vulgar impulse to gloat when Rosalind, still single, had returned to Kent. Sarah's amusement had been short-lived, however, when she discovered the next step in Rosalind's campaign. She alone had been able to see how deliberately Rosalind had turned her ankle and stumbled as she emerged from church just in front of the Marquess of Cranleigh. Harold, rushing gallantly to her side, had been the recipient of such a warm, melting look that he had been startled out of his usual fog of complacent self-importance. If it had not meant that Rosalind would intrude on her life more than ever, Sarah would have been amused by it all, as Harold, utterly helpless in the face of such determination, had been played like a fish on a line. His sister, put off as she was by his unbounding conceit, even found it in her heart to feel sorry for him as she watched Rosalind gather every aspect of the marquess's life into her own dainty hands, establishing complete control over him.

"A few select guests—Lord Edgecumbe and his wife and

daughters, the Duke and Duchess of Coltishall, the Chevalier d'Evron, the Earl of Burnleigh," Rosalind's voice broke into her sister-in-law's reverie.

"The Earl of Burnleigh?" Sarah exclaimed involuntarily.

"Why, yes. He is a coming man in political circles and a friend of Richard's. You may have even met him, for he has visited Richard at Tredington several times," Rosalind replied with studied casualness.

Yes, Sarah certainly did remember the Earl of Burnleigh. No one who had laid eyes on him was likely to forget the tall, athletic figure, the lean, aristocratic features, and gray eyes that surveyed the world with a cynical contempt for humanity and all its failings. Oh yes, Sarah remembered Alistair, Lord Farringdon, Earl of Burnleigh.

Who could ignore or forget one of the most renowned rakes of the *ton*? Rumors of his conquests had even reached their quiet part of the world.

It was only natural that someone of such libertine propensities should be a crony of Lord Tredington's, for Richard, though not much in the petticoat line, was ripe for any other sort of mischief. In fact, Sarah recalled far more about the Earl of Burnleigh than she cared to. The most potent image she retained of him—one that simply would not go away—was of the earl and Rosalind the night of the masquerade ball at Tredington Park. Sarah, escaping the stuffiness of the ballroom and in search of fresh air, had gone for a walk in the gardens and had come across them, Rosalind and Lord Farringdon, locked in a passionate embrace on a secluded bench. They had been so involved that they had not the least thought of anyone or anything else while Sarah, transfixed by the scene, had stood for what seemed ages before making her escape unnoticed by the lovers.

It had been shortly afterward that Rosalind and Harold had announced their engagement, and Sarah, who usually scorned love and romance as figments of silly girls' imaginations, could not help asking herself how someone who had been wrapped in the arms of a man like Lord Farringdon could marry a man like Harold. She would have been astonished to know that Rosalind, in the few moments of unwelcome thought that would intrude in spite of her best efforts to ward them off with parties, flirtations, or the acquisition of the latest fashionable kickshaws, wondered very much the same thing.

However, Rosalind had been given very little choice in the matter, for the Marquess of Cranleigh had been the only one to offer her his name, his ancient title, and an establishment of her own—not that Rosalind was the least grateful to him for it. Unfortunately, the very fact that Harold had been so quick to give her those things made him appear stupid and weak to the woman who had manipulated him so easily. No, Rosalind could not admire, could barely even like such a man, but then men like the Earl of Burnleigh would never allow someone else to lead them as she had led Harold, and they certainly would never have offered marriage.

"But Richard can see to it that Al . . . er, Lord Farringdon is sufficiently amused. I do need your assistance in seeing to Lord Edgecumbe's daughters and to Lady Amelia who is rather shy despite being daughter to the Duke of Coltishall," Rosalind continued, redoubling her appeal. "And, as I believe that Edgecumbe's daughters are considered to be rather blue, I am persuaded you will know just what to say to them. I never have the least notion." The marchioness shrugged helplessly as though rational discourse were as foreign to her as Arabic or Hebrew, Sarah thought.

"I shall do my best," Sarah replied listlessly. The idea of entertaining strangers at such a time was less than attractive, but at least these particular guests seemed to offer more of potential interest than most of Rosalind's acquaintances did.

"Good. I depend on you." With a satisfied smile the marchioness, eager to put her plans for amusement into action, rose and hurried from the room, leaving her sister-in-law to her own speculations concerning the forthcoming festivities.

Chapter Four

The ensuing days involved a whirlwind of activity for the Marchioness of Cranleigh, but they were not so busy that they distracted her entirely from her plans for securing Lady Willoughby's fortune for her own use. After all, festivities of the sort she was planning were not free, and Rosalind refused to be forced by a lack of sufficient funds into putting on paltry affairs. Consequently, Lord Richard Tredington was surprised to receive a visit from his sister less than a week after the reading of the will. It was not that Rosalind was not fond of his company—everyone enjoyed the company of such a gay blade as Richard—but she usually made him dance attendance on her at Cranleigh rather than exerting herself to make the trip to Tredington Park.

"Hello, Roz, you're looking very dashing. What's all this about?" Her brother greeted her jovially as Rosalind, noting that the cushions and carpets were even more frayed and faded than when she had left, draped herself across the least threadbare of the chairs in the drawing room.

"Really, Richard, cannot a sister visit her brother without being subject to an inquisition?"

"Yes, but not this particular sister and not this particular brother. You have some scheme cooking in that pretty head of yours, I'll warrant, or you would not have come all the way over to see me. Tredington Park may be a dust heap, but it is private. You must have something to say to me that you don't wish Melford to overhear." Smiling quizzically at his sister, Richard threw himself into the chair opposite her.

"Not Melford, Richard, Sarah."

"Sarah?" Richard was nonplussed. It was exceedingly rare that his sister concerned herself with the welfare of anyone besides the Marchioness of Cranleigh, much less that of her sister-in-law.

"Yes, Sarah. She is most upset by her grandmother's death. Harold and I do not know what is to become of her. She is such an odd little thing, you know—practically a recluse—and with Lady Willoughby gone she has no one for companionship." Rosalind sighed and raised a hand to her brow. "Harold and I are at our wits' end as to what to do with her."

"Do with her?" Richard looked amused rather than sympathetic. After years of living with his sister, he was inured to her theatrics. "Why should you *do* anything with her? I always found Sarah to be a capable little thing, well able to manage anything. Just you wait and see. This has knocked the wind out of her, but she'll be all right and tight in no time."

Rosalind frowned. Really, Richard could be so provoking with his lackadaisical disregard for everything, and at the moment he was being particularly obtuse. "You don't have the least sensibility, Richard. The poor thing is desperately lonely. She needs the comforting presence of an old friend. You could provide that comfort."

"I?" If Richard had been amused before, he was flabbergasted now by the role his sister was casting him in. As the adored son and the youngest child in a household bent on amusement, Lord Richard Tredington had never had to do anything even remotely uncomfortable. Playing comforter to a bereaved young woman, no matter how well he knew her, struck him as a distinctly unpleasant task, and he was not about to do it. "I have not the least knowledge as to how to help her; furthermore, I don't have the least interest in doing so," he admitted frankly.

"Oh, but you must. She is so unnerved by the entire thing, heaven knows what she will do or what will happen to that enormous fortune she inherited," Rosalind protested.

"Ah." Obtuse Richard might be, but he was not stupid, and he knew his devious sister's mind well enough to catch the drift of this increasingly upsetting conversation. A darkling look settled over his handsome countenance. "I have known Sarah Melford for years, and I like her as well as I like any female, but I refuse to be leg-shackled to her," he began in an ominous tone.

Rosalind smiled up at her brother, coyly batting her eyelashes. "Leg-shackled? Who is forcing you to do such a thing? Richard, how can you—"

"Think such a thing of you?" her brother finished her sentence for her. "Because I know you, Rosalind, and I tell you I won't do it."

"Richard." The sweetness vanished instantly as Rosalind fixed him with a stare that would have made a more intrepid man quake. "You will do this because I gave you the money that kept you out of debtors' prison." Seeing that this telling argument was not having the desired effect, she allowed her voice to quaver ever so slightly and tears to well up in her eyes. "Because I sacrificed myself to this loveless marriage so that you could keep our family home."

"Now, Rosalind, that is doing it much too brown. We both know you married Harold because he was the only one who came up to scratch, and it was to your advantage as well as mine." Richard refused to fall victim to his sister's wiles, but a note of uncertainty had crept into his voice. After all, his sister had looked out for him, in her own fashion, since they had been children. And it was true that the minute she had hooked the Marquess of Cranleigh, she had made him cough up the ready and enough of that to repay all Richard's debts—for the time being.

"Richard, think!" his sister pleaded. "You can't remain single forever. You must carry on the Tredington name, and you have known Sarah for ages. What with her fortune you would never find yourself under the hatches again."

Her brother rubbed his nose thoughtfully. What Rosalind said was perfectly true. He knew he had to marry; it was just a question of when. Thus far he had managed to postpone this unhappy fate, but his debts had begun to cut significantly into the estate, and Tredington Park was beginning to look very much the worse for it.

Richard was no fool. He knew that he was not a particularly eligible *parti*. After all, he had his sister's example before him, and even with all her undeniable charms Rosalind, with no dowry and a debtor for a brother, had been unable to catch anyone but Harold. Certainly he liked Sarah well enough and was comfortable with her. She would not be forever pestering him to take her to London or even to escort her to local assemblies. She, who appreciated fine horseflesh as much as he, would not complain if he were to concentrate his energies on setting up a truly good stable, which was something he had always longed to do but had lacked the wherewithal to accomplish. Suddenly, his sister's idea did not seem as farfetched as it had at the outset.

Seeing that her brother was weakening. Rosalind was quick to press her advantage. "And if you were to marry Sarah, you would not have to spend a great deal of time in London, haunting balls and routs, trying to make yourself agreeable to a bevy of young misses who would expect you to flatter them and dance attendance on them from morning until night."

Richard shuddered.

"Precisely." His sister looked smug. She had felt certain that Richard would come around to her point of view if she presented it well enough. Now all that remained was to convince Sarah. Rosalind was far less sure of the outcome of that part of the plan. That, however, was Richard's affair.

Gathering up her gloves, Rosalind rose to go. "I know I can depend on you to set her mind at ease as to the future. After all, she must marry as well, and she has no more liking of balls and assemblies than you do." Knowing her brother's tendency to put off anything that demanded effort, she continued, "But you had better do it immediately while she is still feeling the death of her grandmother, else you might lose your chance to have a comfortable bride who will not demand assiduous attention in return for her fortune. Believe me, most heiresses are not so careless of their worth as Sarah." And with that parting shot, the Marchioness of Cranleigh sailed majestically from the room, leaving her brother to stare blankly at her retreating figure.

Richard remained rooted to the spot for some time, then, uttering a snort of disgust, poured out a generous glass of brandy and threw himself into a chair. He downed the brandy in one gulp and sat staring fixedly at the pattern in the carpet. It was not that he did not like Sarah; he was actually quite fond of her. It was just that he had a strong distaste for responsibility of any sort. But Richard knew his sister, and he knew that all peace was at an end until he did what she wished. Rosalind could make one's life most uncomfortable if crossed, but she usually knew what she was about. Besides, Richard, as little as he was inclined to put forth the effort of thinking of someone else, felt sorry for his sister, leg-shackled to a stick like Harold. If he himself could improve her life by doing something that was to his advantage, well, then, he would do it.

Thus it was that a good deal later in the afternoon, well fortified by numerous reviving drafts of brandy, that Richard rode over to Cranleigh. "Lady Sarah, please." He peered owlishly at Nettlebed, the butler, who opened the door almost the moment he presented himself on the doorstep. Nettlebed had seen him ride up and, knowing Lord Tredington's propensity for banging the knocker loudly and repeatedly, had hurried to forestall him.

"Good afternoon, my lord," Nettlebed murmured. "Lady Sarah will be down directly." The butler led him into the library and, seeing that his lordship was already considerably castaway, refrained from offering any spiritous refreshments, sending word instead for a pot of strong tea to be served.

"Hello, Richard." There was a note of surprise in Sarah's greeting. It was rare that Lord Tredington called on anyone, especially a lady. Ordinarily, if Richard wished to see Sarah, it was to ride with her, in which case he sent a note over, instructing her to meet him somewhere.

For once in her life, Rosalind had accurately gauged someone else's feelings, Richard thought. Sarah did look as though she were having a devil of a time, and she certainly did not look as though she had just come into a tremendous fortune. She was pale with fatigue as though she had been sleeping poorly. Her face was drawn, and there were shadows under her eyes, making them look enormous in her pale face. He felt a stab of pity for her that was almost strong enough to reconcile him completely to the unpleasant task at hand.

Sarah eyed her visitor curiously. His calling on her was unusual enough, but he also appeared to be more than usually well to live. It must be important if he had had to fortify himself to the point of being foxed before calling on her. She was accustomed to the whiff of spirits on Richard's breath, but generally he only imbibed to the point of gaiety. Now his movements were uncertain, and he appeared to have trouble focusing on her. She waited to hear the reason for his visit, but he continued to sit, staring at her, a bemused expression on his face. Finally, Sarah could bear the suspense no longer. "You wished to see me, Richard?"

"Oh, er, yes, that is, very sorry to hear about your grandmother and all. Know you will miss the old . . . I mean, I know you will miss her." Richard shifted uncomfortably under her clear-eyed gaze. Sometimes Sarah saw entirely too much, and sometimes it made a person most uncomfortable to be with someone who was awake on every suit.

"Yes, I shall miss her. It is very kind of you to call." Sarah continued to regard him inquisitively.

Richard shifted uneasily. There was no avoiding it. She knew there was something in the wind. "Well, you see . . . I mean, the fact of the matter is that you are alone now . . ." Richard ran a finger inside his neckcloth, which had suddenly become exceedingly tight. Where was his sister now when he needed her? It was all very well to put him up to this, but he was the one that had to go through with it, come up with the words as Sarah sat there calmly waiting and watching him struggle. Come to think of it, why didn't Sarah help him out? She was so damnably clever, she probably knew exactly what he was thinking. After all, she was supposed to be his friend. A friend would never let him flounder like this. Richard drew a deep breath and plunged ahead. "The thing of it is, I thought you might like to get married."

There was dead silence while Sarah looked blankly at him. "Thought you might like to marry me, that is," Lord Tredington continued helpfully.

Lady Sarah's lips twitched, and for the first time in weeks she actually wanted to laugh. "Rosalind put you up to this, did she not?"

Richard, looking mightily uncomfortable, nodded sheepishly. "But she could not have made me do it, mind you, if I did not think you were a great gun, Sarah." Then, seeing her devoutly skeptical expression, he added hurriedly, "It is not the money. You know that I don't need the money." The skeptical look deepened. "What I mean is, I shall always be under the hatches, but I shall live the same way whether I have money or not—been doing so for years," he concluded cheerfully. "I just thought you might be wanting a . . . you might be lonely what with Lady Willoughby gone and all."

Sarah smiled fondly at him. For all his wild and reckless ways, Richard truly was her friend and, until the arrival of her grandmother, he had been her closest friend. Lord, the adventures the two of them had had! They had been forever returning home muddied, with clothes torn, the constant despair of nurses and grooms. "Thank you, Richard. It is very kind of you, but you do not really wish to get married, you know." It was with great difficulty that Sarah restrained herself from bursting out laughing at his heartfelt sigh of relief. "And, what is more, neither do I."

"You don't?" Lord Tredington sat bolt upright.

"No."

"I thought all females were desperate to catch some poor fellow in the parson's mousetrap."

"Not I." Why would I want someone who thinks he has a right to tell me how to live my life when I am having a perfectly good time doing precisely what I please?" There was a defensiveness in Sarah's tone that made it apparent to even the most unsuspecting of listeners that she had been forced to voice this opinion many times before.

"Why should you?" Richard was much struck by this. There was a moment of silence while he considered this surprising bit of information. He should have known Sarah would see things the way he did—she was a regular Trojan and always had been. He sighed. If only other females saw things as sensibly as she did, he would not half mind associating with them, but most of them were like his sister, all smiles, dimples, and fluttering eyelashes with motives so deep and dark and hidden that a fellow didn't have the least idea of them until he found himself in the middle of doing something he didn't want to do. At the thought of his sister a gloomy expression descended over Lord Tredington's brow. "But Rosalind, she will never . . ."

"Leave Rosalind to me," Sarah responded soothingly. "I shall make her see that we just do not suit." And I shall stop her meddling in my affairs once and for all, she muttered fiercely to herself.

Chapter Five

However, poor Richard was not to be so lucky. Rosalind, more than familiar with her brother's lack of stamina where such things as duty and responsibility were concerned, was lying in wait for him. She had contrived to deliver instructions to the housekeeper, Mrs. Dawlish, and to Nettlebed in the vicinity of the library so as to be aware of her brother's departure, and she immediately sent Nettlebed to summon Richard to the drawing room almost before he had closed the library door on Sarah.

"Well, Richard, am I to congratulate you, then?"

Lord Tredington, looking extremely conscious, laughed uneasily. "Oh, we decided that we should not suit after all." He spoke with an air of bravado that he was far from feeling.

"You what!"

"Sarah said that we were far too good friends to be man and wife, besides which she does not wish to be married."

Rosalind's finely penciled brows snapped together, and her lips pursed in a dainty pout. Such signs of displeasure had been known to send strong men to their knees, but suddenly Richard was tired of it. His sister had been telling him what to do for years, and it was invariably something that she, not he, had an inclination for. The air of bravado that he had struggled to assume suddenly became real as Richard continued, "And I should not try to persuade her to do otherwise if I were you, Roz. You'll catch cold at that. Sarah knows what she wants and what she does not want. She will not thank you for meddling in her affairs. If you want a fortune, go find someone else's. Sarah deserves every bit of hers, and she has every right to dispose of it as she wishes." And without further ado, he turned on his heel and headed for the door, leaving his sister staring after him dumbfounded.

Equally surprised by this show of independence was Lord

Tredington himself. The effects of the quantities of liquor he had consumed to bring himself to the sticking point were wearing off, and he began to reflect seriously on the entire episode. He was amazed at his own temerity. It had never really occurred to him to resist his sister's demands before, for he had always been fearful of the consequences. Now he could not get over how simple it had been. Of course now, having set himself up against her wishes, he was bound to continue or she would make mincemeat out of him.

In a way, Richard would rather miss having her tell him what to do; after all, in some ways, life had been easier with her making all his decisions. But if he were to show himself weakening after this little display of assertiveness, it would be all over for him. She would make his life truly uncomfortable with her demands. That's what comes of sobering up, my boy, Richard muttered to himself as he descended Cranleigh's imposing staircase to the gravel drive where a groom was walking his horse up and down. You start taking responsibility for your own actions and there's no telling where you'll end up— Richard threw a leg over his mount and took the reins. You need a drink, my lad, before all this clear thinking gets you into trouble. With that thought to spur him on, Lord Tredington clattered off home, leaving behind him two women wrapped deep in thought.

Sarah sat for some time staring out of the library windows at the green expanse of lawn. She had always loved Cranleigh. Indeed, it was more her home than it was Harold's, for she had spent far more time there than her brother had, and she cared a great deal more for all the people on the estate than either he or Rosalind did. Now, however, she felt as though she no longer belonged. Harold was back for who knew how long and with him Rosalind who, as always, was bound and determined to have things her own way. This was only natural; after all, she *was* the Marchioness of Cranleigh. However, being mistress of the estate did not give her the right to dictate to her sister-in-law. Sarah had attained her majority. She was in command of a fortune in her own right, and as far as she could see, was perfectly justified in disposing of this fortune in whatever manner she pleased, provided she did nothing that truly threatened anyone else's welfare.

The corners of Sarah's mouth curved into a mischievous smile. What a novel perspective that was. Upsetting as Lady

Willoughby's death had been, it had freed her in a certain way, with no one else for whom she truly cared to consider, Sarah was at liberty to live as she liked, within reason, of course. And all of a sudden, the idea of running her own establishment seemed like a perfectly practical idea.

Sarah knew that Rosalind did not much look forward to Sarah's presence among them anymore than Sarah looked forward to Rosalind's. The servants, though they deferred to the marchioness, usually did so only after consulting with Sarah. Harold was constantly frustrated because she refused to pay any serious attention to his never-ending prosing, and she was equally frustrated at being expected to do so in the first place. A move to a house of her own would solve a myriad of difficulties, and Sarah knew just which house she wanted.

For some time Ashworth, a small manor house not far from Cranleigh, had stood vacant as the last in its direct line of owners, a reclusive spinster who never went about much, had succumbed to old age. It was rumored that the property had gone to the wife of a wealthy baronet in Yorkshire who had not the least interest in the house or the land. For her part, Sarah had always loved the Jacobean manor house with its many fancifully twisted chimneys and diamond-paned windows. Its location also appealed to her, set back far from the road amongst a grove of trees, with lawns sloping off toward the marsh and, in the far distance, a strip of blue that was the sea. The house itself was nowhere near as large or imposing as Cranleigh or Tredington Park, but the rooms were well proportioned and laid out in such a way as to make the place appear both gracious and comfortable.

Yes, the more she considered it, the more Sarah was enamored of the idea, and a plan began to formulate. To quiet the inevitable objections of her brother and sister-in-law and stop any possible gossip concerning this eccentric behavior, she would ask Miss Trimble, her former governess, to join her as a companion. Sarah knew that this estimable lady had gone as governess to the family of a wealthy manufacturer near Birmingham and sorely missed not only the lush Kent countryside, but the luxury of teaching a pupil who was not only well behaved, but genuinely interested in learning.

That decided, Sarah went immediately to her desk to pen a note to Miss Trimble and to the solicitor who handled Ashworth and its affairs.

Meanwhile, in the drawing room the Marchioness of Cranleigh herself was subject to some startling and unsettling revelations. Ever since she could remember, she had been able to dominate her younger brother, or at least direct him as much as it was possible to direct someone whose behavior was as blithely erratic as Lord Tredington's. This was the first time he had ever even questioned her superior intelligence, much less refused to do her bidding. For someone who had spent all her adult years ordering the men around her according to her every whim, this was indeed a most upsetting state of affairs. However, even more distressing were the implications of her failure to accomplish her goal of keeping Lady Willoughby's fortune at the disposal of the Marchioness of Cranleigh.

All her life Rosalind had struggled to keep up appearances while Tredington Park fell into decay around her, her father, and her brother, both of whom remained undismayed by their pecuniary difficulties and both of whom continued to make mice feet of their inheritance at every mill, every race meeting, and every gaming table within a fifty-mile radius of Tredington Park. Rosalind had barely been able to find the wherewithal to give herself a Season, but, having inherited at least some of the family disregard for insolvency, had managed to order a good deal of her wardrobe on credit built on the strength of her matrimonial aspirations. Even the most hardheaded among London's modistes had been certain that a young woman with a face and a figure such as Rosalind's was bound to contract a brilliant marriage.

It had come as something of a shock to Rosalind to discover that the unfortunate financial situation and ruinous propensities of the Tredingtons was such common knowledge among the *ton,* and it was even more of a shock to learn that her suitors, no matter how smitten they were with her charm and beauty, retained enough sense to avoid committing themselves to filling the bottomless pockets of the Tredingtons.

Knowing that she had only one Season in which to accomplish her goal, Rosalind had begun to feel quite desperate as the Season came to a close. The idea of returning to Kent without having snared any one of the wealthy and eligible bachelors everyone expected her to was more than her pride, let alone her financial circumstances, could bear. Then, on her last evening in town, she had looked down from her box in the theater and spied Harold. She knew what she had to do, and her campaign to become Marchioness of Cranleigh had begun the very next day.

To be sure, it had been difficult to give up hopes that her more dashing admirers would rescue her from life at Tredington Park. After enjoying flirtations with some of the *ton*'s most accomplished bucks, conversation with the stolid and self-important Harold had been boring in the extreme, but it had to be done. The one saving grace was that the Marquess of Cranleigh, in addition to possessing an ancient and well-known title, a significant estate, and a respectable income, stood to inherit a vast fortune from his grandmother. Focusing on the thought of all that wealth, Rosalind had steeled herself to accept his clumsy caresses, to bear with his overweening confidence in the infallibility of his opinions, and to smile in spite of the inevitable comparisons she knew people were making between her dull husband and the scores of fascinating men who had paid court to her.

Rosalind had borne it all with such grace that no one had guessed how it galled her to be seen with someone who had only his own high opinion of himself to recommend him, and she had set about with such energy to remedy her situation that within the space of a few months she and Harold were back in the metropolis where she was more fêted and admired than ever before.

The Chevalier d'Evron and the Earl of Burnleigh had done much to compensate for the numbing dullness of her husband, but even they had not offered the consolation that lady Willoughby's fortune had. With more than ample resources at her demand, Rosalind knew she would never have to fear obscurity again. Possessing exquisite taste and style, and supported by limitless pin money, she would always be a leader in the fashionable world. A woman in command of sufficient wealth could remain dazzling far longer than one of more moderate means.

Lady Willoughby's will had dealt a blow to these hopes and dreams, but Rosalind, accustomed to a lifetime of living beyond her means in a style which she could not necessarily afford, was nothing if not resourceful, and she had quickly developed an alternative plan to participate in Lady Willoughby's estate. Of course Richard and Sarah would have been the chief beneficiaries of that plan. Sarah was so unassuming and unprepossessing that she never spent anything except on books and horses, neither of which would make the least dent in her inheritance even if she were to purchase an entire library and a stable full of thoroughbreds. Richard was more expensive, but far more easily influenced than Sarah, and Rosalind had had great hopes of being able to relieve him of much of what would become his should he marry Sarah. But now even this hope was dashed by the younger brother who had heretofore been guided by his sister in all the important aspects of his life.

Rosalind very rarely gave in to despair—a most unproductive emotion—but at this moment she felt very nearly like doing so. She dropped her head in her hands, sighing dispiritedly. What was she to do? Never in her life had she felt so alone. Richard and her father had never been terribly concerned for her welfare, or anyone else's, but they had at least offered the support of a common heritage. Now her father was gone, and Richard had betrayed her. Harold was no help; he was such a dolt that he constantly required her guidance. Rosalind had never possessed any female friends—competition in the marriage mart being what it was—and Sarah, the only woman who did not appear to care for such things or to envy and dislike Rosalind for her beauty, disliked her for other reasons. Oh, she was civil enough, but the marchioness knew that her sister-in-law disapproved of her; she even knew that Sarah had guessed how easily her brother had been maneuvered into a marriage where all the advantage was on the bride's side. Ordinarily, Rosalind did not give a fig for Sarah's poor opinion of her, but at this moment, when she felt so bereft of any comfort, it was just one more cause for distress.

Sarah! Rosalind, her face brightening with a sudden happy thought, raised her head from her hands. Of course, Sarah should pay for the maintenance of Cranleigh and every other expense connected with it. True, Lady Willoughby had been contributing to the upkeep of Cranleigh before, but Sarah could be made to pay for that and everything else—new furnishings, refurbishments that Rosalind had been planning, and a host of other expensive projects. After all, she was the one who enjoyed all the advantages of living there. Why should Harold, who spent the majority of his time in London, have to support it from his own pocket? As Marquess of Cranleigh he was, of course, entitled to the income from the estate, but the expense of keeping Cranleigh habitable was a considerable drain on his finances and one from which he benefited very little. Yes, that was at least a partial solution to the unfortunate consequences of Lady Willoughby's foolishness. Freed from the enormous costs of Cranleigh, the marquess and his lady would have a great deal more to spend on themselves. It was so beautifully simple, Rosalind wondered that she had not thought of it before. Considerably cheered by her own cleverness, she rose, first to go in search of her husband, and then to begin plans for entertaining guests. Faced with the prospect of extra income and the attentions of the Earl of Burnleigh and the Chevalier d'Evron, Rosalind felt equal to anything and quite like her old self again.

Chapter Six

It was a considerable time before a propitious moment arose for Rosalind to broach the subject of Sarah's contribution toward Cranleigh to her husband, but at last she was able to speak to him as he was going through his correspondence one morning in the library. At first, Harold, rigid upholder of the established order of things, would have none of it. "Give the care of the estate into the hands of a woman?" he huffed indignantly. "That sort of thing just is not done, my lady. *I* am Marquess of Cranleigh and Cranleigh belongs to me, not to Sarah, whatever else she may have inherited," he finished peevishly.

"I know, my lord, I know," Rosalind soothed. She had expected this sort of resistance and had prepared her arguments accordingly. "But just think how little time you spend here and how very expensive it is. Sarah loves Cranleigh, and she has come into a fortune that is rightly yours; why should not some of her inheritance be spent taking care of a place she loves?" Rosalind paused before adding triumphantly, "And I am sure she would agree with me." She then continued in her most practical tone, "Freed of the burdens of these expenses, think of how much more you could do to the house in town, how much more we could entertain on a lavish scale. You know how important that is to your career. A politician of your stature cannot live as shabbily as we have done."

In truth, Harold had not thought that they *had* lived shabbily, but his wife did have a point. They would have to practice far less economy if they were able to put all of their income toward the establishment in Berkeley Square. The more he considered it, the more Harold found that the idea appealed to him. They really did need a smarter carriage, and a few more footmen would certainly add to their consequence. Rosalind had been begging for a barouche that would do her justice when she rode out in the park. Yes, it did seem an excellent solution. Of course, he had already been thinking very much the same thing himself; Rosalind was merely the first to articulate such a notion.

His wife, well aware of the tortuous thought processes unfolding in Harold's head, gave him a moment to digest the concept and appropriate it as his own before concluding, "Then you will speak to your sister directly, will you not, for the more quickly it is settled, the better. We shall have guests arriving quite soon, and given that one of them is Lord Edgecumbe, I feel that we should spare no expense."

"Ah, er, yes, well I suppose so." Harold hemmed and hawed.

"I think *now* would be a good time, Harold." The marchioness's tone was sweet enough, but there was no denying the forcefulness with which she uttered these words nor the determined light in her eyes.

Harold shifted uncomfortably in his chair. At last he sighed and reached for the bellpull. "Very well. I shall send for her." Giving it a tug, he stared gloomily at the papers on his desk until Nettlebed appeared. "Ask Lady Sarah to come to the library," he ordered with such a lack of enthusiasm that the old retainer subjected both of the room's occupants to a penetrating but unobtrusive glance before replying, "Very good, sir."

Something was in the wind for certain, the butler thought. To a man, the staff and the tenants of Cranleigh had been delighted at the disposition of Lady Willoughby's worldly goods, as much because it was a slap in the face of *His Pomposity*, as Harold was known below stairs, as it was good fortune for the young mistress whom they genuinely loved.

In theory, the marchioness was mistress of Cranleigh, but it was to Lady Sarah that they all looked for guidance. She might be a quiet enough little thing, but she was clever, with a hidden strength that would surprise one. Not a thing went on that she did not know about, and she was not too high in the instep to share her knowledge with the rest of the world.

Nettlebed knew that everyone under his command as well as the rest of those on the estate was eagerly awaiting the departure of the marquess and his lady, for each of them made life much more difficult for everyone. His lordship's bumbling attempts to establish his command merely bungled and confused things that had previously run very smoothly by themselves, and her ladyship's whims and incessant demands caused a great deal more work for everyone from the housemaid who had to heat her bathwater to just the right temperature to the handsome young footman required to run countless errands for her in the village.

Nettlebed bowed and shut the door behind him, his brain working furiously. They had both looked so smug that they must be up to something. His lordship did look rather uneasy, therefore it must have been the marchioness's idea, whatever it was. She was much quicker than her husband. If the staff at Cranleigh had not disliked her so much, what with her vain and selfish ways, they would have been extremely diverted at the way she managed her husband. She was forever out-thinking him and then making him believe that everything he did was of his own conception. But Rosalind, though she was no worse than many other mistresses, thought of no one but herself and demanded the same abject service from her servants as she did from her admirers. Consequently, the sympathies below stairs were all in favor of his lordship—not that the self-important marquess did not deserve to be led a merry dance by his beautiful wife.

Mulling all this over carefully, Nettlebed went in search of Lady Sarah. He hoped that those two in the library were not going to make her life miserable. She was such a gentle thing, and her brother and sister-in-law were as selfish as they could be. While it was true that Sarah's quietness did not stem from a weak nature and she did stand up for what she thought was just and fair, the butler did not like the idea of her being put to such a test.

Nettlebed rapped gently on the door to Lady Sarah's chambers. Lady Sarah opened it herself. "His lordship wishes to see you in the library."

"Oh, dear." Sarah sighed, a rueful grimace wrinkling her brow. "Is it very bad, Nettlebed?"

"I could not say, my lady," was the reply. Then, dropping the dignified pose of Cranleigh's most respected retainer, he whispered conspiratorially, "It does appear, however, as though they are up to something."

"Thank you, Nettlebed, I shall be on my guard." Having known the butler all her life, Sarah was well aware that as the source of all information at Cranleigh he was possessed of an uncanny ability to read the implications in even the most ordinary of situations. If he suspected the motives of her brother and his wife, then it behooved her to move cautiously.

Whatever could Harold and Rosalind be concocting? Sarah had no idea, but she could hazard a well-educated guess as to its general purpose. It undoubtedly had something to do with her newly acquired fortune. She had never wished for such a windfall, in fact, it had never occurred to her that her grandmother might leave it to anyone except Harold, but it had been worth any trouble that might ensue just to see the expression of horror and disgust on her brother's face when the will had been read.

The preposterous proposal from poor Richard had alerted Sarah that she was not going to be allowed to enjoy her inheritance in peace, and she could not help but wonder what Rosalind's latest scheme was for diverting the fortune from Sarah to herself. Like Nettlebed, Sarah, well aware of the limits of her brother's mental powers, had no difficulty in identifying the true inspiration behind all these machinations.

"You wished to see me?" Sarah could have laughed aloud as she entered the library, so obvious was it that the pair were up to something. Her brother looked distinctly uneasy while his wife's dark eyes had a triumphant sparkle that boded no good for anyone except the Marchioness of Cranleigh.

"Yes, er . . ." Harold struggled to adopt a suitably impressive expression, which only made him appear more absurdly pompous than ever. "As you no doubt are aware, Sarah," he began majestically, "the duties of Marquess of Cranleigh are many and varied. They have been handed down from one generation to another as a most sacred trust, which the Melfords have always fulfilled with the utmost of distinction. As the years have passed, these duties have only increased in number and complexity. I, as my father before me, was raised to fulfill these ancient and honored obligations and have always endeavored to do so with the utmost of my abilities." To the profound relief of his listeners, Harold at last stopped to draw breath. In doing so, he made the mistake of looking at his sister to reassure himself that she was suitably affected by his words, only to find her regarding him with such blank curiosity that he entirely lost the thread of his long and tangled speech.

"What Harold is trying to say," Rosalind interjected swiftly before her husband could gather his befuddled thoughts, "is that the costs of maintaining Cranleigh are positively ruinous, and what with his political obligations your brother is in a most difficult situation. His duty to the nation requires that he keep up a good appearance in London, which, as you know, is shockingly expensive." Fortunately, Rosalind, even though she never gave a thought to anyone else's opinion, did not look at her sister-in-law, for she could not have failed to detect the ironic twinkle that appeared in Sarah's eyes at the thought of Harold, forced by loyalty to his country to support a fashionable wife and live in the best possible style.

Rosalind proceeded to make her point. "And as you are the main reason that Cranleigh is kept open and fully staffed . . ."

But here Sarah, by now well aware of the direction the conversation was taking, hastened to interrupt. "And I appreciate Harold's concern for my welfare. However, he need worry himself no longer, as I have been making arrangements to purchase Ashworth and shall therefore no longer be a charge on him in any way." It was with some difficulty that Sarah kept the acid note out of her voice. It was not as though she had been such a great burden to her brother after all. In fact, her presence had spared him the necessity of having to keep such a tremendous staff, and it had been Sarah, not Harold, who had discovered that the former bailiff had been pocketing a goodly portion of the rents due the marquess. If anything, she had saved Harold considerable expense rather than incurring it. If Sarah had not become inured to her brother's self-centeredness, she would have been furious rather than amused at his feeble attempts to claim a share of what was left to her by her grandmother. As it was, she was enjoying herself immensely as the full implications of her proposal sank in. Harold's expression of horror and outrage were perfect.

"Set up your own household? Why, I have never heard of anything so absurd, or improper! As your guardian I will not allow you to ruin yourself in such a way!" her brother shouted.

Sarah rose, smiling sweetly. "I thank you for your solicitude, Harold, but as I am of age, my welfare is none of your affair, and, as you so correctly pointed out, it is high time that I look after myself instead of expecting you to support me. Miss Trimble has agreed to join me as my companion, and I have already engaged a staff to see to my needs." This last was not entirely true, for there had not yet been time for Sarah to hear from her former governess, but knowing the woman's affection for her, she felt reasonably assured of the reply. As to the rest of the staff, she was more than amply provided for and in fact had been forced to refuse those from Cranleigh who had begged to come with her when they heard of her plans. With that parting shot she quitted the room, leaving her brother and his wife dumbfounded.

Rosalind was the first to recover. "Of course you will stop her, my lord. This latest queer start of hers is the height of eccentricity and extravagance. It will ruin her," she hissed fiercely.

Her husband, meanwhile, could do nothing but sputter helplessly. He knew very well that Sarah had remained quietly in the country and, with the exception of her unfortunate tendency toward intellectual pursuits, conducted herself with reasonable propriety simply because she wished to and not in obedience to any dictates of his. In fact, for all that she was serenely good-natured, Sarah had a will and a mind of her own, which were both far stronger and infinitely superior to her brother's. At last he gasped, "Outrageous! You must do something, my lady. As a female you understand the importance, nay, the *necessity* of a spotless reputation. I leave it to *you* to reason with her, if reason can be applied to such a ridiculous notion." And, having spoken, the marquess stumped furiously from the room, abdicating to his wife, as always, the responsibility for remedying the situation.

When in doubt, Harold usually blustered, and it usually had its desired effect, which was to leave observers so intimidated by his annoyance and his exalted position as Marquess of Cranleigh that they took care of whatever was upsetting him. Such was not the case with his wife, but Rosalind, knowing the truth of the matter, was well aware that it was up to her to discover a solution whenever her husband was unequal to the task, which was most of the time.

Sighing, Rosalind pressed a hand to her forehead, which truly was aching now, and tried desperately to think of what to do next. In truth, she rather envied Sarah, who had so blithely and easily freed herself from Harold's annoying presence. She also knew that once Sarah had made up her mind, nothing and no one could change it. The best Rosalind could do, as she saw her dreams slipping away and her schemes going sadly awry, was to put a brave face on it and make the best of it. At least with Sarah at Ashworth she would be spared her presence which somehow, for reasons she could not begin to explain, made Rosalind feel the tiniest bit inadequate. The marchioness knew she was far more beautiful, far more sought after than her sister-in-law, but Sarah's very lack of interest in such things robbed her of a sense of superiority. It was Sarah's quiet competence, her unruffled attitude toward everything, coupled with the fact that no matter what order Rosalind or Harold issued, the servants always confirmed it with Sarah that contrived to make Cranleigh's new mistress feel just the slightest bit of relief that Sarah was going.

Rosalind sighed again and rose from her chair. Feeling sorry for herself would do nothing for her; in time she would figure something out. She always got her own way in the end, and this would be no different. Besides, she had a house party to plan and the attentions of two of the *ton*'s most dashing gentlemen to look forward to. After all, who had need of a fortune when one had wealthy admirers to lavish one with beautiful tokens of their esteem. True, she could hardly take Lord Farringdon or the Chevalier d'Evron to London's most fashionable modiste and order a new wardrobe, but a clever and beautiful woman could manage, and she, Rosalind, Lady Melford, Marchioness of Cranleigh, was just such a woman.

Her spirits somewhat restored, Rosalind went off in search of Mrs. Dawlish to give the housekeeper instructions regarding the guests soon to descend on Cranleigh.

Chapter Seven

Some days later in distinctly bachelor quarters in Mount Street, a dark-haired gentleman sat, a glass of brandy in one hand, a gilt-edged invitation in the other, and a sardonic smile on his face as though he were relishing a private joke. In fact, he was. Alistair, Lord Farringdon, Earl of Burnleigh, well known for his own brazen behavior, could appreciate such recklessness in someone else, and this invitation from the Marchioness of Cranleigh was just that. She must be quite thoroughly bored if she were willing to risk gossip among the town tabbies by inviting *him* to Cranleigh. He had enjoyed a discreet but passionate flirtation with Rosalind, but it had been over for some time and quite forgotten until now. Though young, she had been so beautiful and so accomplished in every trick designed to make a man's pulse race that Alistair had been more attracted to her than he had been to any woman in quite some time. In fact, the only flaw in the entire affair had been the young lady's insistence on marriage or nothing, a proposition that Lord Farringdon, one of London's most dedicated bachelors, had regretfully declined.

Of course, he had soon found consolation in the arms of a lively widow whose principles were not nearly as nice as Rosalind's, but then, neither had she been as enticing as the lovely young miss who had taken the *ton* by storm that Season. Being much sought after by ladies of every station, Alistair had not repined over his loss; he had even had the magnanimity to feel a little sorry that such a very talented coquette as the new Marchioness of Cranleigh should be forced to accept a life with someone as dull and respectable as Harold. However, Rosalind had craved social cachet and a secure place in the *ton* more than anything else. As Marchioness of Cranleigh she certainly had these. Giving her credit for having gotten what she wanted, Alistair consoled himself with the thought that rank and wealth outweighed Harold's lack of style or personality.

However, now it was obvious to Alistair that such was not precisely the case. The young miss, intent on securing a place for herself in the fashionable world, had now become a dashing young matron determined to make up for a husband completely devoid of éclat by taking advantage of the freedom that her married status conferred upon her.

Rosalind, like so many others who had married for worldly advantage, was not about to sacrifice romance and delicious dalliance—she had merely deferred them. If he had not been so amused by the transparency of the lady's machinations, Alistair would have been just the slightest bit disgusted. She had dropped his acquaintance quickly enough when it became apparent that he had absolutely no intention of making her his countess. Now, however, it appeared that once again he could be useful to her, and she was more than ready to acknowledge him again.

Alistair chuckled drily. He had no objection to being exploited in such a manner. After all, he never had been under any illusion that he had ever meant more to Rosalind than did her fashionable gowns or her jewels. He was merely another accoutrement for an incomparable to flaunt before the envious eyes of the *ton*, another indication of the power of her attractions. He had known that from the outset and enjoyed her accordingly.

Lord Farringdon glanced again at the invitation. He was also willing to bet any amount of money that the Chevalier d'Evron, another of Rosalind's cicisbeos who had refused to come up to scratch, had also been invited to this particular house party. For Alistair, the probable presence of the charming Frenchman was a far greater reason for heeding the summons from Cranleigh than the beauteous Rosalind.

For all that Rosalind was lovely and exceedingly skilled at the art of dalliance, she was one among many, and the chance to feast his eyes on the creamy skin, voluptuous figure, and perhaps kiss the tantalizing lips of the marchioness was not enough to lure him from the arms of his current mistress or the smiles of his latest flirts; however, the opportunity to keep an eye on the Frenchman was.

The Chevalier d'Evron had appeared in London some years before, about the time that Bonaparte had assumed the role of

First Consul. Armed with the story of an escape to Switzerland at the height of the Revolution, the chevalier maintained that the stolid respectability of the Swiss had driven him mad with boredom, thus forcing him to flee once again. Determining that England was the only place fit to live for a man of his cultivated tastes, he had made his way through Bavaria and Prussia and at last to London, or so his tale went. However, unlike most of the émigrés who had barely escaped France with their lives, the chevalier seemed to lack nothing as far as pecuniary resources were concerned.

He had taken a handsome suite of rooms in Curzon Street, gotten himself proposed as a member of White's, where he won just enough to be a player worth taking on and lost just enough to remain on good terms with everyone. In general he had made himself so agreeable that no one, with the exception of Lord Farringdon and one or two others, had thought anything about it.

Alistair, however, always more alert than the rest of society, had wondered at it all. Almost without exception, the other noble refugees lived in genteel poverty, forced to support themselves as best they could, while the chevalier lived in as much style as any wealthy young Englishman. His suspicions aroused, Lord Farringdon had made discreet inquiries among the French population in London and, not much to his surprise, had discovered that though the chevalier was well enough known now, no one seemed to claim an acquaintance with him that had existed prior to the Revolution.

This was enough to convince the Earl of Burnleigh that the chevalier bore watching. Of course it was possible that he had been able to smuggle a huge fortune out of revolutionary France, but it was highly unlikely. No other émigré had been able to do so. Alistair could only think that the young Frenchman was so plump in the pocket because it was being filled regularly by someone—someone such as Napoleon Bonaparte. Lord Farringdon was more than well acquainted with men in the pay of the Corsican upstart. The Earl of Burnleigh had been making it his business for the last eight years to learn everything he could about the people who were collecting intelligence for the Emperor. After so many years spent watching such people, he had gained a sixth sense for men who were not what they appeared to be.

Eventually, Alistair himself had become one of those who

was not what he appeared to be, and at last had found something that had satisfied his yearning for a purposeful yet invigorating existence. Wild and adventurous to a fault, and having won all the curricle races, seduced the most courted opera dancers, and dallied with the brightest diamonds of the Upper Ten Thousand, Lord Farringdon had become bored beyond belief with life in the *ton* when, fortunately for him, the Treaty of Amiens was signed. This gave him the opportunity he had been waiting for.

Eager to escape the same old routine of routs and balls, days spent betting on absurdities in the clubs along Saint James's, he had been one of the first to hurry over to France to learn for himself what had happened after the Revolution. Courting excitement in his usual way, he had frequented areas that others with a more healthy respect for their own skins might have avoided, and he had sought out people from every level of society in order to discover more about life under Napoleon. The more he had learned about Bonaparte, the more fascinated he had become with the man—his drive, his ambition, his brilliant tactics, and his organizational genius. It was during the course of all this that Alistair became aware of the leader's *Bureau d'Intelligence*. This formidable force of one hundred and seventeen men devoted to ferreting out intelligence about England and France's other enemies was something that England could not compete with. Its existence worried Lord Farringdon, who could see that it would not be long before England and France were again at each other's throats.

When he had returned to London, Alistair had gone directly to friends in Whitehall with all the information he had gleaned. However, the powers that were did not take readily to his suggestions that they set up a corresponding organization similar to the *Bureau*. "It sounds to me like spying, lad," one beefy-faced general had blustered, "and spying is only the slightest bit less dishonorable than being an out-and-out traitor."

As this disdainful attitude appeared to exist throughout the government and the military, Lord Farringdon had begun to despair of anybody's heeding his concerns, but at long last one day at Tattersall's he came across a relatively distant acquaintance, Lieutenant Colonel (as he was then) Sir George Murray, a man of excellent capacities whom Alistair dimly remembered as having a passion for information and organization. Latching on to the lieutenant colonel, Alistair had hurried the man back to his chambers in Mount Street, where he had plied him with port and all the intelligence he had been able to gather in France.

Unlike his peers, Sir George had listened closely and intently, seemingly receptive to Alistair's suggestions. Unfortunately, however, he had disappeared from the scene soon after that, leaving Lord Farringdon to conclude that he was as unenlightened and disappointing as all the rest and that Napoleon with his superior organization would walk all over the British, who preferred retaining their honor at all costs, even if it meant defeat at the hands of the Corsican monster. When Murray resurfaced later, it was to invite Alistair to call on him in his rather obscure office high on the top floor of Whitehall, where he proceeded to acknowledge in a roundabout, almost apologetic way that, following the suggestions of Lord Farringdon and other interested parties, he and others had set up a Depot of Military Knowledge. Furthermore, Murray, who knew that he and many members of the Depot were likely to be called into active service at any time, asked Lord Farringdon if perhaps he might be interested in helping them out.

It was a heaven-sent opportunity, though at the time Alistair had not recognized quite how fortuitous it was. Bored though he was with life in the *ton*, he had found nothing that truly sparked his interest. He had a superb bailiff who looked after his estates in Somersetshire, besides which, country pursuits had never held the least allure. Lord Farringdon found his rural neighbors, though they were decent and upright folk, to be lacking in any spark of curiosity or originality. They in turn viewed him as full of outrageously revolutionary ideas, too much of a libertine in his pursuits, and far too attractive to be allowed near wives and daughters.

Nor did the military, though it offered a far more challenging and adventurous existence, interest the earl, who discovered that, to a large degree, it resembled nothing so much as a herd of bluff hearty sheep. They were good, courageous fellows, all of them, but without a unique thought or personality among them, and never encountered in groups of less than three or four boisterous fellows all devoted to following commands unquestioningly, no matter how stupid or how blind the person who issued them.

Such regimentation was not for Lord Farringdon. Having spent a lonely and isolated childhood virtually forgotten by worldly parents, who, possessing nothing in common with one another except the number and variety of *affaires de coeur* with which they sought to amuse themselves and compete against each other, Alistair had been forced to depend on himself for everything—amusement, education, and guidance. By the time he was packed off to school at a tender age, he was far too individualistic to be accepted easily by his fellows. They were highly suspicious of someone who thought for himself without bothering to take a consensus. He, in turn, was scornful of those who did not dare to attempt anything on their own without first checking the acceptability of their actions among their peers, and then constantly seeking approval while carrying them out.

The same sort of situation prevailed when he entered the *ton*. In truth, the only group who had accepted him wholeheartedly and with a great deal of appreciation was its female members, none of whom, old or young, married or in their first Season, seemed immune to his dashing good looks or his reckless charm. Alistair had reciprocated their appreciation with flattering attention to all of them. He had a ready wit and a genuine interest in everyone from the most stately dowager to the demurest young miss, which made him a most amusing partner for a quadrille, a tête-à-tête, or something even more intimate. The only criticism that could be leveled at him at all was his singular aversion to matrimony, but his charm was such that very few ladies could even hold this against him for long.

However, one could not make a career, or even a life out of dalliance, or at least no one as intelligent and energetic as Alistair could. Thus, hungering for something more out of his existence, he had been delighted with Murray's invitation to help them out at the Depot of Military Knowledge.

Espionage suited Lord Farringdon to perfection. Scorned by most of society as a most dishonorable occupation, its reliance on iron nerves, quick thinking, careful observation, deduction, cool resourcefulness, and a willingness to act on one's own initiative made it a profession ideally suited to the Earl of Burnleigh. With his connections among the *ton* and acquaintances in the sporting world, he was able to move with ease in a variety of spheres, watching and listening for any conversations, any actions that might be in the least suspicious.

Murray and his fellow officers at Whitehall were well aware

that French agents swarmed along the coast, especially in Kent, disguised most frequently as smugglers. What they were less certain of was where these agents were procuring the information that was being sent back to France. Someone with access to the highest levels was passing along intelligence to these men, and though Murray's organization was perfectly capable of hunting down these individual spies, it was an exercise in futility until the major source of information was stopped. The identification of the traitor or spy with access to such vital secrets was the task that Murray had assigned to Lord Farringdon. After months of diligent appearance at every function likely to attract government officials and military men, and months of careful scrutiny, Alistair had at last come to the conclusion that somehow the Chevalier d'Evron was behind it all.

What remained to be done was to catch the chevalier in a compromising situation, a situation preferably that would reveal as much as possible of his organization so that those in the Depot could, in one fell swoop, eradicate it entirely. Now it seemed that a perfect opportunity was presenting itself. Rosalind's invitation had mentioned the possible presence of Lord Edgecumbe, a man of so much power and importance in the affairs of state that it behooved anyone who wished to know the true disposition of the government toward any issue to spend some time in his company.

Alistair smiled broadly. Yes, the odds were excellent that the chevalier would also be putting in an appearance at Cranleigh, but even if he were not, the chance to reconnoiter the Kentish coast for suspicious activity and divert himself with the fair Rosalind were attractions enough to lure him there. After penning a note to the marchioness, Alistair instructed his man to prepare them for a trip to the country. It would be pleasant to see Richard again, too. Lord Tredington was making mice feet of his inheritance, but he still was most amusing company and ripe for any mischief should Rosalind's little house party prove dull.

Chapter Eight

By the time Lord Farringdon arrived at Cranleigh, the rest of the party had gathered. Indeed, the first person he laid eyes on as he tooled his curricle up the sweeping gravel drive was the Chevalier d'Evron, strolling in a leisurely manner through Cranleigh's celebrated rose garden. His gleaming dark head was bent attentively over his companion, whose countenance was obscured by a charming parasol. One glance at the elegant figure beneath this frothy confection was enough to identify her as the mistress of the house. Alistair grinned. His hunches were rarely wrong, and after months of observing the chevalier and his dalliance with Rosalind, he had developed a sixth sense as far as the actions of both of them were concerned. He would have been willing to bet all of his worldly goods that he would find the two of them here in just such a private conversation.

Not wishing to encounter Rosalind until he was good and ready, the earl urged the horses up the drive toward the massive stone portico where the butler, alerted to his arrival by a sharp-eyed stable boy, was awaiting him.

A few minutes later, following the housekeeper to his chambers, Lord Farringdon was struck by the size and impressiveness of Cranleigh. It was clear that there were compensations to be had for marrying the pompous Harold. Cranleigh was certainly one of the finest estates in England. A brilliant shaft of light fell across Alistair's path, and without even thinking he glanced quickly toward the source, an enormous window in what appeared to be the library. Framed in the glow of the afternoon sun which touched the golden highlights in her hair was a young woman standing, book in hand, poring over the text in front of her.

So absorbed was she that she did not even stir or look up as the housekeeper and Lord Farringdon, their footsteps echoing in the vast hall, passed by. Her intentness on the work in her hands was revealed in every line of her slender figure, from the head bent eagerly over the pages to the hands gripping the book, and Alistair, accustomed to the women of the *ton* whose attention was most often fixed on the effect they were having on those about them, was struck by the almost palpable concentration of the woman in the window.

He was intrigued. Never in his life could he remember having seen a woman read anything deeper than *La Belle Assemblée*, and certainly it was never with the interest of the young lady in the library. It was so rare that anyone of Lord Farringdon's acquaintance expended any energy on anything that the image of the solitary reader, brief though it was, impressed the earl and remained with him as he followed Mrs. Dawlish to his chambers. Who was the woman? What was she reading that made her so oblivious to her surroundings? Did she approach everything in her life with such dedication, or was there something so important about that particular book? Having had infinite experience with women of all sorts, Alistair was surprised to come across one who did not readily fit into any of the usual patterns he recognized. He looked forward to meeting her and discovering more about her.

In the meantime, while one of her guests was busy with his speculations, the hostess herself was being subjected to a most interesting, though not necessarily comfortable examination in the rose garden. What Lord Farringdon had assumed to be a delicious tête-à-tête, and what Rosalind had expected to be a delightful interlude from her duties as mistress of Cranleigh, was turning out to be a great deal less delightful and a great deal more threatening than she could have possibly foreseen.

Bending down to gaze deep into the dark eyes shaded by the parasol, the Frenchman smiled enigmatically at her as he spoke. "Yes, my dear Rosalind, as I previously mentioned, I believe that we can be of enormous help to one another."

Rosalind eyed him doubtfully. This was not the way things were supposed to be. Men were supposed to aid and protect women, not the other way around. She laughed lightly. "Oh am sure I do not know what you mean, Chevalier; how could I, helpless female that I am, possibly do anything for you?"

The chevalier's smile broadened. Flutter her eyelashes and flash her dimples though she might, the marchioness was not the least bit helpless. One look at the determined expression in those deep brown eyes and the sound of the steely undertone in the soft voice were proof enough that she was a woman to be reckoned with. But the chevalier had been dealing with far uglier customers than the Marchioness of Cranleigh for the better part of his life, and he was not the least bit daunted.

"Why, I find myself in a most desperate situation, my lady," he continued smoothly. "There are those in France who would dearly love to be rid of me, and, though they are on the other side of the Channel and at war with us, they have a very long reach, long enough to dispose of me when and where they will."

"No!" Rosalind gasped in horror and clapped a dainty hand to her mouth. "You are under the protection of English law now."

The chevalier smiled grimly. "Law, I assure you, has little to do with it when men are this determined." He did not bother to enlighten her as to the reasons behind their menacing behavior, which involved his betraying the secrets of those who had saved him from the guillotine.

"You could save me, Rosalind," he murmured softly.

Her eyes widened. "I? I have no knowledge of such things."

"No, you are much too lovely, much too delicate even to know that such wickedness exists, but you do know much that could be of value to me." She stared at him blankly as he elaborated. "Come now. Your husband is an important man in the government. Surely, he must tell you many things that would be of interest to my tormentors, information that I could trade for my life."

The marchioness, still gazing at him in patent astonishment, shook her head slowly. The idea of Harold's discussing anything intelligent with her was ludicrous in the extreme. Of course his ostensible reason for confining himself to the most mundane topics of conversation with her was that she should not trouble her charming head with such weighty affairs, but leave them to men such as he to sort out. However, the real reason was somewhat different. Rosalind knew, and she imagined that her husband suspected, that she was a great deal cleverer than he. In some areas this superiority did not matter, but politics was not one of them. The Marquess of Cranleigh liked to think himself an authority on affairs of state, and he was not about to threaten that position by discussing them with his wife. "No." With an effort Rosalind concealed her relief at being able to deny all knowledge of Harold's affairs. She was not a prude or a prosy Methodist, but what the chevalier was proposing did not sound entirely honorable. "No, he never speaks of such things to me."

"However, I am sure that Lord Edgecumbe, so much more perceptive a gentleman than your husband, realizes that you are quite intelligent enough to understand whatever he may confide in you as to the latest problems that are pressing him," the chevalier persisted smoothly.

Rosalind sensed that they were reaching rather dangerous ground. Suddenly, it seemed as though the eyes of the chevalier, which had been fixed so intently upon her, were menacing rather than admiring. She had always been rather attracted by his intensity; now she found it quite unnerving—she was not so helpless a creature as to call it frightening, not yet anyway.

Rosalind laughed gaily. "Oh really, sir"—she fluttered her eyelashes—"you know men do not wish to speak of such things with me. They prefer to speak of things far more interesting than dull politics, a topic that I assure you I find to be excessively boring." She smiled up at him archly.

At this point another man would have been unable to think of anything but her ripe red lips parted so invitingly or the sparkle of dark eyes, the voluptuous bosom that heaved under the thin silk of a gracefully draped French scarf. In fact, in the white-and-black striped India muslin walking dress made tight to her shape and artfully ornamented with jet bead trimmings, the marchioness was the picture of female beauty. However, all this was lost on her companion, whose relentless pursuit of his own concerns was making her distinctly uncomfortable.

"Perhaps you do not discuss things with your husband and Lord Edgecumbe now, my dear marchioness, but I should like to suggest that you do so in the future. You are the only one to whom I can turn. Believe me, dear lady, my life is in your hands." The chevalier's dark eyes smoldered with passion, and he snatched one gloved hand to raise it to his lips. No woman ever before had been able to resist the idea that she alone had power over his destiny.

But Rosalind, despite being breathlessly aware of his fervent gaze and not entirely unaffected by his impetuous plea for help, possessed a strong sense of self-preservation, and this sense was now telling her that no matter how charming the supplicant, or how desperate the cause, betraying one's country was not good *ton,* and Rosalind never did anything that was not good *ton.*

Summoning as much regret as she could muster, the marchioness sighed gently as she replied, "I am distressed beyond measure to hear that you are in such difficulties, sir, but I am, I fear, a poor person to rely upon for such assistance. No one tells a woman anything of any consequence; you know that."

The warmth in the chevalier's eyes disappeared to leave them gleaming hard and dark as obsidian. The mobile mouth thinned unpleasantly into an unyielding line. "I think, my dear lady, that you *will* help me. It does not matter whether or not they offer to confide in you; you will make them do so. No"—he raised an admonitory hand as Rosalind opened her mouth to protest—"I feel confident that you will do most excellently well. And, if you do not"—his voice grew softer and even more menacing—"you will find that your brother's reverses at the gaming table will be so well known that he will be in utter disgrace."

"Richard?" Rosalind tried to laugh carelessly, but there was a rising edge to her voice. "He is always under the hatches. The Tredingtons are that way, you know. We are very expensive."

"In debt, yes," the chevalier continued silkily, "but not ruined, yet. I have in my possession the vowels for all of his gambling debts, the sum of which is many times the value of Tredington Park. A gentleman without money is one thing, but a gentleman without a home is quite another."

"You would not!" Rosalind gasped. All attempts at coquetry were gone now, and the dark eyes glistened with unshed tears, but the chevalicr was as unmoved by the marchioness's distress as he had been by her flirtatiousness.

"No, I would not, or, I shall not, if you supply me with the information I must have."

There was a long silence. "Very well. Tell me what you wish me to do," the marchioness replied listlessly.

The chevalier quickly suppressed a triumphant grin. "Oh, I am certain that you will get the knack of it very soon. I wish to know anything on troop movements, changes in command, increases or decreases in forces, information on French agents who are being watched for the moment or have been caught—any number of things can be of great interest to me. You are a clever woman, my dear; I have no doubt that you will be able to elicit precisely what I wish to know, and"—he wagged a playful finger at her—"do not doubt for one moment that I will know when you are holding something back on me. Now, I am delighted that we have come to this understanding of ours. I thank you for sharing your lovely garden with me, but I have some letters that I must write, and I do believe that I heard a carriage in the drive. I shall leave you to attend to your guests."

With one more enigmatic smile and a quick bow, he headed toward the house, leaving Rosalind to sink helplessly onto a low stone bench, her heart thudding violently. She had expected her walk with the chevalier to quicken her pulse, but not quite in this particular way. Odious man! How could she ever have thought he was the least bit attractive. There was nothing for it, but to do as she was asked. She could never let the man expose Richard—think of the scandal of it all—she would never survive it. The *ton* would never forgive her for having a brother so disgraced.

Rosalind sighed and headed into the house herself. Things were not turning out at all the way she had planned. She paused on the threshold. Alistair! For a moment, in her shock and distress over the chevalier's ungentlemanly behavior, she had forgotten Lord Farringdon. How clever you are, Rosalind, she congratulated herself silently, Alistair will help you.

The Marchioness of Cranleigh had always felt that it was most expedient for a woman to possess more than one admirer, and now she was about to prove the correctness of this belief. She was still left with one gallant to enliven the house party for her and to offer her the amusing interludes she had planned for herself and, quite possibly, he also represented the solution to her difficulties. Somehow the Earl of Burnleigh appeared to be the sort of person able to deal with such creatures as the Chevalier d'Evron. There had always been an air of energetic resourcefulness about Alistair that was so noticeably lacking in the other bucks of the *ton*. Though Rosalind had seen him at work only in the drawing rooms and ballrooms of the fashionable world, charming one diamond or another, or heard of his curricle races and his prowess on the hunting field, she had always sensed in the man a strength and a forcefulness that was capable of overcoming anything. She was certainly in dire need of such a man now.

That was it. She would throw herself on his mercy and beg

him to help her. This thought was so reassuring that Rosalind could almost smile again, but she quickly adjusted her expression. If she was to follow through with her plan to request Alistair's assistance, she must not look too carefree. There was nothing that enhanced a woman's attractiveness so much as an air of mystery or of sorrow nobly borne. Smoothing her skirts and adjusting her shawl into a more enticing drape over her bosom, the marchioness went in search of her recently arrived guest.

Chapter Nine

Unlike her sister-in-law, Sarah had spent a good deal of the day trying to put the thought of the Earl of Burnleigh and his imminent appearance at Cranleigh entirely out of her mind. In previous weeks she had avoided all thoughts of the impending gathering by throwing herself into her removal to Ashworth, which had proven to be less unsettling than she had feared it might be.

In the first place, she loved the house itself. The warm brick manor house with its many windows and cozy rooms was far more welcoming than Cranleigh. She loved the distant view of the sea afforded by the windows in her bedchamber and the library. In fact, once she had arranged all her books and a few favorite pieces of furniture, Sarah realized that she felt happier and more comfortable than she had felt in a long time. To be sure, she had lived her entire life at Cranleigh, and she and her grandmother had overseen the running of the great house, but neither her brother nor her father had ever allowed her to feel that she was more than a temporary inhabitant there, a fixture until she was married off.

When Rosalind had come to Cranleigh, Sarah's sense of being extraneous had only deepened, so it was with great relief that Sarah crossed her own threshold, secure in the knowledge that she belonged and that she and only she had the right to be there. The house was solely her responsibility. She actually looked forward to seeing to its upkeep and all the repairs that were needed after it had stood empty for so long, and she threw herself into a myriad of tasks with more interest and vigor than she had felt for some time.

But as always, her delightful solitude was short-lived. In the end Harold had given in, not that he truly had any choice, and allowed her to move, provided she return to mingle with the guests so as not to appear too eccentric. Sarah's attendance at

Cranleigh had been required the very instant the first guests had arrived, and she had been given the responsibility of looking after Lady Edgecumbe and her two daughters.

Lady Edgecumbe was not so bad as Sarah had expected. Unlike Harold's and Rosalind's other fashionable acquaintance, she could not have cared less about the *ton*. Descending from her enormous traveling coach, clad in a carriage dress that even Sarah had recognized as being outmoded, she had given Sarah one quick appraising look, announcing in a forthright manner, "You look as though you have some sense about you; tell me, do they rotate the crops here at Cranleigh or let the fields lie fallow for a year?"

Lady Edgecumbe's manner was somewhat rough, and her constant interrogation could be a trifle exhausting, but in the main, Sarah had found her to be a great deal better than she had feared. At least the woman wished to discuss something seriously, even if agriculture remained the single topic of her conversation.

The two of them had rubbed along in a tolerably companionable manner as Sarah, though not as enthralled by husbandry as her guest, was sufficiently knowledgeable to converse intelligently with her. The daughters, on the other hand, were another matter. Great awkward girls both of them, Cordelia and Lucinda had inherited their mother's coarse features, high color, and sense of self-importance. They, however, also possessed some pretension to fashion and were delighted to discover that Sarah was far less conversant with the *ton* than they. Rosalind had not been entirely correct in labeling them bluestockings, for their lack of social graces stemmed from a complete absence of wit and a tendency to talk at length about their own concerns rather than any interest in more erudite matters.

Both of them, in addition to having frequented the local assemblies in Buckinghamshire, had had a Season and were consequently more than happy to patronize their less worldly hostess with stories of their flirtations and their conquests. Unfashionable though she might be, Sarah was well enough aware of the refined tastes of the *ton* to be certain that the Edgecumbe girls had probably not been accorded all the admiration they considered their due, but she did not challenge their superiority, allowing them instead to think that she believed entirely their overblown estimation of their social success.

In fact, Sarah was more amused than anything else at the airs of Lucinda and Cordelia, whose overbearing attitudes only added to their physical gracelessness. Galling though it was to acknowledge it, Sarah admitted to herself that living with Rosalind had taught her what to expect from a true incomparable.

Sarah had also been mildly diverted at the sight of the obvious and utterly useless lures the girls had thrown in the chevalier's direction the moment he had arrived. His lack of enthusiasm was plain to see, but he had borne their assault with good grace, and his Gallic charm was such that neither Cordelia nor Lucinda was aware that he was anything but delighted to lavish attention on them. Observing all this, Sarah could only imagine the effect the Earl of Burnleigh's presence would have on the two of them.

To be sure, the chevalier was good-looking enough with his mobile countenance and dark eyes that gazed with intense concentration and appreciation when he was addressing someone. However, the effect he had, Sarah knew from personal experience, was nothing like that of Lord Farringdon.

She was provided with ample opportunity that evening to reconsider the effect of Lord Farringdon as he was present at dinner, and, though he was seated at the far end of the long mahogany table, Sarah was immediately and uncomfortably aware of his presence. Even Rosalind had not dared to seat him on her right, which was reserved for the Duke of Coltishall, but he was not far away, placed as close to the marchioness as possible and next to the duke's retiring daughter, Lady Amelia.

The Earl of Burnleigh was no less magnetic now than he had been before at Tredington. It was not just that the man presented such a pleasing appearance. Sarah was not one to be impressed by his athletic physique or the bold good looks conferred by a firm jaw, high cheek bones, and enigmatic gray eyes under dark brows. It was the energy and alertness about the man that caught her attention and set him apart from the rest of the world.

There was no doubt about Lord Farringdon's legendary charm. Sarah observed even Lady Edgecumbe's rugged features soften into smiles and laughter as he had led her into dinner. Now Lady Amelia was speaking to him in the most confiding manner. Sarah knew for a fact that that young woman only conversed in monosyllables, if at all, even when addressed by someone as unalarming as Sarah. Earlier that evening, exhausted by her agricultural discussions with Lady Edgecumbe and out of patience with the petty vanity of her daughters, Sarah had done her best to make Lady Amelia feel welcome, but the girl was so shy it had been a considerable effort. Each question had been more difficult than the last, and Sarah found it impossible to sustain a conversation when the other participant responded with a soft yes or no. It was, therefore, with a great deal of curiosity mixed with a begrudging admiration that she watched the Earl of Burnleigh put the young lady at her ease, enough to elicit a smile from her and eventually conversation that was almost animated. There was no doubt that the man had considerable address, Sarah remarked to herself as he turned to answer a question posed by Lady Edgecumbe in a manner that made her outrageously turbaned head nod vigorously in approval.

Mesmerized against her will and fascinated by this adroitness, she became a reluctant spectator as Lord Farringdon entertained the females at his end of the table. So engrossed was Sarah by the entire performance that she was less alert than usual, and the earl, glancing up from his companions for a moment, caught her in mid-stare.

Alistair, inured to languishing looks and plaintive sighs from females of every age and rank, was somewhat taken aback. Here was a woman observing him, not as though she were attracted to him, but as though he were a rather curious scientific specimen. However, his ever-present sense of the absurd asserted itself and he quirked one dark eyebrow humorously at her.

To her consternation, Sarah felt a hot blush rising to her face, but she too was struck by the ridiculousness of the situation—really the man had no shame—and an answering smile, quickly and ruthlessly suppressed, tugged at the corners of her mouth.

"And what did you think of the article in *The Edinburgh Review* on the government of India," a pleasant cultured voice broke into Sarah's disordered thoughts.

She started, colored even more fiercely, and turned to the vicar, who was regarding her with a twinkle in his eyes. "A rare treat for us rustics to observe the *ton* at such a near remove, is it not?" he remarked, nodding in the direction of the gay little group at the end of the table. By this time Rosalind, unable to bear the loss of the earl's attention for more than a few minutes, was entertaining her immediate dinner partners and those within earshot such as Lord Farringdon with a scintillating recitation of the latest *on-dits*.

"Yes, I suppose, if one is diverted by that sort of thing," was Sarah's bemused reply. How utterly embarrassing! It was bad enough that such useless fribbles as Lord Farringdon should even attract her attention, much less to a degree that was noticeable to her longtime friend, the Reverend Thaddeus Witson. It was the vicar who had shown her how many other things there were in the world on which to focus her energy and intellect besides the social milieu, and it was he, along with Lady Willoughby, who had made Sarah feel as though she was a person of value in spite of her distaste for the flirting and coquetry at the local assemblies. Thaddeus Witson had devoted hours of his time to her education long after her governess had departed. That he should catch her gawking like the veriest schoolgirl at a man who from all accounts had quite enough women lavishing attention on him already, was disconcerting in the extreme.

Sternly calling herself to task, Sarah turned to her dinner partner. "Yes, I did read the article, though I confess to being no more enlightened now as to the management of India than before, though I do feel it imperative to employ indigenous peoples in that endeavor as much as possible."

Thaddeus smiled warmly at her. "Certainly that is an opinion that does you great credit." And thus, safely over the awkward moment, the two of them launched into a spirited political discussion so absorbing to them both that the rest of the party receded into the background. Alistair, stealing another glance down the table at the woman who had subjected him to such a cool appraisal, discovered himself completely ignored as she immersed herself deep in earnest colloquy with the scholarly looking gentleman seated to her left.

Everyone else around the earl was speaking with more or less animation to their fellows, but somehow the particular conversation he was now observing appeared to be different from the others. Where those around him were desultory, this was intense, the topic obviously of a serious nature and entirely absorbing to both of them. Unlike so many other exchanges he had witnessed over the years, the lady in this one was as fully engaged as the gentleman. Ordinarily, it seemed to Alistair that in conversations between the men and women of the *ton* the male expounded while the female nodded encouragingly, smiling where appropriate. It was either that or a female who chattered flirtatiously to an admiring masculine audience. This interchange, however, appeared to be a true trading of ideas with the lady as involved as the gentleman and, more unusual yet, each one stopped to listen respectfully to the other.

His interest fairly caught, Alistair resolved to drift closer to the pair when they adjourned to the drawing room for, from the look of it, they were immersed in a debate that was likely to continue for some time, and he was most curious to hear what the lady had to say.

However, when the men joined the ladies in the drawing room, Lady Sarah—Alistair had at least remembered the identity of the observant young lady—was deep in conversation with Lady Edgecumbe. Edging closer to the two women, the earl could just catch the words of the older woman. ". . . rotate the crops in each field and I would highly encourage you to do the same," as well as the reply. "Yes, we do that at Cranleigh, but it is difficult to convince the older farmers of the wisdom of that practice no matter how effective it is proven to be. I do ride out to discuss it with them, but . . ."

"But they are a thick-headed lot." Lady Edgecumbe snorted.

Alistair seized the moment of silence following her remark to interrupt. "And as I recall from my previous visit in this neighborhood, Lady Sarah, you are an exceptionally fine horsewoman. Tell me, do you still have your Ajax? He was a most impressive animal as I remember."

Sarah was taken aback that the earl should insinuate himself into the conversation without so much as a by-your-leave. The nerve of the man was incredible! He seemed to think that she was as readily bowled over by good looks and easy address as her sister-in-law and the Edgecumbe girls, all of whom were watching Lord Farringdon's every move with varying degrees of obviousness. Still, she could not help being impressed, and even the tiniest bit flattered that he remembered her. "Why, thank you," she replied coolly. "Yes, I still have Ajax, who remains a most loyal and excellent mount." Sarah calmly surveyed the earl, refusing to initiate further conversation. If the man wished to intrude upon them, then let him take responsibility for the discussion.

He did. After a brief appreciative glance at Sarah—the lady appeared to be awake on all suits—Alistair launched into a series of informed remarks and questions concerning estates and their management. Soon the conversation was flowing as smoothly as if it had never been interrupted.

It was some time before Sarah noticed what had happened, and not until the middle of her description of draining a field at Cranleigh a few years back that she realized that somehow, instead of ending their discussion, the earl was actually enlivening it. He did have an inquiring mind and a felicitous turn of phrase that seemed to inspire even Lady Edgecumbe into something like vivacity. Loath though she was to admit it, Sarah became aware that she was actually enjoying herself.

For his part, Alistair was equally struck. He did feel inordinately pleased with himself for having won over the most difficult person in the room. Having interpreted, with a fair degree of accuracy, Sarah's initial categorization of him as a creature of the *ton,* he had set out to prove to her that she could not dismiss him so easily. Oh, he could tell that she disapproved of him as a rake and a libertine, and she did not consider him worthy of serious attention, and he could not help being irked by it. That she should so obviously look down on him, and then equally obviously enjoy the company of the unassuming vicar made her something of a challenge to Lord Farringdon.

Besides, the earl was tired of women hanging on his every word and trying to entrap him into intimate conversations. There was something about Sarah that appealed to Alistair. She appeared so serene, so quietly self-assured among the rest of the ladies, all of whom were vying for attention in one way or another. Glancing around to check on everyone else's reactions, laughing or smiling, always with an eye to who was observing, they never let their gazes settle on anyone for more than a second. And in the midst of all this was Lady Sarah Melford, quietly and unconcernedly being herself.

Alistair could not immediately call to mind anyone, especially a woman, who demonstrated such an air of self-possession, and he found it rather attractive. He had been taken by it, in fact, from the moment he had entered the drawing room. To be sure, his pride, piqued by a woman who was visibly unimpressed by him, had also urged him into speaking to her, but it was more than that. For some inexplicable reason

Lord Farringdon wanted to become acquainted with Lady Sarah in a way that was deeper and most unlike his customary flirtatious relationships with women. As he conversed with her, the Earl of Burnleigh resolved privately to discover more about her customary habits so as to seek out Lady Sarah at moments when they were not being so closely and critically observed by everyone.

Chapter Ten

Oddly enough, it was Rosalind who, luring the earl into a stroll along the terrace some time later, gave him his first information about her sister-in-law. As they left the drawing room, the marchioness sighed, laying a white hand on his sleeve and gazing up at Alistair, her eyes wide and her expression one of hidden sorrow. "I am so glad you were able to come to Cranleigh." there was another gentle sigh. "My life has been rather difficult of late, and your presence is one of the only pleasures I have had this age."

Rosalind paused briefly, waiting for encouragement, but as none was forthcoming, she continued. "Harold has not been himself at all, what with this dreadful business over Lady Willoughby."

This was not the conversation Alistair had expected, and forgetting that he had resolved not to let himself be pulled into anything, he echoed in surprise, "Lady Willoughby?" and then cursed himself for a fool at being so easily led into what was bound to be a situation that required some assistance from him.

"Yes, Harold's grandmother had led him to believe he was her heir, and then left everything to Sarah. Who could have foreseen such a thing? It is beyond thinking of—a tremendous fortune all for a young woman who cares about nothing except reading and tramping around the countryside—when Harold has so many things he could do with it.

"Lady Sarah, an heiress?" Certainly the quietly dressed unobtrusive person Alistair had observed that evening acted nothing like the heiresses he had known.

"Yes. And with all of that wealth, she has only become odder than she was already, setting up her own establishment at Ashworth and distributing money to the poor without the least though for her family. You cannot conceive how embarrassing and distressing it is to Harold. In addition, for someone in his position to be forced to live on the income of Cranleigh, which is the merest pittance, is . . . well, you have no notion how lowering it is." Rosalind pressed a hand to her brow and allowed just a hint of tears to glisten in the dark eyes.

Alistair was not particularly certain as to where the conversation was leading, but knowing Rosalind, he felt sure it would eventually involve his helping her out somehow or at the very least being forced into a sympathetic response that would lend spice to an existence that appeared to be boring her. However, as he did wish to learn more about Lady Sarah Melford, there was nothing to do but listen and nod. He could see that Harold deprived of a fortune would hold no attraction whatsoever, and he did feel sorry for Rosalind, but not sorry enough to want to entangle himself in her clutches. The situation required some delicate maneuvering.

Standing there with the light of the waxing moon washing over her and making her eyes appear enormous, the soft breeze gently blowing dark curls against her soft white skin, she was undeniably enticing, but Alistair was inured to her charms, and they no longer held any allure for him. The marchioness was so obviously needy, so patently desperate for an attractive man to solve her problems that he felt not the slightest bit of passion toward her, only pity and the certain knowledge that she would take considerable advantage of any compassion he might exhibit.

Delicately, Alistair removed the hand that was again clutching his arm and turned to face her. A good deal of tact and diplomacy was called for because he wished to remain on good enough terms with her to glean further information about her sister-in-law and about the Chevalier d'Evron, yet he did not want her to cast him in the role of either her savior or her latest flirt. "How very distressing for you," he murmured sympathetically, gently propelling her back toward the doors to the drawing room. "But you are such a leader in society now that everyone follows your example without the least thought of your fortune. You have an elegance of style and a grace that have nothing to do with something as vulgar as money or lack thereof. You are an incomparable now, Rosalind." He spoke her name as though it were an invocation of all that was delicate, refined, and in the first stare of fashion. "And as to your sister-in-law, what is it that she does that could possibly reflect upon you?"

"What does she not?" Rosalind sighed. "In addition to behaving without the least sensibility, she immerses herself in the most inappropriate pursuits—politics and local affairs. Why she reads newspapers and journals as though she were a man. She is forever prosing on about such things with the vicar, and she rides about the countryside in the most indelicate manner on a horse not fit for a lady, without even a groom to accompany her. And to set herself up as mistress of her own establishment! Why, people will say that she is a bluestocking, or worse."

Now that his suspicions were confirmed that such a notable horsewoman as he remembered Lady Sarah to be would be bound to roam about the countryside and was thus easily encountered alone, Alistair was more than ready to rid himself of Rosalind's company. "Surely, no one would think that such behavior had the remotest connection with such an exquisite creature as the Marchioness of Cranleigh. No, I am assured"—here Alistair directed a smile at Rosalind that was at once reassuring and admiring—"that no one blames you in the least. Rather, they have the utmost sympathy and respect for you and all that you are forced to bear."

They had reached the drawing room, and Rosalind was left with nothing to do but thank the earl for escorting her to get a breath of air. "For I am such a poor creature that the closeness of the room was making me feel quite faint." She spoke just audibly enough to be heard by anyone who might have questioned the absence of a beautiful woman and an attractive gentleman on such a lovely evening.

Alistair merely nodded politely. By acquiescing in her wish for a moonlight stroll, he had run a grave risk, the risk of becoming involved once again with Rosalind, but it had proven worth it. He had gleaned useful information about Lady Sarah and had then managed to extricate himself before the marchioness could make the situation more intimate. The earl could see, however, that now he would have to be on his guard. Rosalind was obviously unhappy and equally obviously looking for a man who would dispel that unhappiness. Alistair had not the slightest wish to be that man. If he remained aloof, she would be forced to depend on the chevalier, a solution that would suit the earl to perfection.

Acting on his hunch the next morning, Alistair had his horse saddled up for an early morning ride and, having ascertained from the stable boy the location of Ashworth, he headed off in that direction, keeping a weather eye out for solitary riders.

It was not long before he saw one, and by what he could tell at such a distance from the way the rider sat the horse, it was a female, and a female who rode better than most males, he thought as horse and rider sailed gracefully over a rather daunting hedge. The earl urged his own horse forward, and soon they were directly in the path of the oncoming rider.

Startled at the sight of someone else out at an hour when she could usually count on having the countryside to herself, Sarah reined in hard, bringing her magnificent gray to a screeching halt, his sides heaving. Lady Sarah Melford on horseback was far more impressive than Lady Sarah Melford in the drawing room. Her dress the previous evening had been virtually shapeless, devoid of any style or detail. Now her slate gray habit, severely tailored, fit her to perfection, revealing a lithe, slim figure that seemed molded to the enormous gray stallion, who was snorting with impatience to be off again. The pert little hat emphasized the classic lines of her features while the dull gray of her attire called attention to a flawless complexion glowing with exertion.

The green eyes, however, were colder than they had been the previous evening, regarding the intruder with guarded suspicion. Lady Sarah did not look to be best pleased by this interruption in her day, and for the briefest of moments, Alistair found himself at a loss as to how to proceed. So accustomed was he to alluring glances and welcoming smiles that it took him a moment to adjust to the idea that lady Sarah considered his presence to be an impediment rather than an addition to her appreciation of the fineness of the morning.

You have become an insufferable coxcomb, Farringdon, Allistair muttered under his breath. Blessed with a rather sanguine view of himself, he had often dismissed the women who flocked around him as being governed more by fashion than by actual attraction to his person. Lord Farringdon was rumored throughout the *ton* to be a sad rake, and therefore women did their very best to confirm this reputation. Now, however, he was confronted by one who thought for herself, and things were rather different. Apparently, Lady Sarah neither knew nor cared about his many vaunted attractions. Alistair grinned ruefully. It certainly was a challenge, and there was nothing the Earl of Burnleigh thrived on so much as a challenge.

He leaned forward in the saddle. "Good morning, Lady Sarah. I apologize for intruding on your morning's ride. Had I known how much you treasure this time alone, I should not have accosted you." Alistair was rewarded by a flicker of surprise in the eyes that regarded him so warily. Good! At least he had provoked some reaction besides a general disinclination for his company.

Indeed he had, and more than he realized. That morning Sarah had already been berating herself for her conduct the previous evening. That she had even allowed herself to pay attention to this arrogant coxcomb was bad enough, but actually to enjoy his conversation was beyond belief, especially when he, clearly irked by her lack of appreciation, had sought her out to prove himself at her expense. Lord Farringdon was obviously accustomed to charming women as easily as he breathed, and she had allowed him to do the same to her. Why, she had been no better than the silly Edgecumbe girls, who had thrown themselves at his head. Actually, she was worse, because she was an intelligent, skeptical woman, uninterested in vulgar flirtation, yet she had allowed herself to be won over by a disarming smile and easy address. And now, she could feel the same thing beginning to happen all over again. How provoking!

Alistair had been correct in assuming that Sarah treasured the peace and solitude of her early morning rides. The appearance of anyone who threatened this would have annoyed her, but to have it be the person who had exerted a disconcerting effect on her was upsetting in the extreme. The previous evening she had been immediately aware of the absence of her sister-in-law and the Earl of Burnleigh. She had observed them carefully as they returned to the drawing room and had been unable to suppress the image that so constantly intruded itself on her consciousness where Lord Farringdon was concerned. It was the image of his dark head bent low over Rosalind as he enveloped her in a passionate embrace. No doubt the two of them had been doing much the same sort of thing on the terrace. As always, the thought of it made her knees weaken and her stomach flutter in the oddest way.

Now here was the same man who had caused that effect on

her the night before, looking even more dashing, more vigorous, more vital astride a horse than he had in evening attire. She had known it was Lord Farringdon even when he was too far away to identify his features. There had been no mistaking the athletic figure and the proud bearing of the earl. It would have been cowardly to avoid him so she had steeled herself to meet him, resolving that she would exchange only the briefest, coolest of greetings and then be off. But he had confounded her with his apology. Somehow he had divined her thoughts and acknowledged them with a ready sympathy that utterly disarmed her. Sarah was left with nothing to say except, "Good morning, my lord," with as good a grace as she could muster.

Having surprised her this way, the earl took advantage of Sarah's momentary confusion to continue. "Actually I was in pursuit of much the same solitude as you were. I find that an early morning ride is the best way to reflect on things and work out problems." The look of astonishment on his companion's face was so patent that Alistair could not help but chuckle. "I know that to someone of your serious turn of mind it is inconceivable that a useless fribble such as I should even think, much less consider solving things."

Sarah blushed uncomfortably. Really, dealing with this man was as frustrating as trying to hold water in one's hand; one could never tell the direction he would go in next. Suddenly, she went from being justifiably annoyed at him to feeling rather guilty for having judged him so quickly and on such superficial evidence, dismissing him in precisely the same unthinking way she condemned most of the fashionable world. "I, ah, I mean, I did not, that is . . ." Sarah stammered.

"Don't apologize. In the main it is true; I am a useless fribble and I prefer that most of the world look upon me that way. Admitting to having serious thoughts and concerns makes one most vulnerable, and as I have no wish to share those thoughts with the rest of the heedless world, I do my best to keep that side of me well concealed. You, on the other hand, have chosen a far more sensible course. You remain here in Kent, away from a frivolous and selfish society, in your own establishment where you have no need for such dissimulation, free to be yourself. I am sure that it is a much better way to be."

Now where had that speech come from, Alistair wondered. He had most definitely meant to win her over, but not to the extent of sharing feelings he barely knew he possessed. There had been something in her eyes as she was stammering out her apology, a look of sympathy, that had made him blurt out more than he had meant to. She seemed to see him as a fellow human being instead of in the role society had cast for him, and that little bit of understanding had made Alistair wish to confide in her somehow.

All his life people had been viewing him as a symbol rather than a person. To his parents he had been the bothersome reminder of an unhappy marriage they were doing their best to ignore, an unwanted responsibility and a constant proof that they were growing older. To women of all types he had represented a challenge; his attention to them was an indication of their attractiveness. He was something to amuse them or to make another man jealous. To men he represented the daring life and the freedom they all wished they had, but were either too weak or too cowardly to pursue. To his servants and the tenants on his estate he was a remote godlike figure who, though rarely present, was responsible for all the decisions that governed their lives. But to no one was he just plain Alistair, except, perhaps to the young lady who was regarding him quizzically at this very moment, head tilted slightly to one side, her forehead wrinkled in thought.

"I had never quite considered it that way," Sarah replied slowly. "I never had any interest in the sort of life led in the *ton* so I simply ignored the fashionable world altogether." She paused for a moment before adding, "However, that does not mean I have been completely free to pursue my own interests. People in the country are no less inclined to gossip than those in town. There are just fewer of them. I am regarded as being most eccentric, you know."

"So I have heard." The earl grinned. "And that reputation affords a certain protection in itself. When no one knows quite what to make of a person, they generally leave that person alone. You undoubtedly have become a law unto yourself around here."

It was Sarah's turn to smile. There was something mischievous yet intimate in Lord Farringdon's expression that she could not help responding to. "I suppose I have." Not since Lady Willoughby had died had she shared her private view of the world with anyone in quite this manner. To be sure, there was Thaddeus Witson, who participated in so many of her interests, but he did not possess the same rebellious nature that she did. If he noticed the rest of the world at all, it was in the vaguest sort of way, and he certainly did not care how it related to him. Sarah did notice and she did care, not enough to change herself or to sacrifice her independence, but enough to feel anger at the narrow-mindedness and pettiness of most of society at large.

They both fell silent as they sat gazing over the rich green fields dotted with sheep and the marshes beyond. It was a comfortable silence, the silence of two people at ease with one another's company. Sarah was the first to break it as, glancing at the sun which had risen considerably higher over the treetops, she sighed. "Oh dear, I fear I have stayed away too long. Mr. Dallow is coming to see me about some sheep, and I must not be late." She nodded to the earl, wheeled, and was off before he could so much as think up a reply.

Alistair remained watching her until she became the merest speck in the distance heading toward what appeared to be a rose-colored manor house set in a grove of trees. So that was Ashworth. He smiled to himself. She was a rather taking little thing in her own way and, with her prickly independence, a delightful change from Rosalind and so many other women he had had over the years. He had not done too badly with her; in his presence, and in the space of half an hour she had gone from barely concealed hostility to something like friendliness. Lady Sarah Melford was a challenge, to be sure, but it was a challenge the Earl of Burnleigh was more than equal to.

Chapter Eleven

Riding back to Ashworth, Sarah, like Lord Farringdon, was also marveling at how the earl had been able to transform her dislike of him so easily into something less hostile. How odd, she had felt more at ease with Lord Farringdon than she had with anyone in a long time. Fool, she muttered to herself as she took a low hedge. He is legendary for his charm. You are just another victim of that charm—and a willing, credulous victim at that, she concluded furiously. But she could not really bring herself to believe that. He had been too honest, too open to be leading her on. He had not flattered her with admiring remarks on her physical characteristics or her costume as did most men bent on offering Spanish coin—not that she had been the recipient of such comments, but Rosalind had so often regaled her with stories of which admirers had said what that Sarah was very well aware of what passed for flirtation in the *ton*. Lord Farringdon had certainly not subjected her to any of that. No, in fact, he had treated her as though she were an equal and a friend, which was precisely what was so pleasant about it all and why she found herself drawn to him, however unwillingly.

And that, Sarah muttered furiously to herself, is exactly why he is so dangerously attractive; he adapts himself to the temperament of the company in which he finds himself so that Lady Amelia is as comfortable with him as Rosalind is, and none could be more different than those two. The man is nothing more than a chameleon. However, she could not help being intrigued by him. Undoubtedly the Earl of Burnleigh was a rake, but he was certainly a very clever rake and far more entertaining than anyone else she had encountered in quite some time. In spite of herself, Sarah could not help looking forward to her next visit to Cranleigh just to see what he would do this time.

Thoughts of Lord Farringdon continued to intrude upon Sarah during the rest of her day, making her less forceful than usual in her dealings with Mr. Dallow.

Even Miss Trimble, despite her failing eyesight, noted Sarah's abstracted air. The former governess, now in failing health, had been delighted to hear from her pupil, and so excited at the prospect of being useful to her that she had hurried to Ashworth, completely ignoring her infirmities. In fact, Sarah had been appalled to see how much the lady had aged, but she had allowed herself to be assured that a sojourn in a household with her former charge was just the thing the governess needed. Indeed, Miss Trimble had seemed to move more quickly and look a good deal more stout after a few days at Ashworth, and though she would actually not have been of much help should Sarah's virtue have been seriously threatened, her presence was enough to protect her former pupil's reputation.

Guessing from the few details that Miss Trimble let fall that hers must have been a rather narrow and poverty-stricken existence, Sarah was only too happy to be able to offer her every possible luxury she could think of. The poor woman was pathetically grateful. "So kind, always so thoughtful, even as a little girl," she murmured over and over again as Sarah would lead her to a chair in the sunlit library, bring her a shawl, or read her the latest news from *The Times*.

Actually, Sarah was rather enjoying having someone to look after. It brought a warmth and a sense of usefulness, a sense of belonging that she had sadly missed in her life without Lady Willoughby. To be sure, she continued to involve herself in the welfare of the villagers, helping the younger children to learn their letters, occasionally settling disputes among the older ones, taking food to the sick, and generally interesting herself in the problems and difficulties that beset her less fortunate neighbors. Though they appreciated all that she did and frequently sought out her advice, the villagers still stood somewhat in awe of her. To them she was the lady of the manor and consequently a being from another realm entirely. To Miss Trimble she was one of the few kind and genuinely concerned people the governess had encountered in her life.

It did Sarah a great deal of good to feel needed, to feel as though she meant something to another person. For much of her life she had been rather extraneous to anyone's existence.

Certainly, she had never been anything but an encumbrance to her father and her brother, if they stopped to think of her at all. And Lady Willoughby, though she had delighted in her granddaughter's companionship, had done far more for Sarah than Sarah could do for her grandmother. While it was true that Rosalind was demanding Sarah's help right now, the marchioness had made it abundantly clear that had there been anyone more fashionable and more amusing than Sarah to call upon, she certainly would have done so.

No, when Miss Trimble's face lighted up as she entered the room, Sarah experienced a glow of happiness, knowing that her mere presence was so important to someone. The idea that someone was even thinking of her gave her a sense of well-being such as she had never felt before.

Sarah would have been astounded had she known herself to be the focus of someone else's thoughts, someone far less feeble, far less helpless than Miss Trimble. Lord Farringdon continued to contemplate Lady Sarah Melford all the way back to Cranleigh, and even after that as he sat down to a hearty rasher of eggs. She is a funny little thing, he thought as he paused in the meal to take a great gulp of coffee, quiet and seemingly happier alone than in company, yet she was not at all shy. Sarah appeared ready to discuss topics that most women would customarily have avoided. Unlike almost all the females he had encountered, she was quite capable of conversing intelligently about something other than herself—a rare trait, indeed. He looked forward to speaking further with her. Certainly, she offered a distinct contrast to Rosalind and the Edgecumbe girls, all three of whom made him feel positively hunted with their interest in him, hunted to the degree that it was a delightful relief to enjoy the early morning hours without fear of their pursuit, safe in the knowledge that they had probably not yet arisen and would be at their toilette for some time after that.

This sense of security was short-lived, however, as Rosalind, after a morning spent closeted with her maid, appeared around noon, a vision of loveliness that demanded masculine attention and admiration. Nothing would do but to have both the attractive men in the household dancing attendance on her. To this end she organized a trip to Folly Hill, the local promontory that afforded a commanding view of the countryside and required the use of several carriages. If she could have had things her way, Rosalind would have sat alone in the barouche with either the chevalier or the earl, but given the impossibility of this, she invited Lady Amelia and her mother to join her as they offered the least competition for masculine attention. Besides, a gentleman riding attentively alongside could carry on just as intimate conversation as one seated in a barouche.

Another barouche containing Lady Edgecumbe and her daughters made up the party while the chevalier, Lord Farringdon, and Lord Tredington accompanied on horseback. Sarah, hastily summoned from Ashworth and loath to be confined to a carriage with either her sister-in-law or the Edgecumbe girls, was also mounted, a circumstance that caused Cordelia and her sister to exchange knowing glances at yet another example of her unbecoming lack of femininity, but since Sarah limited her conversation to the Reverend Mr. Witson and posed not the slightest threat to any of the women bent on attracting the attention of either the chevalier or the earl, she was soon forgotten in the rush to see which carriage would command the escort of which man.

Wishing to avoid further importunities from the chevalier, Rosalind was quick to call Lord Farringdon to her side with the first comment that came to mind. "What a truly splendid animal, my lord. I am persuaded that you must find it very tame sport to accompany us at such a snail's pace when you are accustomed to risking your neck at every possible chance."

Sarah, who was close enough to be within earshot of this transparent bid for attention, snorted to herself at the idea that Rosalind would recognize any quality about a horse beyond its color and the fact that it possessed four legs. Unfortunately, she was also able to hear the earl's reply, which was equally fatuous. "But what is speed compared to the opportunity to feast one's eyes on such loveliness?"

What a coxcomb! All Sarah's dawning respect for the man evaporated in an instant. How he could empty the butter-boat over her sister-in-law in such a fashion with a straight face was more than she could fathom. Unable to stop herself, she stole an incredulous glance at Lord Farringdon only to discover that he was looking straight at her and, what was worse, the man had the audacity to wink at her in a most conspiratorial manner!

Of all the . . . ! Sarah's hands tightened on the reins, causing

Ajax to sidle and toss his head, which only deepened the amused expression on the earl's face. And then there was Rosalind, so accustomed to masculine adoration that she accepted such barefaced flattery without a blink, not even questioning its sincerity. As far as she could see, the two of them deserved one another—both were so convinced of their fascination to the opposite sex that it never occurred to either one to doubt its potency for even a moment.

Still, the earl had appeared to be a reasonable creature both this morning and the day before. For some inexplicable reason, Sarah discovered that she did not want to think of Lord Farringdon as one of Rosalind's flirts, but why that was she could not say precisely. He had seemed too cynical and too intelligent to be taken in by a lovely face and practiced coquetry. Yet now he was leaning over the marchioness as though enthralled by her every word. There remained, however, an air of wry self-consciousness about the man when he caught Sarah observing. Did he think he could win Sarah over as well? She shook her head in disgust. Almost, she had come to enjoy the man's company, but she should have known better after witnessing that passionate embrace years ago. He was just as much interested in dalliance as Rosalind was. Sarah sat stockstill for a moment, struck by yet another, even worse possibility—perhaps he was truly in love with her sister-in-law.

No. Somehow that idea was even more upsetting than thinking of him as a rake. Surely, he would have married Rosalind if that had been the case. His family was as ancient and respectable as the Melfords and his fortune a good deal larger than Harold's. And why was she wasting all this thought on the Earl of Burnleigh anyway, Sarah chided herself. He was nothing more than a Bond Street beau who spent his life in pursuit of excitement and amusement, not the sort of person she would have ordinarily wasted a second thought on. It was with relief that she turned to the vicar, who broke into her thoughts.

"I am happy that the marchioness was able to lure you along on this expedition, for I now have the opportunity to enjoy intelligent conversation as well as a beautiful day. I have been meaning to ask you what you think of this Burdett business?"

Sarah was grateful for the distraction. There was something about Thaddeus's pleasant, open countenance that made one instinctively like and trust him. There was certainly nothing of the deliberate charm that made people such as the Earl of Burnleigh so upsetting. She sat in silence, gazing at the flowering countryside and considering this difference. Then, with a start, she realized that she had not answered the question addressed to her. "Burdett? I admire his convictions; however I am not at all certain I understand all the fine points of this latest contretemps with Parliament. Certainly he is a zealous reformer, a man who acts to protect the rights of those people who have few, if any, to speak for them."

"And yet he opposed our efforts to rid Europe of the most absolute demagogue the world has seen in some time," a deep voice spoke behind them.

Sarah whirled around to discover Lord Farringdon regarding her quizzically, one dark eyebrow raised and a crooked smile tugging at one corner of his mouth. Blast! Was she never to be allowed to forget the man's presence? Why did he not stay fawning over Rosalind and the Edgecumbe girls? They deserved his attention; she did not, especially when she was trying to have a serious discussion with Thaddeus. Men like Farringdon did not possess a serious bone in their bodies, and yet here he was presuming to pass judgement on a man who devoted his life to that most weighty of subjects—political reform. "I believe Sir Francis Burdett to be a most estimable man, a champion of rights for those who are unfortunate, a tireless worker in the cause of justice, and a believer in liberty for all men—a belief, which though it may lead him to oppose war with France, makes him nonetheless admirable," she responded with close-lipped annoyance.

"The man has a most devoted defender in you, Lady Sarah," Alistair responded, a twinkle of amusement lurking in the gray eyes. The lady was irritated with him, and he knew precisely the reason, having provoked her deliberately. But it was worth it. She did look magnificent with the brilliant color staining her cheeks and righteous anger sparkling in her eyes. "And he would most certainly think highly of you as well, an earnest young woman who devotes her life to good works in the surrounding countryside, eschewing the empty amusements of the *ton*."

Somehow, Sarah felt more exasperated than flattered by this encomium, nor did it help to have Thaddeus rush loyally to her defense. "Lady Sarah is an example to us all. She concerns herself not only with the welfare of those at Cranleigh and

Ashworth, but in the larger neighborhood as well. She has made sure that a school has been established to teach girls as well as boys their numbers and letters, and even helps out there herself. The parish is most fortunate to have her," he concluded enthusiastically.

It was with an effort that Sarah maintained a serene, detached expression under the earl's ironic gaze when really she longed to scowl most dreadfully at him. Drat the man! He seemed omniscient. Something in the way he was looking at her made her realize that he was well aware of the conflicting thoughts and emotions she was experiencing. Ordinarily, Sarah would have been more than happy to acknowledge her interest in the welfare of the villagers and in politicians who were working to effect changes in the broader scheme of things for such people. Ordinarily, she would have scorned anyone who was not concerned with such important affairs, dismissing that person as not being worth the time of day. But, perversely enough, at this particular moment she did not wish to be thought of as one of those very dull, very blue ladies who went around boring everyone with their constant talk of their own good works. On the whole, such creatures were humorless and unattractive, and for some reason Sarah did not wish to be put in a class with them, especially when her sister-in-law was looking so ravishing in a dove gray carriage dress of the new corded muslin with a black lace shawl draped gracefully around her. The Marchioness of Cranleigh might be in half-mourning, but she looked enchanting, and certainly far more alluring and interesting than someone attired in a severely cut slate gray riding habit that was years out of fashion.

Sarah gave herself a mental shake. What was wrong with her, anyway? She had never admired Rosalind in the least and had even less desire to compete with her, but neither did she wish to be dismissed as an antidote who had nothing to do with her life except help around the parish. Nor did she wish it to be thought that her sole admirer was the local vicar. Somehow the tone in Lord Farringdon's voice and the expression in his eyes implied all that. Worse yet, she was bothered by it. Why she should care what some arrogant Corinthian thought of her was more than Sarah could fathom. Now the arrogant Corinthian was addressing her again. "I beg your pardon? I was not attending," Sarah was forced to confess with some confusion.

"I know." Alistair grinned at her. Then, in a complete about-face, he grew suddenly serious. "I do beg your pardon. I have been teasing you. You flew so fiercely to Burdett's defense that I could not help myself. In truth it is people like Burdett and like you, people with wealth and conscience who take their social responsibilities seriously that ensure that we do not have a revolution such as the one that brought Napoleon to power in the first place. Burdett was right in defending the Napoleon who began with republican principles, but he does not understand that the Emperor's victories all over Europe have given the man such enormous power that his judgement has become clouded. Now he subjects peoples to the sort of tyranny that is rampant in Spain and Portugal, not to mention the misery that war in general has brought to the populace."

Sarah regarded the earl with astonishment. Sitting there on his superb horse, flawlessly attired in jacket of dark blue Bath superfine, snug breeches, and boots so highly polished one could see one's face in them, he looked the picture of a fashionable Corinthian who knew nothing and cared less about the state of the world. Yet here he was making passionate observations about it.

"Whew." Alistair chuckled. "I had not meant to go on like a regular jaw-me-dead, but the situation in the Peninsula seems to me to be extraordinarily grave and so few people here pay the least attention to it."

"Perhaps," Sarah replied thoughtfully, "but I did read in *The Times* just the other day that Canning is planning an examination of the campaign in Parliament." In spite of herself Sarah could not help being drawn into the discussion. It was entirely possible that he was flattering her as much as he flattered Rosalind, catering to her pride in her intelligence very much the same way he catered to Rosalind's pride in her beauty. But it did not seem as though he was dissembling. Furthermore, Sarah never had been one to resist a good conversation no matter who was involved in it. Ruthlessly ignoring her doubts and suspicions, she allowed herself to become totally immersed in a thorough analysis of the situation in the Peninsula.

Chapter Twelve

Meanwhile, the Peninsular Campaign was also under discussion among other members of the party, though not with quite the same patriotic fervor. Responding to the subtlest of glances from Rosalind, the chevalier had approached her carriage the minute the earl had left it. The marchioness had not been best pleased at the casual manner with which Lord Farringdon had abandoned her, but it would never have done to reveal her annoyance in front of the Edgecumbe girls, who had been keeping a close watch on Rosalind and the Earl of Burnleigh. Unsophisticated though they were, Lucinda and Cordelia had spent enough time in the *ton* to gloat over such patent desertion on the part of an admirer. Observing the meaningful glances the sisters had exchanged at Lord Farringdon's departure, Rosalind thought that she almost preferred the company of her sister-in-law, eccentric rustic that she was, to that of Cordelia and Lucinda. Sarah for all her oddities was not unkind, nor was she someone who competed for attention and admiration in the way women of the fashionable world did.

Turning around, Rosalind spied another potential admirer, and, wishing to inspire envy in the jealous breasts of the Edgecumbe sisters, the marchioness smiled ever so slightly at the chevalier. He responded with flattering alacrity, but his first words sent a disquieting chill down her spine that Rosalind did her best to ignore. "I see that your husband and Lord Edgecumbe do not join us. Can it be that they are back at Cranleigh, discussing political affairs?"

Rosalind shrugged and replied airily, "Oh, Lord Melford is not one for these outings." But there was no mistaking the tenor of his question nor the meaningful expression in his dark eyes, which flickered briefly but significantly toward her brother riding directly behind the other carriage and then back to the marchioness.

Rosalind's heart sank. She had hoped, however vainly, that the chevalier would forget all about the little proposition he had made in the garden the other day. Actually, it had been more of a threat than a proposition, and Rosalind had no more idea what to do about it now than she had had at the time. She had intended to enlist Alistair's aid, but somehow she had not had the opportunity to bring it up. She had meant to beg his assistance during the evening stroll on the terrace, but the moment had slipped away before she had been able to broach the subject—a subject that required the utmost delicacy in its presentation, for she was not at all certain what his reaction would be.

The Earl of Burnleigh, for all his reckless ways and devil-may-care attitude, was not an easy man to know. He had hidden depths that could quite take one by surprise. Rosalind had had occasion to discover this one evening some time ago when she had made an offhand remark about the French emperor's being the merest adventurer and upstart and thus not a serious cause for concern. It had been the wrong thing to say. The gray eyes that had been warmly admiring the moment before had become as hard and cold as slate, and the smiling lips had compressed into an unyielding line. "You and all the rest of the world are fools for underestimating him," Alistair had snapped. That was all he had said, but it was enough for Rosalind to see very clearly indeed. Nor would he discuss these issues further with her. Her inopportune remark had been made before Austerlitz, Jena, Wagram, and Marengo. When these stunning victories had proven Lord Farringdon correct, she had tried to bring up the topic again, but he had neatly sidestepped the discussion with flirtatious banter and flattering remarks about her appearance.

No, Alistair could not be approached for assistance without careful preparation. In the meantime, there was no denying the purposeful expression on the chevalier's handsome countenance. Perhaps, Rosalind hoped optimistically, she could avoid being alone with him and thus forestall future demands, but his next words put an end to such wishful thinking.

"He is a busy man, is my Lord Melford. I saw the dispatch rider arrive this morning from London. It is a great shame my lord has no time to enjoy such a lovely day with his beautiful wife, *non*? I am a poor second as a companion, but I would greatly enjoy a further tour of the gardens of Cranleigh given by its mistress."

This time there was no denying the menace in his tone. Rosalind shuddered ever so slightly, and then, summoning up a smile that could have hardly have been less enthusiastic, she responded mechanically. "Of course, I shall be happy to show them to you, Chevalier." She was trapped, and there was nothing she could do. If she refused, Richard would be ruined, and his sister could not help but be tainted by the ensuing humiliation. However, the alternative of giving the information to the Frenchman was not particularly attractive either.

It was not so much that Rosalind was concerned about betraying her country as much as she abhorred scandal. If it was ever discovered that she had passed along secrets to the chevalier, she would never be able to hold up her head in the *ton* again, and to the Marchioness of Cranleigh, society and her position as one of its leaders were the breath of life. Nothing else gave her such a sense of satisfaction or pride as the envious glances of the women and the admiring ones of the men. Without these, she would be nothing, no one.

Now all of this, so carefully sought, so bitterly won, would be destroyed by her foolish brother and her dull-witted husband. Life was hard. It was all because of Richard in the first place that she had been forced into marriage with the uninspiring Harold, which was, Lord knows, trial enough for a clever, beautiful woman. If Richard were not so very improvident or if Harold were not such a self-important fool that he insisted upon attaching himself to rising politicians instead of being satisfied with enjoying his role as the husband of one of the *ton*'s most brilliant young matrons, she would not be in this fix. In her agony of self-pity Rosalind forgot entirely that it was she who had pushed Harold to seek out more lofty political circles than those in which he had been moving before marrying her. It was enough to make one's head ache. Certainly Rosalind's was throbbing now, and the bright sunshine was only making it worse in spite of the fetching parasol she held tilted at such a becoming angle.

"Then let us agree to take a stroll in the gardens later on, as I am sure we shall have a great deal to discuss, which would only bore your lovely companions." The chevalier turned to include the Duchess of Coltishall and Lady Amelia in a brilliant smile. "But come, we have arrived, and we must ask our fair guide to point out the noteworthy landmarks in the distance. It is a splendid vista, *non*?"

For the remainder of the outing the marchioness's mind was in a whirl. Whatever was she going to do? However was she supposed to find out anything of use from Harold, and what was it that she was supposed to find out? What if she could not discover anything? Would she be ruined anyway? Surely, the chevalier would not be so cruel. That was it! She would tell him that she had been unable to discover anything, that her husband had refused to discuss such things with her; after all, she was only a woman. Men did not discuss affairs of state with women.

However, at that very moment, another man was discovering, much to his surprise, that a man could discuss such things with a woman, and that furthermore, the experience could be just as enlightening and certainly far more charming than debating such topics with men. Pursuing her own comment concerning Canning's activities in Parliament, Sarah had turned toward the earl to remark, "From your expression it appears that you do not look for much from the parliamentary inquiry into the situation in the Peninsula."

Alistair grimaced. "I very much fear that the Whigs will soon come into power, and undoubtedly one of their first actions will be to demand the withdrawal of our troops from Portugal."

"But surely, since Napoleon has made it clear that he himself plans to lead an attack on Lisbon, they would not dare do such a thing," she suggested.

"Perhaps," the earl acknowledged, "but there are strong sentiments for peace, what with the poor harvest last year and the closing of the European market to British goods."

"However, now that Spain has turned against France, there must be a need for British manufacturers that did not exist before."

It was a telling point, and Lord Farringdon, much struck by it, was thoughtful for a moment. He so rarely had the opportunity to thrash out such complicated ideas with anyone, especially someone who could broaden his thinking, that he found himself having to stop and consider very hard indeed before his next reply. "Yes, but it is all a question of the final result, you see. If we lose, we have spent a great deal of money and many lives for nothing—worse than nothing, because a victorious Napoleon is sure to exact harsh penalties from the losers. He has been so invincible up to this point that such an outcome is within the realm of possibility, and now that he has allied himself with Austria, it is even more so." Alistair paused for a moment, looking out over the expanse of green that ended in the shimmering sea, his expression speculative. "If, however, we can form the Portuguese into an efficient fighting force, incorporate them into our army, and inspire the Spanish, why then we may just win."

"I can see that is the approach you favor," Sarah commented.

He grinned. "Is it so obvious, then?"

She could not help smiling in response. "There is no mistaking the vigor in your tone, my lord. It is a grave risk, however, and . . ."

"But I feel certain that in time, other nations, inspired by the Spanish revolt, may follow suit and try to throw off the yoke of the Continental System, leaving us free to trade with anyone. Then our victory would be complete. I do beg your pardon; I did not mean to interrupt . . ."

"However your convictions are very strong," Sarah finished for him. "I do not mind in the least. Your opinions do you credit, but can they be supported by the men and supplies to see it all through?"

"I believe so," he began carefully, glancing around as he did so. The chevalier was deep in conversation with Rosalind, and everyone else, with the exception of the inoffensive Thaddeus, was out of earshot. "Napoleon has succeeded thus far because he has been highly organized and efficient, throwing thousands of men into pitched battles before the enemy has a chance to collect itself. He is a superb leader and has devoted and well-trained forces, but his methods of supplying those forces by living off the countryside work against any lengthy campaigns, especially in such unforgiving terrain as there is to be found in the Peninsula. The army rapidly exhausts the resources of an area, inspiring the animosity of its inhabitants, and then is forced to move often. The world thus far is reeling under his onslaught, but I do believe it is now beginning to collect itself, and the tide will eventually turn."

Sarah regarded the earl with new respect. Either he was a complete dreamer or he was very deep indeed. Given the assurance with which he spoke, it seemed as though the latter were the case. She had only the briefest of moments to wonder how he came by his information before Thaddeus broke in.

"That may be all very well, but as the emperor has just allied himself with Austria, there is certainly little likelihood of that country's allying itself with anyone but France."

Lord Farringdon looked grim. "That is true, for the moment at least, but it will also very likely push the Russians into a more antagonistic stance toward Napoleon. Even now it appears as though Alexander looks upon Tilsit as more of a truce than a true alliance between Russia and France."

"And I suppose that ultimately any country, at the slightest show of weakness on Napoleon's part, is bound to turn against him. Although he is a brilliant general and perhaps even a brilliant leader, he is still an upstart in the eyes of the monarchs of Europe, and his republican origins are bound to make them uneasy." Sarah spoke meditatively, almost as though she were thinking aloud rather that addressing her two companions.

The earl smiled approvingly. It was a provocative idea and certainly one worthy of discussion. He had not been wrong in his first impression at the dinner table—conversation with Lady Sarah Melford was indeed stimulating. But at the moment she did not look like someone who had scored a telling point. If anything, she looked to be seriously annoyed with a frown on her face that spoke considerable displeasure. Alistair regarded her curiously.

The earl was entirely correct in his reading of her expression; Sarah was miffed. There had been something so patronizing in Lord Farringdon's attitude, as if she were a clever child who had suddenly, and most unexpectedly come up with the correct answer. Why should it be so surprising that she had contributed a sound theory? She was as intelligent as most people after all, and she read the newspapers and reviews as much as anyone. It was more than Sarah could stand. "I fail to see why you are so taken aback at my opinion, my lord. It seems a most obvious conclusion for a well-informed mind to reach," she muttered stiffly before clamping her mouth firmly shut.

Now he would certainly laugh at her if he were not laughing inside already. Any other woman, say Rosalind for instance, would never have gotten into such a deep discussion in the first place. If she had, she would have gracefully laughed off the earl's air of superiority. All that Sarah had done by being so prickly was to make herself open to derision from the sort of man who was accustomed to delicious flirtations with women instead of political debate. She stole a glance at Lord

Farringdon, who, oddly enough, was not laughing at her at all; in fact, he looked rather grave.

"I stand corrected, Lady Sarah," Alistair apologized. "I was a coxcomb. While it is true that I never have had the pleasure of conversing with a truly intelligent and educated woman before, that should not give me the right to make assumptions about a particular woman from my general experience."

Sarah studied him carefully, but there was not a hint of mockery in his expression. He was serious to the point of being contrite, and she found herself warming to him in spite of her annoyance. There was something rather disarming about a gentleman who is willing to admit his faults.

A teasing smile tugged at the corners of the earl's mouth. "But you *will* allow me to say in my defense that you are most unusual. I have never encountered a woman such as you, and I must say that I am finding it to be a most delightful and illuminating experience."

The rogue. Undoubtedly he was just saying that, but Sarah flushed with pleasure all the same. "Why, why, thank you," she stammered.

Alistair cocked a quizzical eyebrow. "Well, you are welcome, but I had nothing to do with it. You are a rare creature, Lady Sarah."

For a moment she could do nothing but stare at him, mesmerized by the half-teasing, half-admiring glint in his eyes. It was, for a brief second, as though they were the only two people in the world. The rest of the party, even Thaddeus, ceased to exist as they sat there gazing at one another. For an instant they both sensed a depth of communication that went beyond words—a mutual recognition and understanding that had nothing in common with the ordinary social interchanges of the rest of the world. Then Lord Tredington came riding up, and just as quickly as it had appeared, the moment was broken—so quickly in fact that Sarah was not entirely sure that it had happened at all except that Lord Farringdon seemed to be something more than he had been before. He was not just a man of fashion whose only interests were wine, women, and song, but someone who hid graver interests and concerns under a careless exterior. Furthermore, she wanted to think that the same sort of revelations had occurred to him about her, and he, too, had come to a deeper understanding of her.

Chapter Thirteen

There was not much opportunity for further conversation. Lord Tredington, who had sought out Alistair to question him about his mount—"Stunning animal, get him at Tatt's?"—rattled on at length about London, its clubs, and the endless games of chance he had won or lost, mostly lost, there. It was a rather one-sided exchange, and the earl, not being called upon to respond except with an occasional "Oh, really?" was free to observe the rest of the party.

As usual, Rosalind was commanding the attention of the most attractive man, and the rest of the group, with the exception of Lady Edgecumbe, who was taking careful notes of crops and livestock, was watching Rosalind and the chevalier. But oddly enough, this appeared to be bringing Rosalind little pleasure. Ordinarily, the marchioness would have been all smiles and fluttering eyelashes to a gallant as practiced and charming as the chevalier, who appeared to be hanging on her every word.

Instead, she seemed to be concentrating more upon the passing scenery than on the gentleman. It was a curious thing, most curious indeed, and the earl, his instincts heightened wherever the chevalier was concerned, resolved to keep a weather eye on both the chevalier and the lady on whom he was lavishing attention.

The earl was quite correct in his assumptions. Rosalind was not enjoying herself. In fact, she was as uncomfortable as she ever remembered being when the chevalier, leaning close to the carriage so that only she could hear him, murmured, "I suggest that you speak to your husband about the news brought by today's dispatch rider before we have our promenade in the garden."

"I shall," the marchioness snapped. Her dark eyes flashed dangerously, but their rebelliousness was belied by the unhappy pout of the full red lips. Rosalind was caught in an impossible situation and she knew it. There was nothing she could do, no one to whom she could appeal without disgracing herself. A quick glance at the chevalier's implacable countenance was enough to convince her that he would remain merciless in his pursuit of information. A barely detectable sigh escaped her as she patently avoided his eyes fixed so intently on her, and she turned to survey the lush green fields and burgeoning hedgerows on either side of the carriage.

As instructed by the chevalier, Rosalind sought out her husband almost immediately upon the party's return to Cranleigh. The marquess was in the library, seated at his desk, frowning heavily at some papers in front of him. If he had been a perspicacious man, or even one who was ordinarily aware of others than himself, he would have been surprised at his wife's intrusion, for the marchioness tried to spend as little time with him as was humanly possible. But Harold was too distracted by the matters at hand even to notice such a thing.

It was an opportune moment for Rosalind. "More dispatches from London, my lord?" she inquired brightly.

"Mmmm."

"It is a great deal too bad that you are forced to spend your time on them instead of enjoying the day."

"One cannot indulge in frivolity when the fate of the nation is at stake, my lady. I leave such pleasure to others," the marquess replied with a gravity of demeanor calculated to make the observer think that the future of the entire kingdom rested upon his shoulders.

Privately, Rosalind thought that if the affairs of the nation were truly in her husband's hands, Napoleon would have added England to his vast empire long ago, but even she, bored as she was by politics, had more faith in England's leaders than to believe they would allow the Marquess of Cranleigh anything but the most harmless minor role in the true workings of the government. "You are very diligent, my lord, but surely nothing can be that urgent?" Rosalind inquired encouragingly.

At last her husband looked up. "Now there you are wrong, madam," he began ponderously. "Why, just this morning I have received notice of the imminent departure of troops for the Peninsula."

"Truly?" Rosalind was awed. "I do hope they are not any of

the regiments in which we have acquaintances. Sir Reginald Farquhar is in, is in . . ."

"The Royal Horse Guards. No, they have not been sent, only the Thirteenth Light Dragoons, a battalion of the First Foot, a battalion of the Coldstreams, and one from the Third Foot." Harold paused for a moment, a frown of concentration wrinkling his brow. "Oh yes, a battalion from the Royal Scots and one from the First Staffordshire," he concluded triumphantly. There, that should prove to his wife that she was not the only clever one in the household. It was quite a feat of memory to recall all of those regiments from a dispatch that was so secret Lord Edgecumbe had allowed him only the briefest of glimpses at it.

"Oh my." Rosalind acted suitably impressed, but her brain was feverishly committing these particulars to memory. For the moment, she remembered them all, but if she did not write them down soon, she would quickly forget. "You are busy." Rosalind tried to sound impressed. Harold beamed in a superior fashion. "But do not work too hard. Surely, you will join us for some refreshment. It is such a beautiful day we shall be out on the terrace. I myself am going to put on something more suitable." With that she hastily made her exit to go in search of pen and paper before changing her costume into something even more flattering than the carriage dress she now wore.

The other members of the party had also retired. Most of the ladies, except Sarah, who had returned to Ashworth, had repaired to their chambers to refresh themselves, and the gentlemen had either continued on with their exercise or gone to get out of their riding clothes. The earl was one of the latter group, and it was some time later as he was toweling himself off after a refreshing splash of cold water that he happened to glance out of the window to the gardens below, where he caught a glimpse of Rosalind hurrying to meet the chevalier, who was seated on one of the stone benches, idly swinging his quizzing glass.

That seemed odd. Given the lady's apparent lack of relish for the gentleman's company earlier that afternoon, it was strange that she would now agree to an assignation. However, it did not appear to be much of one, for after the briefest and coldest of exchanges, she thrust a piece of paper into the chevalier's hand and hurried off. How very strange.

Until this moment Lord Farringdon had been observing Rosalind and the chevalier with the idle curiosity of one who was amused by the machinations of two people expert in the art of dalliance, but now he straightened, frowned, and slowly began to pace the floor of his bedchamber. This meeting had taken on the complexion of something far more serious than a mild flirtation, and the more he considered it, the more Alistair began to wonder if the ever so gallant chevalier was perhaps blackmailing the lovely marchioness. And if he was blackmailing her, what was he blackmailing her for? Were they political or personal secrets he was dealing in? Rosalind with her desperate need to be a leader in the *ton* would be vulnerable on both counts, what with the fashionable world's horror of scandal.

The situation demanded careful observation. Though he had long ago broken off with the beautiful mistress of Cranleigh, the earl bore her no ill will. In any case, he did not wish to see her hurt. However, it was the political rather than the personal that truly interested Lord Farringdon, and since Rosalind's husband, obtuse though he might be, was connected with powerful men in the government, and since Cranleigh was so close to the Kentish coast, it was a perfect environment for a French agent to operate in, and thus bore looking into. The earl smiled grimly to himself as he completed his toilette. Things were working out just as he had suspected they might.

Alistair kept a close eye on Rosalind and the chevalier for the rest of the afternoon and evening, but learned nothing further. The chevalier was as punctilious as ever, offering flattering compliments to the Edgecumbe girls, running to retrieve the Duchess of Coltishall's shawl when she left it on the terrace, complimenting Harold on his magnificent estate and efficient staff, in short, making himself as agreeable as possible to all and sundry.

Rosalind was a slightly different matter, however. She flirted gaily with Lord Edgecumbe, dimpled charmingly at the Duke of Coltishall, and engaged Alistair in a witty conversation about their mutual acquaintances in town. To all intents and purposes she was her usual vivacious self, but the earl sensed that she was putting a great deal of effort into appearing carefree. To a close observer, and one who knew her as well as Lord Farringdon did, the lines of strain around the luscious mouth and a hint of worry in the dark eyes all indicated that the Marchioness of Cranleigh was perturbed about something. Alistair also noticed that her eyes followed the chevalier everywhere he went in a manner quite unlike the coquettish Rosalind, who was more accustomed to being watched by everyone else rather than the other way around.

Yes, the earl concluded to himself as he leaned against the mantel in the drawing room that evening, there was definitely something going on between the Chevalier d'Evron and the Marchioness of Cranleigh, and it was not of a romantic nature.

Lord Farringdon barely had time to register this thought when his attention was attracted to another part of the room where Sarah, at the request of her brother, who liked to show off his sister in what was, according to his opinion, the one socially accepted role in which she could shine, was seated at the pianoforte. The earl had been vaguely aware of the strains of country airs emanating from that part of the room, but now he heard a Mozart sonata being executed with such skill and depth of feeling that he broke off a rather desultory discussion with the Duke of Coltishall, who had approached him to debate the merits of the various horses running at Newmarket, in order to concentrate his attention on Sarah's performance.

Alistair had already accepted the notion that Lady Sarah Melford was an unusual female. In fact, she was an unusual person, and he was ready to acknowledge that she appeared to be as intelligent as anyone he had ever run across. Now it seemed that she was something of an artist as well, for the technique of her performance and her interpretation of the music easily rivaled what he had heard from professional musicians.

No one else in the room was paying the least attention to her playing. All of them, busy with gossip or flirtation, or both, were too intent upon trivialities to allow themselves to be swept up in the power of the music. Only Sarah, her blond hair gleaming in the candlelight as she bent intently over the keyboard, seemed to be the least bit aware of its beauty. She was completely caught up in it, her entire body reflecting the ebb and flow of her playing. Other women had been taught above all to look decorative at their instruments, the musical execution being only secondary to the picture they presented. Not Sarah. She was too wrapped up in the melody to be aware of anything.

Intrigued, the earl nodded in a genial manner to the duke

and made his way unobtrusively to the other end of the drawing room. Propping one broad shoulder against a convenient pilaster, he watched with interest as her hands flew over the keys. The smooth white forehead was furrowed in concentration, her cheeks were flushed with the exhilaration of producing such exquisite sound, and she was so totally absorbed in the music that she was completely oblivious to the hum of conversation around her or the presence of an interested observer.

Thinking it over, Alistair realized that he had never seen quite that look on any woman's face, and in his vast experience he had certainly witnessed a panoply of feminine expressions from coquetry to lust, from anger to coyness. However, he had never encountered a woman so truly unself-conscious, so intense, so caught up in something that she had no thought for her surroundings. Lord Farringdon found this oddly compelling, attractive even. Surely, a woman capable of such single-minded passion in one endeavor was capable of it in many others.

It was strange how many woman, with their fluttering eyelashes, alluring smiles, and lascivious glances did their best to hint at such depths of passion, but how few of them actually seemed to feel anything of the kind once they had attracted a man's attention with their ploys.

This brought to mind the Marchioness of Cranleigh in particular. Rosalind was a woman whose every move was carefully calculated to drive a man wild with desire, but when she finally allowed herself to be embraced, she remained curiously unaffected by the ardor she inspired. Alistair could still remember the scent of her, the feel of her soft curves under his hands as he had kissed her in the gardens at Tredington several summers ago. He had rained kisses along the soft white neck and the delicious hollow at the base of her throat only to discover that her pulse was beating no faster, her breathing coming no harder than if she were seated by the fire, reading a book.

In fact, as he had emerged breathless from the embrace, she had smiled absently and carefully patted her coiffure to ascertain if anything had been disarranged. It was lack of emotion, more than his distaste for matrimony or her brother's ruinous propensities, that had kept Lord Farringdon from making Rosalind Countess of Burnleigh. From that point on, he had taken rather cynical notice of the promise of coquetry in a woman's eye in relation to her subsequent actions and had come to the conclusion that whether they were opera dancers or highborn ladies, they rarely felt the desire implied by their flirtatious looks. On the contrary, these looks were far more likely to have been motivated by a calculated wish to trap him into a relationship that would benefit them socially or monetarily, or both, than they were inspired by any physical longing.

Now, however, the earl was beginning to wonder. Perhaps there did exist a woman who could experience the depths of passion that he had hoped for. If any could, he was willing to bet that Lady Sarah Melford might be just such a woman. It would certainly be most intriguing to find out. And with that, almost as though she had divined his thoughts, Sarah glanced up from her music to discover the earl's eyes fixed upon her.

The intensity of his gaze was somewhat unnerving, yet at the same time it seemed to be questioning her. Well, let him look as much as he liked, she would not be put out of countenance. Sarah's hands paused over the keys and she stared back at him steadily, unblinking, until Lord Farringdon, a wry grin tugging at the corners of his mouth, strolled over to the pianoforte. "I beg your pardon, Lady Sarah. I did not mean to be impertinent, but I could not help admiring your playing."

Her cool smile expressed such patent disbelief at his words that he felt like the rawest youth. Damnation! "Truly, I had not thought to hear such a performance outside the concert halls of London." Worse and worse. He sounded like the veriest coxcomb. Her delicately arched eyebrows rose a fraction of an inch, and the green eyes glinted scornfully.

"I know you suspect me of offering you Spanish coin, but I am not." Alistair paused, then smiled ruefully. "Believe me, I would never do such a thing to you. After all, it would not do me the slightest bit of good." There, he could see the faintest beginnings of an answering smile hovering around her lips. "I am particularly fond of Mozart, who, I believe, has depths and complexities that are often overlooked by less skilled musicians and audiences."

That was unanticipated. Sarah had not expected someone like the earl to notice her playing, much less identify her repertoire. She looked at him with some surprise.

"I am not a totally useless fellow, you know." Despite his best efforts, Alistair could not help sounding piqued. Why should he not be just as cultured as she was, after all? Did he look like such a barbarian? Too often she made him feel rather like one. Lord Farringdon shook his head. More and more he was determined that she know the real man behind his public facade.

Sarah continued to study him, her expression slowly changing from one of purest skepticism to one of dawning curiosity. The man *did* seem to be in earnest—not that Sarah was well versed in the ways of rakes and libertines, but she fancied herself a good enough judge of human character to recognize true interest when she saw it. "Perhaps you are not," she conceded cautiously, "but you must know that your reputation is not one that would encourage a person to take you seriously."

Alistair remained thoughtful for a moment. "True. But then I do not wish for most people to think that they can take me seriously." The gray eyes did not waver from hers as he gazed down at her, willing her to believe him.

Suddenly, Sarah felt slightly breathless, almost giddy. It was the oddest sensation. She had never experienced such a weakness before. Perhaps it was the closeness of the room, but no, the French doors on the other side of the fireplace were open, and she could see the flames of the candles flicker slightly as the gentle breeze wafted in.

"I hope *you* will take me seriously when I say I admire your skill," Alistair continued. "You must have had a very fine teacher."

"I did." The moment was past. Sarah took a deep breath, steadied herself, and began to describe her good fortune in receiving instruction from a court musician who had barely escaped France with his life when the Revolution came. Soon she was talking easily, and the conversation turned to safer channels: her study of music, composers in general. They discovered their tastes in music to be quite similar, and a most stimulating discussion ensued, so much so that they quite forgot their surroundings.

However, such happy obliviousness was not enjoyed by another member of the group. Rosalind, while appearing to hang on Lord Edgecumbe's every word, was stealing suspicious glances at her sister-in-law and Lord Farringdon. Almost imperceptibly her eyes narrowed and her lips tightened. It was not that she feared in the least any competition from someone as unfashionable as Sarah—oh no—but she did not like to have the attention of the most attractive man in the room fixed on anyone but herself. It was high time she did something about it. That little tête-à-tête had been going on far too long.

Excusing herself from Lord Edgecumbe, who was deep in an elaborate description of a recent parliamentary debate in which he had distinguished himself, the marchioness glided toward the pianoforte. "Now, my lord"—Rosalind shook a playful finger at Lord Farringdon—"you must not distract our fair performer. You are depriving her listeners. Besides, Sarah confines her mind to higher topics than mere gossip."

The first part of the marchioness's remark was demonstrably untrue. Not a single person in the room, with the exception of Rosalind, had even noticed Sarah's music, much less her silence.

The earl turned to Rosalind. "Forgive me, my lady. It was exceptionally rag-mannered of me. I am at your service. If you will but engage me in conversation, I promise to leave our musician to her playing and the rest of the company to their enjoyment of it." But Alistair did not allow himself to be led away before he had sneaked a conspiratorial wink at Sarah.

Left alone with her music, Sarah sat motionless at the pianoforte for a moment before resuming her playing. She had been somewhat taken aback, but inordinately pleased by Lord Farringdon's last gesture. It was infinitely reassuring to know that he was not completely under Rosalind's thumb. In spite of herself, Sarah had rather come to enjoy the man's company, and it was heartening to see that he appeared to see through her beautiful sister-in-law, at least to some degree. Unbidden, the image of the earl's dark head bent over Rosalind in the garden rose again before her, bringing with it the oddest wish that it had been she, rather than her sister-in-law, who had been locked in his arms. Sarah shook her head vigorously and laid her hands purposefully on the keys. Mozart had a way of calming even the most disordered senses, and hers were certainly disordered at this particular moment.

Chapter Fourteen

Physically, Alistair might have been separated from Sarah, but his thoughts remained with her for the rest of the evening. Even after he had retired to his bedchamber, he stood for some time, gazing out of the window at the gardens below and thinking about her. What a rare person she was, so unlike any other woman he had ever known. Where the others were all artifice and superficiality, she was serenely herself, quiet, with hidden depths, surprises at every turn.

Her company was both restful and stimulating at the same time: restful because one did not feel pursued the way one did with so many other women, and stimulating because she was interested in so many things beyond the empty trivialities of the latest *on-dits*. How delightful it was to be with someone who did not want anything except to share ideas, who did not appear to expect him to say or be anything but himself.

Most women cared about the earl only in relation to themselves—how he flattered them, what his interest in them would do for their status in the *ton*, or what his patronage would do for them in the demimonde, but Sarah actually listened to what he had to say, pondered it and responded. That sort of interaction, Lord Farringdon had discovered, was equally or even more exciting than the most reckless of affairs he had pursued. Oddly enough, it was also in many ways more intimate because they were exchanging ideas that were the products of their personal reflections rather than the empty responses of the standard flirtation. Strange though it was, Alistair felt closer to Sarah in many ways than he had to others with whom he had shared more physically intimate liaisons or even those with whom he had had romantic connections.

Loosening his neckcloth, the earl drew a long breath of the cool night air. He had not thought this deeply in quite some time, and he was rather enjoying the quiet moment of reflection as he surveyed the moonlit countryside. Suddenly, a rhythmic thud broke the peacefulness of the evening. Instantly alert, Alistair pulled back into the shadow of the drapery and squinted in the direction of the sound. Sure enough, in a few seconds, a horse and rider emerged from a clump of trees off in the direction of the stables. Of course the earl could not positively identify the Frenchman's features at such a distance, but the size and shape of the man on the horse were more nearly equal to the that of the chevalier than any of the other guests.

Alistair grabbed the jacket he had just tossed into the chair, struggled back into it, and rummaged in a dresser drawer for a pistol and several neckcloths. It was a pity to ruin perfectly good neckcloths, but at the moment the earl could think of no other way to muffle the sound of Brutus's hooves. No doubt Rogers would have some harsh words for him later, but what were a valet's sensibilities when the safety of the country was at stake?

Stuffing his pistol into his pocket and carrying his boots in one hand and the neckcloths in the other, Alistair crept down the hall, mentally reviewing a variety of excuses should he be caught. He made it safely to the drawing room, whose doors overlooked the lawn, allowing him an easy exit without having to pass by the servants' hall.

The stables presented a problem, as he had no idea whether the stable boys were given separate quarters or were expected to bed down with their charges. Fortunately, when he had first arrived, Lord Farringdon had seen to Brutus's accommodations so he knew right where to find his mount. The horse whickered softly as his master approached. With relief Alistair noted that there were no stable boys in sight, and then hurriedly bound Brutus's hooves, saddled him, and led him slowly from the stables. It seemed hours until they left the cobbles of the stable yard and reached the grass of the park. Pausing briefly, the earl glanced cautiously over his shoulder, but all was quiet. The great house, bathed in moonlight, remained dark, not even one window showing light.

Hastily mounting Brutus, Alistair headed off in the direction in which the rider had disappeared. From his earlier visits to Tredington Park, Lord Farringdon had gained a rough idea of the countryside, which he had reinforced with his ride the previous morning. This knowledge, coupled with the suspicion that the Frenchman was going to meet with contacts from across the Channel, made it fairly easy for him to ascertain the way the chevalier had gone.

It was a relief after the forced inactivity of observation to have his suspicions proven and to be able to act on them. After the social repartee of the drawing room where every word was overheard and analyzed by many ears, every gesture seen and interpreted by many eyes, it was wonderful to gallop across the silent countryside and to be doing something active and constructive at last.

Off to his right rose the dark shape of a manor house. Ashworth, the earl thought, and he wondered briefly about Lady Sarah's opinion of the evening. The road curved around the house, heading toward the coast, and as he rounded the turn, he saw a light flickering from a downstairs window. Evidently, she was still awake.

Soon the scent of salt air stung his nostrils, and Alistair reined in Brutus to a walk as they approached the vast expanse of marsh ahead. He stopped and scanned the horizon, listening intently, but there was nothing except the sound of the breeze stirring the marsh grass, which rippled in the moonlight. Horse and rider advanced slowly, picking their way along the road, which had now dwindled to a narrow track. Alistair leaned forward, trying to pick out the dark shape of a rider against the silvery landscape. The Frenchman had a lead on him, but not that great a lead.

They crept along this way for some time when at last Lord Farringdon saw it, a flicker of light, so quickly dowsed that he almost doubted his own eyes. At least they were on the right track. Leaning even lower over Brutus's shoulders, he urged the horse on while straining to catch the slightest sound.

The wind rustled through the grass, and Brutus flicked an ear, his nostrils flaring as though he had caught the scent of another horse. "Good boy," Alistair whispered, stroking his mount's neck. At last, he, too, was able to detect the faint sound of voices coming from what appeared to be the very depths of the grasses. There must be an inlet close by, Alistair reasoned, a perfect place for landing small boats unobtrusively.

He slipped quietly down off Brutus's back and led him carefully forward in the direction of the voices. Soon he was able to make out the dark shapes of horses and men ahead of him in the high grass. Still too far away to identify anyone or hear anything, Alistair crept forward as quietly as he could, trying as much as possible to make his movements sound like the soft breezes in the grass. At last he was within earshot, and there, sure enough, was the chevalier, his horse standing quietly beside him, in deep conversation with another man.

The chevalier was clutching a small packet and gesticulating furiously while his companion, obviously a subordinate, but also obviously a gentleman, listened intently, nodding emphatically from time to time. A little bit beyond them was a rowboat pulled up into a narrow inlet in the marsh. A third man sat in the middle of the boat, leaning on the oars and staring vacantly off into space.

"Ah." Alistair let out a long silent sigh of satisfaction. It was precisely as he had expected. The Frenchman was passing information to one of his countrymen, who would no doubt slip quietly off to some French ship lying in wait off the coast, and, once across the Channel, ride straight to Paris and the emperor. He had known it all along! Now all Alistair had to do was to prove it, and the Chevalier d'Evron would no longer haunt the salons and drawing rooms of the *ton*.

The earl was so intent on the chevalier, his treacherous behavior, and visions of the man's ignominious downfall that he failed completely to notice a fourth man standing guard a little apart from the others. However, this man did see Alistair, and he made for him immediately, brandishing a bulky pistol and giving a warning shout to the others.

Alistair threw himself on Brutus's back, wheeled, and headed in the direction from which he had come at breakneck speed. Shots rang out, and he heard the sound of pounding hooves behind him. Glancing quickly over his shoulder, he saw that the man, too, had grabbed a horse and was gaining on him, but the man's mount was little more than a pony and no match for Brutus.

Another shot rang out, and the earl felt a burning pain on his right side. Damn and blast! He had been hit. Now what was he going to do? Leaning low over Brutus's neck, he urged his animal forward, soon outdistancing his pursuers, but now pursuit was the least of his worries.

Alistair could feel the warm, sticky blood beginning to run down his side, and he was tiring rapidly. It hurt to breathe, and, what with the excitement and the exertion, he was forced to gulp in great quantities of air, which only exacerbated the pain. Grasping the reins with one hand, he gingerly felt his side, but could discern nothing beyond the fact that he was losing blood. At least the wound appeared to be peripheral enough not to have hit any vital organs, but it still left him with the enormous problem of getting it attended to without attracting any notice. Servants were bound to talk, and he did not want the news that he was suffering from a gunshot wound to reach the chevalier's ears. The earl was reasonably certain that he had been unidentifiable to the men on the marsh, and he preferred to have it remain that way in order to carry out his mission of rendering the chevalier and his colleagues inoperative.

Of all the blessed luck, he cursed to himself. No, actually that was not precisely true; of all the buffle-headed things to do, charging down on them without keeping a careful watch out for sentries. In his excitement at the opportunity to catch the chevalier in action, he had thrown caution to the winds, blundering in as stupidly as a raw youth who had never done this sort of thing before. Ow! He winced, as much from his own stupidity as from the pain that shot through him as Brutus, leaving the soft turf of the marsh behind him, stumbled on a rock in the rough track leading back to the road.

The earl shifted uncomfortably in the saddle, and his eye caught sight of a light ahead of him. Ashworth! Sarah was still up. He sighed in relief. It was the perfect solution. From all that he had seen of Lady Sarah Melford, Alistair felt certain he could count on her to help him. There was something about her cool intelligence, her self-possessed air that made him sense he could rely on her assistance and her discretion.

A great weight was lifted from his mind, and with the happy thought of comfort and aid, he urged Brutus toward the welcoming golden patch gleaming ahead of him in the darkness.

Chapter Fifteen

In the library at Ashworth Sarah sat at her desk, surrounded by books and papers, her pen in hand and a frown of concentration wrinkling her brow. Thaddeus had been urging her for an age to write down her opinions and share them with the rest of the world. At last the perfect opportunity had presented itself in the form of a book by Thomas Broadhurst that had captured her interest, *Advice to young Ladies on the Improvement of the Mind.* It addressed a topic dear to her heart, and in composing a critique of the book for *The Edinburgh Review,* she had seized the opportunity to express her own ideas. Of course she had not used her own name, and only the publisher was aware of her identity. He had obligingly sent her all letters addressed to the author of the review, and it was to one of these that she was struggling to compose a reply.

Sarah was searching for a word that would give her a particular turn of phrase when she heard what she thought was a rap on the window. Do not be silly, she muttered to herself. You have an overactive imagination. It is merely a branch in the wind. But the rapping began again, more insistent this time. She turned around and started in astonishment, for there at the French doors leading to the garden appeared the figure of a man, his face gleaming ghostly pale in the surrounding darkness.

Heart thumping rapidly, Sarah cautiously opened the drawer of her desk and as unobtrusively as possible, extracted a wicked-looking letter opener. Holding it slightly behind her so as to conceal it in the folds of her dressing gown, she crept toward the French doors. As she came closer, Sarah discovered, much to her astonishment, that her mysterious visitor was none other than Lord Farringdon, and that he appeared to be in some distress.

She fumbled with the latch in her haste to let him in. It

yielded at last, and she barely had time to swing one door open before he stumbled through. Sarah reached out and grabbed his arm, steadying him as she led him to a chair. It was only then that she noticed a patch of red staining his side. "My lord, this is an unexpected pleasure; is something amiss?" How she wished for the bottle of brandy that always sat on a side table in the library at Cranleigh.

Alistair's crack of laughter ended in a painful gasp. "A bleeding man invades her home in the dead of night and she asks if something is *amiss*. You are magnificent, Lady Sarah. Any other woman would have screamed, or fainted, or both."

Sarah colored with pleasure at this unlooked for praise, then in a voice unnaturally brisk to cover the self-consciousness she could not help feeling at being caught bare-footed en déshabille, she continued, "Perhaps, but that does not signify. We must see to your wound. If you will wait here, I shall find some brandy and some bandages." With that she hurried from the room, her dressing gown billowing behind her.

In no time she was back, brandishing a bottle of brandy, a glass, and quantities of bandages. Pouring a generous helping of brandy into the glass, she handed it to him. "Here, drink this while I fetch some water." And she headed off again to return a few minutes later with a kettle that she placed gingerly on the dying embers of the fire before turning to her patient. "I am afraid that this is not very warm, but I did not wish to rouse the servants."

"No matter. I am just grateful for your assistance." Alistair tried not to flinch as she eased him out of his coat and then his shirt.

"Hmmm," Sarah muttered thoughtfully as she examined the wound. More unnerving to her than the ragged flesh and blood was the sight of Lord Farringdon stripped to the waist, his broad chest bare, the muscles in his arms and shoulders glistening with sweat. She had never seen a man this way; it gave her the queerest feeling in the pit of her stomach, and she was oddly breathless. Uninvited, the image of those arms wrapped around Rosalind rose again before her. Hastily, she pushed it aside and concentrated on the path the bullet had torn.

"You are lucky only to have been grazed, my lord—badly grazed, to be sure, but at least the bullet did not lodge inside you."

"Yes." Alistair tried not to groan as she wiped away the

blood. "And I was far enough away that the bullet was mostly spent." He gazed down at Sarah gently sponging his side. What a woman! Not only had she not screamed, fainted, or raised the entire household, she had set to the task of nursing him in a most businesslike fashion without one question. Lord Farringdon could not think of a single female he knew who had not demanded an explanation from him for many things far more mundane than appearing injured on her doorstep in the middle of the night; yet beyond asking him if something was amiss, she had made no comment, concentrating instead on the immediate problem of attending to his wound.

"There." Sarah finished winding the bandage around his chest and stood back to admire her handiwork. "Now, if you will have another glass of brandy, I shall see what I can do to repair your coat." And picking up the basin of water, his shirt, and his jacket, she hurried off, leaving Alistair to his own reflections.

Somehow he had known that he could count on her to be this way. There had been something about her air of calm self-possession that had made the earl sense that Lady Sarah Melford was equal to almost anything. He glanced over at the desk where she had been working. It was littered with papers and books—a purposeful, masculine desk, so different from the delicate escritoires he had seen in numerous boudoirs.

Unable to contain his curiosity, Alistair pulled himself out of his chair, wincing as he did so, and made his way over to the desk, where a half-written page lay open, a pen dropped in haste on top of it. "My dear sir," it said, "as I wrote in my article, 'A great deal has been said of the original difference between men and women; as if women were more quick, and men more judicious—as if women were more remarkable for delicacy of association, and men for stronger powers of attention.' I assure you that I have had some experience in the education of both of the sexes and I . . ." Even if he had not known it, he might have guessed the handwriting was Sarah's; it was so like her—neat, but forceful, firm and compact with the words marching purposefully across the page. The topic, *A Reply to Critics on 'Advice to Young Ladies on the Improvement of the Mind'* was just the sort to engage her attention. Lord Farringdon began to read. Having conversed with Lady Sarah, he was not so surprised as he might have been to discover that a female could lay her arguments out in such a clear and telling manner. Really, it was quite good, he admitted grudgingly to himself, and he was sorry when he came to the blank spot at the end of the page. However, it was high time he was back in the chair, where she had placed him for it would never do to be discovered poring over her manuscript.

Alistair made his way back to the chair and poured himself another glass of brandy, swallowing a generous amount before he set the glass down. The immediate pain from the wound was beginning to recede, and he felt curiously comfortable and at home as he sat staring into the fire. He supposed it had to do with having risked trusting someone for the very first time in his life and having that trust fulfilled. Why, he could not have done better himself if a friend in trouble had suddenly shown up at his own doorstep.

It was odd how proud and gratified he felt that Sarah had performed so beautifully. He shook his head. Sarah would call that a rather arrogant way of looking at it—that she had justified his good opinion of her—but he did not really mean it that way. It was just that Alistair had been drawn to her from the outset, had sensed something different about her—an integrity, a fineness of character—and, cynic that he was, he had not truly allowed himself to believe that it actually existed. Now she was proving it all to be just as he had hoped, and Alistair was oddly grateful to her for it.

His reflections were interrupted by the lady herself as she came bustling back into the library, shaking out his jacket and shirt. "There, I have sponged them off, stitched them, and brushed the jacket. They should stand up to all but the most careful inspection; however, you may have to concoct a suitable story for your valet."

Alistair quirked an eyebrow at her. "And what story shall I concoct for you?"

"Why, nothing. What you do is your business. I have no need to be privy to it," she replied simply as she draped his garments in front of the fire to dry. In truth, she seemed far more interested in restoring them in some semblance of repair to their owner than in uncovering the reasons behind his unusual appearance at such an hour.

Alistair shook his head, smiling. What a remarkable person. "But surely you must have some explanation of your own for my . . . oh . . . er, present unfortunate circumstances."

Sarah gave a last twitch to the jacket she was hanging.

"Why I assumed you were smuggling." Her tone was as calm as though she had suggested he were out for a morning ride.

"Smuggling!" Alistair was nonplussed.

Surprised at his vehement reaction, Sarah turned to look at him. "Well, many people do, you know, though most of the men from the village who are involved do it because they are in more desperate straights than you appear to be. However, appearances can be most deceiving."

"You thought I was a smuggler, and you took me in to your house?"

"You were wounded," she responded simply as she poured him another glass of brandy.

Alistair remained silent for a moment, stunned, and just the tiniest bit hurt at her ready assumption that he was involved in some nefarious activity. Did she truly believe that he was that bad, that he was such a loose fish he was dead to all finer feelings? It was a measure of the respect he held for Sarah that he cared so much for her opinion. Normally, he did not give a fig for what anyone thought, most of those around him being so self-centered and so vain that their opinions mattered very little to him, if at all.

But Sarah was different. She was someone who had thought about life and lived it purposefully. Unwilling as he was to admit it, Alistair very much wanted the approval of that sort of a person. A cynical smile tugged at the corners of his mouth. So many women had tried to cast him in the role of their *preux chevalier*, someone who would protect them and work miracles for their sake that he had obstinately resisted these efforts. Several times he had even behaved quite badly, simply to discourage such expectations, yet now he wished to be regarded in precisely that light by a mere country nobody who was not the slightest bit interested in him, and was less dazzling than even the dullest of his flirts. How ironic.

"No, I was not smuggling," he replied piously, "I was spying."

"Spying!"

Ha, that had shaken her out of her serene self-possession. However, she was likely to have even more distaste for spies than she did for smugglers, and Alistair hastened to defend himself before Sarah could jump to any conclusions. "Yes, well someone must stop those blasted French. They keep coming over here, infiltrating our government at the highest circles, and gathering so much vital information that our poor lads in the field do not have a sporting chance."

"Oh," Sarah responded blankly.

"Napoleon possesses a highly organized network of spies that send word of our every plan back to him, and we do nothing. No right-thinking Englishman would dirty his hands in such a nefarious business, so the tactical advantage goes to those who are not hampered by such lofty principles," the earl continued bitterly.

Sarah regarded Lord Farringdon curiously. For once the mask of cynicism and nonchalance had slipped to reveal a man who appeared to care deeply, not only about his country, but even about people's opinions of him. Despite his customary air of ironic indifference and his mocking attitude toward the petty vanities of his peers, he had obviously suffered at their hands or he would not be so defensive now. Sarah quite understood. After all, when she had heard the word *spy*, a vague frisson of disgust had shaken her, and she was less likely to take society's strictures at face value than most. But now, stopping to consider it, she realized that those involved in protecting the military and political secrets of their country and seeking out the enemy who was endeavoring to discover those secrets ran all the risks of injury or death without participating in the sense of camaraderie enjoyed by those in the military, and certainly without enjoying any of the glory or admiration accorded those who paraded around in splendid uniforms.

In fact, Lord Farringdon's seemed an extremely solitary and dangerous occupation with no hope of reward except his own private satisfaction in having done what he could to thwart the enemy. Glancing over at him now as he sat staring into the fire, with lines from pain and fatigue throwing the hawklike nose and high cheekbones into fine relief, Sarah sensed the basic loneliness of the man—a loneliness that was usually well hidden under a devil-may-care exterior. Her eyes softened. Who could know better than she what it felt like to be looked at askance by one's fellow creatures simply for establishing one's own set of values and remaining true to them?

Sarah longed to smooth back the lock of dark hair that had fallen over his high forehead. More than anything, she wished to bundle him off to bed and let him have the good night's rest he so obviously needed, but that was out of the question, not so much for the sake of her reputation as for his. Anyone who was a spy needed to maintain a facade of utmost consistency so as not to arouse the least suspicion. But who was the earl tracking here in Kent, and what had gone wrong? Lord Farringdon did not look the sort to be foolish enough to get caught. Had he been betrayed? And what was she to do with him now?

Chapter Sixteen

As if reading her thoughts, Alistair smiled grimly. "Never fear, as soon as these are quite dry"—he nodded toward his jacket and shirt—"I shall be on my way. You need not trouble yourself that I shall continue to impose my disreputable presence on you any longer than absolutely necessary."

Sarah shook her head, but he had seen the conscious look on her face, even though it was quickly suppressed. "I do not worry for myself," Sarah protested, "but how are you to ride after the shock, after losing all that blood and . . ."

"After drinking all that brandy," he finished with a harsh laugh. "Do not fret yourself. I have found my way home in worse shape than this times out of mind. There is no need for concern."

The bleakness in his voice and the proud, remote look on his face cut Sarah to the quick. He was so ready to believe himself despised, so determined not to care, not to depend on anyone for anything. This air of desolation wrung her heart, and she could not help laying a gentle hand on his bare shoulder. "Indeed, you mistake me. I was but trying to think of some way to convey you to Cranleigh without arousing suspicion, for it would never do to have the chevalier get wind of even the slightest irregularity."

It was the earl's turn to look self-conscious. "The chevalier! How did you know it was he? I must be making a bad job of it indeed if you arrive so easily at such a conclusion."

The faintest hint of a smile played across Sarah's mouth, and there was a mischievous twinkle in the green eyes. "Come now, my lord, I fancy I am more awake on all suits than most. I am not stupid, after all, and being less caught up in the flirtation and gossip than the rest of the world, I am more at liberty to look around me. I fancy that no one else noticed, but what I saw was that while you lavished a great deal of attention on the females present at Cranleigh, you also spent a fair amount of time observing the Chevalier d'Evron."

The earl was silent for a moment, struck by his companion's perspicacity. Lady Sarah Melford might eschew the social milieu, but she was a fair observer and judge of humankind, it seemed. He could not help feeling chagrined. "Still and all, I ought to have been clever enough, or at least careful enough to disguise my interest in the gentleman." But in a way Alistair was glad he had not deceived her, for two reasons. One, he liked it that she was perceptive enough to notice and deduce such things, and, two, the thought of deceiving someone whom he was coming to respect more and more was repugnant to him. "I have not been very intelligent on all counts." He pointed to his bandages with a grimace. "I have become what you thought me all along—an arrogant coxcomb—and now I am paying the price of my overweening of confidence and pride."

"Why, I never . . ." Sarah objected hastily, then catching his eye, she laughed. "Well, perhaps I *did* think that of you at first, but it was not *that* long before I began to revise my opinion of you."

"A thoroughly reformed character, in fact." He chuckled.

"Well, I would not go that far," she teased. Then, seeing him shift uncomfortably in his chair, she at once became serious. "We must see about getting you back to Cranleigh. Perhaps I can ride behind you and support you and—"

"What?" Alistair sat bolt upright in spite of the stab of pain in his side. "And have you make your way back here in the dead of night? You may think me a rogue, but I am not so ungentlemanly as to allow you to do that."

"Nor am I such a weak creature as to need an escort," Sarah retorted spiritedly. "Why, times out of mind I have explored the countryside at night. I am probably a great deal less likely to come to harm than you are. Besides, I assume that the people responsible for your visit here are still roaming about. What if they see you?"

"They won't catch me again." The earl looked grim. "Anyway, what could you do?"

"Run for help." Sarah was exasperated now. He must think her a very poor-spirited creature indeed.

"A fine fix I should be in then." Alistair refused to listen to her logic. "We might as well take out an advertisement in *The*

Times. "Alistair, Lord Farringdon, Sixth Earl of Burnleigh, wishes to announce that he is a spy for His Majesty's government and . . ."

"Well, it would not do His Majesty's government less harm to have you killed!" Sarah shot back, thoroughly irritated with his stubbornness.

That won a reluctant grin. "Touché. You are in the right of it; however, I think that enough time has elapsed now for them to have given up any hope of catching me, and I am certain that they were unable to identify me. I thank you for your concern, but I feel quite equal to making it back to Cranleigh on my own." Sarah still looked doubtful. "Believe me, I *have* gotten out of worse than this—the life of a spy, you know," he added reassuringly.

The earl could not help but be amused by the expression on Sarah's face. She was so obviously torn by curiosity on the one hand and the wish to respect his privacy on the other that she looked for all the world like a little girl begging to be told a story.

He rose carefully, testing to see if his head swam or the bandages pulled, but everything remained just as it had been. "Some other time I shall tell you of my exploits, but for now I must make it back as quickly as possible. I must not appear suspiciously fatigued in the morning. I do not believe that the chevalier has tumbled to me yet, but I must proceed under the assumption that he is watching me as carefully as I am watching him."

For some reason she could not quite fathom, Sarah was loath to see the earl depart. It was so cozy sitting there in the library, talking with him. There was no doubt he was an intriguing character. Every encounter with him was full of interest and never failed to reveal some heretofore unsuspected side to his character. Life had certainly become exciting since he had arrived at Cranleigh.

Until now, she had never been alone with a grown man except for her brother, her father, Richard, who was like a brother, and the vicar, who did not really count. Yet now, here she was in the middle of the night with a half-dressed man standing in front of her fire, his broad chest wrapped in bandages while she sat there in her dressing gown. Sarah smiled to herself as she rose to retrieve his clothes. How people would talk if they knew. She gathered the earl's shirt in her hands feeling to see if it was dry before handing it to him. "It is almost as good as new. Certainly no one except your valet will guess that anything untoward happened to it.'

Alistair reached for it, wincing as he did so.

"Here, let me help." Sarah hurried to take the shirt and hold it so he could slip in with a minimal amount of effort. Her breath caught in her throat as the muscles rippled in his arms and shoulders. She had never been so close to a man before, and the warmth, the scent of sweat and the outdoors, was disconcerting in the extreme. She had the strangest urge to wrap her arms around him to revel in the heat and strength of him. How strange. She had never truly thought about such things before, but somehow the warmth and smoothness of the earl's skin under her hands as she had cleaned and bandaged him had made her experience sensations she had never even known existed. It was with a shock that she realized she was not so immune to the feelings that existed between men and women as she had previously thought.

Until this moment Sarah had observed maids gazing longingly at footmen, or villagers walking out together, and had never fully understood what drew them together. Only the brief interlude she had witnessed between Rosalind and the earl had given her the slightest inkling of what it was all about. To be sure, it was love, or passion, she knew that, but she had never been able to picture herself in such a situation. Now she could, and for a brief wistful moment she almost wished for something she had hitherto scorned as a weakness. It was a most humbling experience. Forcing her breathing under control, Sarah reached for the jacket and held it out with hands that only betrayed by the slightest tremor her inner turmoil.

If was fortunate for Sarah that Alistair was too occupied with the awkwardness of the bandage and trying not to aggravate the stabbing pain in his side to notice his companion's discomposure; fortunate because women so often suffered palpitations when they found themselves in close proximity to one of the *ton*'s most eligible and attractive males that Alistair would instantly have recognized the signs for what they were. But as it was, he accepted Sarah's assistance ruefully but gratefully, hoping all the while that he would be able to carry off his return to Cranleigh as nonchalantly as he had led her to believe he could. It was a novel position for the earl, wanting to live up to a woman's expectations. Heretofore he had always done his best to fall short of them in order to depress female pretensions and discourage the constant pursuit he found himself subject to.

Was he becoming such a coxcomb that he could not bear it if a woman did not fall at his feet? Alistair considered this for a moment. Surely he was not. Surely it was Sarah's quick intelligence, her resourcefulness, and her coolness that attracted him to her rather than the fact that she was one of the few, perhaps the only female he had come across who had not pursued him.

The earl turned and headed toward the French doors through which he had come. Outside, he could see Brutus waiting patiently, tethered to an apple tree. Alistair paused, his hand on the door, and looked down at his hostess. "I cannot thank you enough, Lady Sarah, for taking me in, for seeing to all my needs so efficiently and, and . . ." He hesitated, searching for just the right words to convey to her exactly how much her being there had meant to him.

Alistair could not believe himself. Was the glib flatterer of the fashionable world's most beautiful women at a loss for words? He was stammering like a bashful schoolboy. ". . . and thank you for being . . ." For being what, you nodcock, he muttered fiercely to himself. Out with it, man, or she will think your wits are addled. "For being, for being who you are," he finished lamely. Then taking her hand in his, he bowed low, kissed it gratefully, and was gone, leaving Sarah to stare after him in astonishment, greater astonishment than that with which she had greeted him in the first place that evening.

As the sound of hooves receded into the darkness, Sarah made her way back to the dying fire and sank into a chair. what an extraordinary evening it had been! And how many unexpected things she had discovered, not only about Lord Faringdon, but about herself. She was flattered that he had trusted her enough to come to her for help, though, being realistic, Sarah conceded that she had been his only choice. And though he did express some surprise and admiration at her calmness in handling the situation, at the same time he rather seemed to have expected her to comport herself precisely as she had. Sarah found that expectation more rewarding than all the compliments he could possibly have showered on her.

Oh, she knew that any other woman would have preferred to have him call her beautiful or breathe words of longing and admiration in her ears, but Sarah never had wished to have the butter boat dumped over her. Far more meaningful was his sharing with her, his confiding in her as though she was an equal rather than a flirt. Respect was far more important to Sarah than all the admiring speeches other women craved. To be relied upon by someone whom she suspected rarely, if ever, allowed himself to depend on others was high praise indeed, and Sarah took it as the greatest compliment the Earl of Burnleigh could have paid her.

Yet, for the first time in her life, after her experiences of the evening, Sarah had a glimmer of understanding for all those women who did crave pretty speeches and flirtatious glances. There had been something about the square shoulders and broad chest that had made her heart beat just a little faster, had mad her wish that somehow, incredible though it might be, she could work the same effect on him that he had worked on her. Sarah shook her head firmly, dismissing such absurd thoughts. Far better to be appreciated for one's character than one's beauty. After all, one's physical attractions soon faded, but one's character could only grow stronger with the passing years. Still, it would be wonderful, just for once, to be as beautiful as Rosalind was, and, even more important, to be so certain of that beauty.

Sarah would have been astounded to know that, in fact, the earl was thinking of her in much the manner that she wished he was as he made his way slowly and carefully back to Cranleigh, his mind a jumble of images: Sarah at the door, pale but composed with a letter opener clutched in her hand; Sarah bending over him, bathing his wound with the firelight catching the golden highlights in her hair; Sarah listening to him round-eyed, her eyes dark with sympathy and understanding. He could not remember a time in his life when he had asked anyone for help, had ever really needed anyone, man or woman. Now, when he had, she had been there, calm and reassuring with her gentle comforting touch. Undoubtedly, he could have managed on his own if he had had to, but knowing she was nearby, he had been drawn to her in a way he could not quite explain. His instincts had been right, however, and here he was safely on the road to Cranleigh with no one the wiser and hardly the worse for his wound. At the thought of Sarah, Alistair felt a surge of warmth flow through him. Was it happiness? Gratitude? He did not have the least notion, but he savored it as he slid off Brutus and led his mount carefully back to his stall.

Making his way stealthily back to his bedchamber, the earl wished Sarah could know he had made it back safely. She had not spoken, but her face had been so full of worry and concern when she bid him good-bye that he had longed to sweep her into his arms and reassure her that he would be all right.

Now, secure back in his quarters, Lord Farringdon, too exhausted to undress, flung himself fully clothed on the bed. If Rogers was surprised at his appearance in the morning, he would just allow his valet to think that he had had an assignation with some female. Alistair grinned to himself in the darkness. In fact, that was not far from the truth, except that the female had been more in the way of a nurse than a lover, not that she had not looked damned attractive in that dressing gown.

And recalling the way the flimsy material had revealed the supple figure underneath it, the gentle swell of a perfectly formed bosom, the long slim line of her leg and the delicate ankle that occasionally peeped through the froth of lace at the hem, Lord Farringdon fell asleep with a smile on his face.

Chapter Seventeen

Worn out from his wound and the activities of the night before, the earl did not arise the next day until nearly noon. He cursed himself for being a slugabed. I must be going soft, he muttered to himself as he splashed water on his face. Most of his annoyance was because he had planned to catch Sarah on her morning ride, but a glance out the window at the angle of the sun told him that the opportunity was long gone. Blast! Alistair was surprised at his own eagerness to see her again. By rights he should have been dying to discover all that he could about the chevalier and the precise nature of his connection with the Marchioness of Cranleigh, but instead, he could think of nothing but Sarah.

Alistair struggled to analyze his attraction to her as he carefully pulled off his jacket and shirt. It was not her physical appearance, though that was undeniably appealing, especially when freed from the restrictions of her customarily drab costumes. No, it was the idea of her that drew the earl to her more than anything else. Over the course of the past few days Lady Sarah Melford had come to represent to him a purity, a certain integrity, and a sense of purpose so noticeably lacking amongst the vain and frivolous members of the *ton*. She also managed to retain these qualities without being a sanctimonious or a prosy bore as virtuous people often were. Until now, Lord Farringdon had been as cynical about those who made good works their obsession as he had been about those who wasted their lives in pursuit of pleasure. Neither group had very much to recommend it, each having sacrificed its common humanity and any good sense that its members might have been born with, but not Sarah. Somehow she was different. At first the earl had written her off as yet another dried-up bluestocking devoid of any real warmth or understanding, someone who adopted false scholarship in place of real life, but he had been quite wrong.

Not only did Sarah possess a sense of humor—a rare quality in most people, but especially in those with pedagogical tendencies—she was a passionate person under that cool exterior. Anyone with any sensitivity could sense that from the way she came so hotly to the defense of her heroes or from her absorption in the music she performed so well. Besides, most bluestockings with whom Lord Farringdon was acquainted—as a general rule he tried to avoid them if at all possible—were all superficial without any true understanding. They could recite facts until they were breathless, but were incapable of any true intellectual exertion. Sarah, on the other hand, was not only highly capable of defending herself in a debate, she was more than able, it appeared, to express her observations and conclusions on paper. In short, Alistair found Lady Sarah Melford to be one of the most highly intriguing individuals, man or woman, that he had met in some time, and he was most anxious to see her again.

For her part, Lady Sarah was arriving at much the same conclusion. She had awakened that morning, marveling again at the events of the night before. Who would ever have thought that such a man about town as the Earl of Burnleigh would be involved in something as momentous as spying? True, such a dangerous business was likely to appeal to someone with his reckless attitude. Even in rural Kent the curricle races, the duels, and other outrageous exploits of Lord Farringdon were legend. However, Sarah had never expected such gravity of purpose behind his wild adventures. From the way Lord Farringdon had spoken, both the previous evening and during the outing to Folly Hill, it appeared that he was motivated in all this by true patriotic sentiments and a real desire to end Napoleon Bonaparte's dominance over Europe.

Not only that, but he was prepared to work toward this goal in a way that was not going to win him any personal glory. Not only were his efforts, even if they were successful, unlikely to come to the attention of the world at large, they were in an area of endeavor that most of humanity looked upon as treacherous and dishonorable despite the nobility of the cause. The earl certainly had no illusions about the general disrepute in which spies were held by the rest of society, yet this had not deterred him in the slightest.

Lady Sarah felt a stab of pity as she recalled the bleak look in Lord Farringdon's eyes as he alluded to the scorn reserved for those engaged in the sorts of activities he was, and his apologetic expression as he promised to rid her household of his presence as quickly as possible. She could tell from the tense way he had held himself that he expected her to dismiss him with disgust. When she had not, his relief had been almost palpable. Poor man. That brief exchange had suddenly changed her perception of the dashing Lord Farringdon. She now was certain of the deep loneliness that she had only guessed at before, and she had been struck by the notion, though of course she had no way of knowing whether she was correct, that for all his address, his attractiveness to the opposite sex, and his reputation for being up for any sort of wild adventure, he did not have any true companions.

That was sad. Why even Sarah, isolated as she was, had Thaddeus and, until recently, there had been Lady Willoughby to share her thoughts. Perhaps the earl preferred life alone, what with his cynical view of his fellow creatures, but somehow Sarah did not think that was so. She sensed that if he could have exchanged his superior and ironic view of mankind for a feeling of camaraderie, he would have. There had been just the slightest air of wistfulness about him that had betrayed him to her. Sarah was eager to test out her hypothesis with further observation. Consequently, she made her way over to Cranleigh that morning with a dispatch that was quite different from her usual deferring for as long as possible her encounter with Rosalind and her guests.

It was Rosalind who first caught Sarah's eye as she rode across the fields from Ashworth—Rosalind and the chevalier that is—for naturally one would never expect to find the beautiful Marchioness of Melford without an attentive male by her side. Actually, there were two attentive males. The chevalier was strolling through the rose garden with her sister-in-law on his arm, while on the terrace a level above them, his presence obscured by a hedge that separated the garden from the rest of the grounds, was the earl, sitting on a bench in the shadow of the house. Sarah was too far away to be able to read his expression accurately, but his whole posture suggested that of a man intent on observing the couple in front of him.

Before she could help it, a small sigh escaped Sarah. Was Lord Farringdon still caught in Rosalind's toils, then? Sarah hoped not, for she had grown to respect him, even to enjoy his company, and she did not like to think that he was no better than all of the others who fell for the beautiful face while remaining ignorant of the selfishness and vanity that lay behind it. Sarah's rational mind told her that the earl had experienced far too much of the marchioness's company to be taken in by her flirtatious ways, that instead he was keeping an eye on the chevalier, and Rosalind just happened to be with the Frenchman.

But something else, something that had nothing at all to do with reason, made her fear the worst, fear that Lord Farringdon would once again lose himself in passionate admiration for her sister-in-law and that once again she might run the risk of discovering Rosalind entwined in the earl's muscular arms. That she had just recently seen those muscular arms stripped to the flesh only served to make the whole idea that much more unsettling. What was wrong with her? She was acting like some milk-and-water miss sighing over a handsome face. Heretofore such thoughts had never entered her mind.

Sarah shook her head resolutely and turned Ajax toward the stables, where some minutes later as the groom was helping her dismount, she heard a deep voice behind her. "Good morning, Lady Sarah. You must have enjoyed your ride this morning. I confess to having slept to an unconsciously late hour. However, if you will walk with me in the gardens, I shall be delighted to take that as my morning exercise."

She whirled around to find the earl looking down at her with such a wealth of meaning in the gray eyes that she could only nod her assent.

"Good. Then let us begin." He offered her his arm with such alacrity that no one would have suspected in the least that his side was tightly wrapped in bandages.

It was not until they were out of earshot and approaching the rose garden that he leaned over to whisper softly, "I saw you arrive. As you may have guessed, I was keeping a sharp eye on the chevalier." The dark brows drew together in a frown of concern. "And I very much fear that he was somehow persuading Ros . . . er, the marchioness, to provide him with critical information."

"Rosalind?" Sarah gasped. "But she does not know any."

"No, but her husband does," the earl replied grimly.

"Harold?" The idea of her brother's possessing any vital information was almost as absurd as that of Rosalind's dispensing secrets to the enemy.

"Oh, I am sure that Harold is not privy to the government's deepest strategies, but he does have access to more intelligence about troop movements than the chevalier, and knowing his wife, I am sure she was able to extract this intelligence from him without his being the least bit aware of it."

Sarah's heart sank at the words *knowing his wife,* but she quickly pushed such unwelcome thoughts aside to concentrate on the matter at hand. "But why would Rosalind do such a thing? She is a vain and selfish creature to be sure, but she is not a traitor."

Alistair quickly suppressed a smile. So the demure Lady Sarah had claws, did she? It was not as though he had known any woman who liked Rosalind; she was far too competitive, far too jealous of attention to share even the tiniest bit of it with anyone else, but he had not expected such behavior to bother someone as reclusive and as uninterested in the vagaries of society as Lady Sarah. "No, she is not a traitor," he began, his voice deadly serious, "but she could be made to be if someone possessed damaging information about her or her family. As you say"—he shook his head ruefully—"she is a vain creature. The fashionable world is everything to her, and she will not allow anything to threaten her position in it. The chevalier must have got hold of something that could do so, and it must be of a fairly serious nature, for whatever she is, Rosalind does not lack courage. She has the resolution and charm to brazen out mere rumors and gossip, so there must be solid truth behind whatever is being held over her. I wonder what it is?" The earl paused for a moment, squinting speculatively off into the distance.

Sarah was silent, wondering more about his feelings toward Rosalind than about the secret that her sister-in-law was hiding. From his words it appeared that Lord Farringdon recognized the marchioness's true nature, but at the same time he seemed to accept it, and to acknowledge her immense powers of attraction; so did he still admire her or did he not?

Sarah wished desperately that the entire question was of the supremest indifference to her, but it was not. Ever since Rosalind had returned from school, Sarah had wished for just one male who did not fall victim to Rosalind's spell, and spell it was, for Sarah well knew that the marchioness's air of sweet feminine helplessness was the purest illusion. To be sure, the Reverend Mr. Witson was one male who was no more interested in the Marchioness of Melford than he was in the person of any of his other parishioners, but he did not count. Sarah very much doubted that the earnest vicar had any more notion of human female attractiveness than her horse, Ajax, did. To Thaddeus people were all the same, differing only in their varying needs for spiritual guidance. It was a highly admirable way of looking at the world, though not at all satisfying for someone such as Sarah, who was hoping for reassurance of some sort.

Now, there was the earl. Sarah found herself wishing desperately that he, of all people, saw through Rosalind, though she really did not want to examine precisely why she felt that way, except that he appeared to possess such a cynical view of the *ton* that it seemed impossible that he was not aware of her true character.

"Whatever it is," Alistair concluded, "I pity her. The chevalier is a man accustomed to having his way with everyone, especially women, and he will not tolerate anyone's keeping him from his goals, no matter how charming she is."

Sarah felt a sharp pang of disappointment. Did he not understand that Rosalind was precisely the same? To be sure, she preferred to coax people to do her bidding instead of threaten them, but when pushed, she could turn quite nasty. Sarah had seen this vicious streak more times than she cared to remember, and she could only hope that once in a while Rosalind was the recipient of such treatment herself. It seemed only fair.

Sarah had no idea how much her face reflected her thoughts, but Alistair, looking down at her, had not the slightest difficulty in reading them. He was both amused and touched by what he saw there: amused that his opinion of Rosalind should matter so much to Lady Sarah, and touched by the wistful expression in the green eyes. Undoubtedly, Sarah had seen Rosalind bending people to her will for more years than most, and it must have galled her to see anyone wasting sympathy on a woman who always got what she wanted. Well, almost always, he amended silently. After all, Rosalind was not the Countess of Burnleigh.

"I know it seems incredible that anyone should feel concern for your sister-in-law," he began gently, "but consider what she is, a creature of the *ton*. She has nothing but her beauty, which is undeniable." He held up an admonitory hand as Sarah opened her mouth to protest. "I know; beauty that does not extend to the soul is at best transitory. When the Marchioness of Cranleigh loses her beauty, she will lose the power to attract men, her power to arouse envy in the minds of other women; in fact, she will lose everything. She has only a short time before that beauty fades, until someone younger, someone who is fashionably fair instead of fashionably dark, becomes all the rage. When that happens, what does she have? Nothing. Small wonder that she is willing to take enormous risks to postpone the day when she is no longer the toast of the *ton*. Small wonder that her fear of oblivion, of powerlessness, blinds her to the immorality of what she is doing, if she is doing anything, which I have yet to prove. At the moment, all I have are my suspicions."

Sarah regarded the earl in astonishment. She had never considered her sister-in-law in that particular light. Viewed that way, she did seem an object of pity, for what did Rosalind take pleasure in but the admiration of the fashionable world? Furthermore, Sarah had inherited, albeit reluctantly, the fortune that Rosalind had married the Marquess of Cranleigh to gain. Sarah was under no illusions as to her brother's character, and she knew that nothing but the fear of being an ape-leader, the allure of an ancient title, or promises of vast wealth could have made any woman, no matter how desperate she was, shackle herself to someone as stupid and self-centered as Harold.

How odd; she had always been so envious of Rosalind's attraction that she had never really thought very clearly about her. And why had she even been envious of her at all when, in fact, she did not covet in the least the things that Rosalind had won with her manifold charms, except perhaps one thing. Even now Sarah was not willing to admit to herself what that one thing was or to acknowledge that the shivers that had gone through her when she discovered the Earl of Burnleigh and Rosalind embracing in the garden had sprung from her own wish to be in Rosalind's place. Surely, it was not.

What had upset her about Rosalind was that everyone was so taken with her. To discover that the entire world assumed there was an equal amount of beauty and charm of spirit underneath the carefully cultivated exterior when there was nothing of the sort, was what had always bothered Sarah about Rosalind. She was certain of that. At least she now felt convinced that Lord Farringdon appeared to be under no illusions as to her sister-in-law, for no one could suspect a person of passing along state secrets to the enemy and maintain a very high opinion of her character.

Again Sarah's expression was a mirror of her thoughts, and Alistair suppressed another smile. So she really did care what he thought of the Marchioness of Cranleigh. Why on earth should he find that so gratifying? The earl shook his head. "Now," he began briskly, "that leaves us with a great deal to do."

"Us?" Sarah blurted in surprise. But she was no proof against the surge of happiness that rose within her at his wishing to include her in whatever adventure was in store for him.

Chapter Eighteen

The earl grinned. "You do not think I am such a selfish lout that having plunged you into this affair without so much as a by-you-leave, I would then keep all the rest of the excitement to myself, do you? I am not so poor a fellow as that." Alistair congratulated himself at her gasp of delighted surprise. He had gauged her character to a nicety, then. His suspicion that she had a secret longing for adventure was entirely correct.

Lady Sarah looked more pleased to be included in it than if he had told her that she was the most beautiful woman in the world. Her eyes shone, and her entire posture was one of eager anticipation. Alistair could hardly keep from laughing; she looked so much like a hound that had just found a fresh scent. How very dull her life must have been, stuck here in the country with nothing but her books for amusement and her grandmother and the vicar for company.

"Now admire the roses," the earl admonished her. "It must seem as though we have nothing more enlivening to discuss than the different varieties you have managed to cultivate here at Cranleigh." Sarah's gratified smile revealed that he had not been wrong in that assumption either. Of course, Rosalind would have been far too busy cultivating her own beauty to care about a garden, and he knew Sarah's mother had died many years ago, so, with the exception of Lady Willoughby, that left only one possible keeper of the garden.

For her part, Sarah was wondering just how one person, and a gentleman at that, could be quite so perceptive. She supposed, however, that his professions, both as a spy and as a rake, demanded such acute powers of observation. Still, she could not help but feel flattered by the close attention he was paying her.

"We must find out exactly what it is that Rosalind has told the chevalier, and somehow we must convince her to refrain from giving him any more information until we can . . . er . . . *discourage* his presence here in England," Lord Farringdon continued thinking aloud.

"But how ever will you do that? It is not, of course, that I doubt your powers of persuasion, but . . ."

Alistair did not miss the twinkle in Sarah's eyes or the tiny smile that hovered at the corners of her mouth. The little minx! She was teasing him. But even as he noticed it, her expression became more thoughtful. "Why do you not persuade her to give the chevalier more information, only make it the wrong information? That way, she will not be in danger from the chevalier and England will not be either."

The earl regarded his companion with dawning respect. There had never been much doubt that Sarah was intelligent but this was positively clever, and he wished that he had thought of it himself. "An excellent suggestion. You seem to have a veritable knack for this." When he saw how much pleasure this simple response brought her, he was more than happy that it was she who had come up with such a brilliant scheme.

How unappreciated Lady Sarah must have been all her life to be so thrilled with the few crumbs of recognition as he gave her from time to time. Considering that her brother was a blockhead who could not see beyond his own nose and was totally unwilling to acknowledge the existence or importance of anyone besides himself, Alistair decided it was completely understandable.

"Now that you have come up with the solution to our problems, I suppose you are also ready with the suggestions for executing it," he teased.

"Well yes, as a matter of fact," Sarah admitted with an answering smile, "I have."

For a moment the earl's handsome countenance contorted into a rueful grimace. "I can see that I have been relegated to functioning as the merest accessory in all of this." His tone was plaintive, but his eyes gleamed with amusement.

"Not at all. In fact, you are the key, for only you hold enough influence with Rosalind to be able to persuade her to do something."

"You are too kind." There was no mistaking the ironic note in his voice, and Sarah took foolish delight in it. Then he was no longer Rosalind's devoted admirer, despite the sympathy he had expressed for her earlier.

"What makes you think that I, or anyone else for that matter, has any power to control the fair marchioness?"

"Oh, it is not just Rosalind; from what I hear, you can prevail upon any woman to do anything you wish." Sarah laughed at the earl's expression of mock horror. "And I draw this conclusion from what I have seen as well," she hastened to add. "Why, even Lady Edgecumbe is practically eating out of your hand. They all toady to you in the most remarkable way."

"Which you simply cannot understand," he finished for her.

Sarah chuckled, then added offhandedly, "But then, that sort of thing does not interest me."

"And what, pray tell is *that sort of thing*?" Piqued by the superior tone in her voice, the earl was not about to let her off easily. All his life he had chased after beautiful women and, accustomed to charming all of those he pursued; he was not going to let this snip of a girl dismiss him so lightly.

A faint flush tinged Sarah's cheeks, as looking just the tiniest bit self-conscious, she stammered, "Oh . . . you know . . . society . . ."

Alistair knew perfectly well what she meant, but he schooled his features into a look of innocent perplexity.

Sarah tried again. "Well, men, I mean women and . . . oh, call it flirtation." By now she was most uncomfortable, and what was worse, she suspected the earl of maneuvering her into this awkward situation and then secretly laughing at her.

"What? You have never flirted with anyone? Never sighed over a handsome face?"

Unable to speak, Sarah shook her head vigorously.

"Never even wanted to?" he pursued incredulously.

Again she shook her head, though not with quite so much assurance this time. All her life Sarah had scorned lying and deception, but now she was beginning to realize that sometimes it was not such a simple thing to adhere to exacting principles, for while it was not precisely a lie, it was also not entirely true that she had never *sighed over a handsome face*. The images of the earl and Rosalind were far too intrusive in her thoughts for her to ignore.

She had never allowed herself to wonder what the constant presence of that image might signify, and she certainly was not about to now, but given its frequent reappearance in her consciousness, she did have her doubts as to the complete sincerity of her answer. It was definitely time to change the subject.

She drew a deep breath before suggesting, "Somehow, in addition to helping Rosalind pass along incorrect information, we must discover what she has already given the chevalier so that you can pass it along to your superiors and they can change their plans accordingly."

"Whew!" Alistair whistled in admiration. "You are a deep one, are you not? You take to this espionage thing like a duck to water. Are you sure you have never done it before?"

Sarah could not decide whether to be pleased at his admiration for her cleverness or insulted that he could even think she would engage in such nefarious activity. As a result, she wound up looking adorably confused.

It was a most uncharacteristic look, one the earl found oddly attractive. Even more gratifying was the knowledge that it was he who had disconcerted this terrifyingly self-assured young lady. "As you appear to have it all thought out, may I know what the next step in this affair is to be?" Try as he would, Alistair could not hide the edge in his voice. After all, he had been at this game for years, and here was a green girl who had been plunged into it all only a scant twelve hours ago, calmly dictating strategy to him as though she were Colonel Sir George Murray himself.

His pique was not lost on Sarah, who took no little satisfaction from it. She had not the least desire to have the arrogant earl think he could manipulate her as easily as he did the rest of the fair sex. To give the man his due, he appeared to be rather clever and certainly articulate, but he was not the demigod the rest of the female population appeared to consider him. Smiling graciously, she replied. "Why, yes. From now on it is all up to you to get Rosalind to confide in you, which is something only you can do, and I would not dream of suggesting how to go about it. You have your ways, I am sure." Sarah exulted to herself as she saw his lips tighten. She had provoked him after all, and she had meant to. She was not ordinarily a contrary person, but there was just something about Lord Farringdon that impelled her to compete with him, even if it were only verbally. The man was so sure of himself, she could not help taking it as a challenge.

Alistair grinned. "Yes, as you say, I do have my ways, and since I have been doing my utmost to avoid an intimate tête-à-tête with the marchioness from the moment I arrived, it should be simplicity itself to accomplish this next task." He noted the dangerous sparkle in his companion's eyes with smug satisfaction. There, that should pay her back for the tone of gracious condescension with which she had referred to his many flirtations. "Now, don't poker up at me, Lady Sarah, you asked for it. If you continue to treat me as though I were an arrant coxcomb, why then, I shall act like one. I am not at all stupid, you know."

Sarah had the grace to blush. She really had been rather hard on him, but she was still feeling discomfited from his earlier probing about her feelings toward the relationships men and women had with each other.

The earl took pity on her. "And much of the time, I freely admit, I *am* a coxcomb. It is just that I am not accustomed to dealing with people who are competent as well as clever, and I find the whole experience unnerving, though delightful, but unnerving nevertheless. You must forgive me for trying to reestablish my self-respect, which you are so very hard on. Shall we cry friends then?"

The man looked so penitent that Sarah could not help laughing and taking the proffered hand. There was no doubt about it, Lord Farringdon could disarm the devil himself. "Friends. I hope you do not discover anything too alarming when you talk to Rosalind."

He was suddenly grave. "I hope I do not either. She is a vain creature, but she has never had much guidance. Her father and her brother were entirely bent on their own pleasures, and all she could do was go along with them or be left to her own devices. I am not excusing her behavior, but she has been shown only one way to act, and that is selfishly.

"The reputation of the Tredgingtons is such that she could not hope to capture a man wise enough to guide her or strong enough to stand up to her. The end result has been that she has grown only more headstrong as she has grown older. Without the help of her family, she has had to rely upon herself to get what she wanted. Though her goals may not have been admirable, her determination has been. Now she stands a chance of losing much of what she has fought for, and I am sure that she is not about to give it up. I must see that she does not destroy herself in the process."

Sarah regarded him soberly. At least now she was convinced that Rosalind was nothing to the earl. He saw all too clearly what she was. In fact, he saw her more clearly and more objectively than Sarah had heretofore been able to, and she was just the tiniest bit humbled by this. Nor could she help but feel a begrudging admiration for his chivalrous impulses. Apart from his obvious concern that Rosalind was passing along vital information to the enemy, he was genuinely solicitous of her welfare in a purely disinterested manner.

Lord Farringdon certainly did have surprising depths to his character, Sarah concluded. There was no doubt he was a most complex person, who was beginning to exert a rather dangerous fascination on her. It was definitely time to change the subject, change the company, and regain some of her equilibrium. "I have every confidence you will be able to help, not only your country, but Rosalind as well. Now you must forgive me, but I did promise to show Lady Edgecumbe around the village." Lord, she sounded like the starchiest of bluestockings, but she could not think of anything else to say. With a fleeting smile and a brief nod of her head, Sarah made her escape and went in search of her assigned companion, leaving Alistair to his own reflections.

Chapter Nineteen

His reflections were many and complicated. Foremost, however, was his appreciation for her quick-wittedness, her ability to grasp the problem at hand and get right to a solution. Alistair could hardly call to mind any man who did this well, much less a woman. Why, for a moment, even he, who was usually ahead of his fellows, had felt a little slow, but he had not minded too much. In fact, he had experienced a curious sort of pride in her continuing to fulfill his initial belief in her capabilities. Yet for all her intelligence and her mental sophistication, there was a naiveté about Sarah that Alistair found enchanting. On one hand, she could render material assistance without the blink of an eye to a wounded man who appeared on her doorstep in the middle of the night under most suspicious circumstances; yet on the other, the merest mention of men and women and love overset her completely in spite of her insistence that she had no interest in such things whatsoever.

For a moment the earl toyed with the idea of making her fall in love with him. As far back as he could remember, he had never failed to win over even the most resistant of females. Lady Sarah would present a challenge of the highest order, to be sure, and there was nothing that stimulated Lord Farringdon more than a challenge. But somehow he could not do it. Another part of him, the stronger part, wanted to protect her from men who were just like him. He wanted to defend such innocence—no, it was not innocence precisely, because she was well aware of such things—call it purity, against someone who wished to threaten that purity simply for the sport of it.

To be perfectly honest, this hitherto unsuspected chivalrous aspect of his character was, for the first time in his life, making the earl suffer just the slightest twinge of remorse for his previous predatory attitude where the fair sex was concerned.

But had he truly been predatory? No, now that he considered it, he felt compelled to say in his own defense that all the women he had made love to had been more than willing in the end. Any resistance they had shown had been merely for the sake of propriety, to force him into a declaration he did not wish to make, or to make him part with some very expensive proofs of his interest. More often than not, it was he who had had to do the resisting. And it seemed as though he was going to be called upon to do some more resisting at this very moment, for Alistair had just caught sight of the Marchioness of Cranleigh picking her way daintily through the roses in his direction.

"Good day, my lord. I had not thought to see you involved in such tame sport." Rosalind greeted him with a most enchanting smile that gave him ample opportunity to admire the delicious dimples and perfect teeth.

"Why, may not anyone appreciate the beauties of nature, my lady?" The earl responded with a smile equally as intimate and suggestive as that of the marchioness.

"Of course they may, foolish man." She rapped his knuckles playfully with the ivory handle of the delicate lace parasol that was shading her lovely face. "But they are not generally men like you."

"Oho, this is dangerous ground. And what sort of man am I, pray tell?" The gray eyes glinted with amusement, and something else that was far more unsettling.

Observing the earl closely from under long, dark lashes, Rosalind was hard put to identify that something. Being Rosalind, she naturally assumed it to be a passionate attraction to her person; however, there remained just the slightest bit of doubt. The Earl of Burnleigh was in general a rather disconcerting person to know. He never behaved as other members of the *ton* did, and he certainly never behaved as he ought, which was precisely why she had broken off their affair, Rosalind told herself smugly, forgetting entirely that it was Lord Farringdon's gentle but firm refusal to invite her to become Countess of Burnleigh that had been the true cause of the rupture.

The earl's question still hung between them, and with a coquettish smile, Rosalind opened her eyes wide. "What sort of man are you? Surely so many other women have told you that my reading of your character is quite unnecessary and is likely to make you even more top-lofty than you already are."

"I? Top-lofty? Surely, I have never been anything but your admiring slave, my fair one. You must elaborate; you cannot leave me in such an agony of suspense, you know." Alistair persisted in the hope that something she said would leave him an opening to ask the questions he wished to pursue.

"Oh." Rosalind fluttered her eyelashes. "I do not know. However, I do know that you are more an adventurer than an observer. You are far more likely to wrestle with nature than admire it."

"A cantankerous sort, in fact." Lord Farringdon chuckled.

"Not cantankerous, precisely, but . . ." She struggled to find just the right words. "Adventurous, bold. One might almost say that you seek out trouble and excitement." Rosalind bit her full lower lip enticingly. La, she had forgotten just how attractive such characteristics could be, especially when they were embodied in such a handsome figure of a man as the Earl of Burnleigh was. And how very dull her husband and his cronies were.

Admiring the speculatively seductive expression on the marchioness's face, Alistair grinned. Trust Rosalind to turn even the discussion of a man's character into an opportunity to exploit her charms. But he was tired of flirtatious banter, and he was also well enough acquainted with her to know that no matter how long they remained in the garden, tossing provocative remarks back and forth to one another, that is all that would happen. Rosalind enjoyed being a coquette. She was extraordinarily skillful at it, but she did not possess the inclinations to follow such dalliance to its natural conclusion. For her, flirtation was all about power, her power to attract and to influence men. It was not about passion or even about romance, and certainly it was not about love. Alistair had discovered this the moment he had held her in his arms. The marchioness had been about as responsive as the parasol she was now twirling gently on her shoulder.

Lord Farringdon had had enough. There were things he needed to discover, decisions and communications that had to be made. "So I seek danger and excitement, do I? Well then, I shall not disappoint you by running true to form and asking you if the Chevalier d'Evron is importuning you in any way." His bluntness had the desired effect. Alistair saw the brown eyes widen a moment and the delicate nostrils flare before his companion reassumed her flirtatious air.

Rosalind allowed a silvery laugh to bubble up from her slender white throat, giving herself a moment to recover from the shock of such a direct attack. It was just as well she had not married the earl. Really, the man had no manners whatsoever, asking questions like that and staring at her in that intense way. "Whyever should you think such a thing, my lord?" One delicate hand fluttered to her breast.

The earl, however, was not about to be distracted by an enticingly rounded bosom; he was far too experienced to fall for a trick as simple-minded as that. "Cut line, Rosalind," he responded curtly. "I have seen you and the chevalier in deep conversation more than once, and you have looked none too happy about it. Unless I miss my bet, it was not Spanish coin he was offering you, no sweet words of love he was whispering in your ear. You looked far too uncomfortable for that to be the case. Furthermore, you have been doing your best, unsuccessfully, I might add, to evade him. Now the Chevalier d'Evron is an attractive and much sought-after gentleman. It is not like you to avoid someone such as that—quite the opposite in fact." Alistair raised one skeptical dark brow.

Rosalind's mind raced. Really, the man was far too observant for his own good. He could do himself and her a great deal of mischief, pursuing such a line of reasoning. "La." She shrugged in what she hoped was a careless fashion. "He is not so irresistible as he seems to think. Why, the man appears to believe that all he has to do is smile at a woman to make her heart flutter."

As if you do not subscribe to the same notion yourself, Alistair muttered to himself. "Yet, you do not seem to have convinced him of your lack of interest. Now why is that?"

The gray eyes looking down at the marchioness were as cold and gray as a winter sea and they seemed to bore into the very recesses of her mind. There was no putting off the earl when he was determined; Rosalind knew that well enough. After all, she had never planned to allow him to kiss her at all until she had done him the honor of accepting his proposal to make her Countess of Burnleigh. Yet, she had found herself one warm summer evening some years ago, crushed in his fervent embrace before she had been aware of what was happening. No, it would do no good to deny him; it was time for another tactic.

Rosalind allowed one perfect tear to roll down her cheek as she caught her breath in a sob. "You are right. Of course you are right," she whispered so softly that he had to bend close enough to catch a whiff of her perfume in order to hear her. "I do not know what to do. I vow I am driven quite distracted by it all." She squeezed a tear out of the other eye.

"By what all?" Alistair was entirely unmoved by the glistening drop that clung to her lashes.

"Oh, you know, he is so French and he thinks that . . . that, I might be able to help him."

"That you might spy for him, you mean," Lord Farringdon interpolated bluntly.

"Oh heavens, what you must think of me even to say such a thing!" Rosalind was breathing heavily now, her bosom heaving under a thin silk shawl that was carelessly thrown over the low neck of her walking dress. This was not all an act. She truly had been upset by the demands the chevalier was making of her, and she did not know whether to be relieved or distressed at Lord Farringdon's discovery of it all.

"I think you are in a desperate situation," Alistair replied calmly, "and I think you are being forced to supply the chevalier information in order to protect someone, probably Richard," he concluded in a tone as conversational as though he were discussing the weather.

Lord Farringdon's lack of reaction had a steadying effect on the marchioness. Her breathing slowed, and she stopped twisting her parasol so desperately. However, Alistair had not missed the slight widening of her eyes at the mention of her brother. He decided to press on. "What price did the chevalier exact for saving Richard, who, I might add, is going to ruin himself, despite anything you might do to save him."

"Oh, nothing much." Rosalind began twisting the parasol again. "He just wished me to report to him anything I might overhear of Harold's conversations—that sort of thing. As if Harold ever has anything of import to say."

Hearing the scorn in her voice, Alistair almost had it in his heart to feel sorry for the hapless Harold. After all, the poor fellow could not help that he was as stupid as a sheep, nor that he was pompous and self-important. He had been bred that way. Unbidden, the image of Sarah's bright intelligent face rose before him, and for a brief moment, before he returned to the question at hand, he considered how unfair life had been to her in making Harold instead of Sarah a member of Parliament and master of Cranleigh. A smile quirked the edge of the earl's mouth. "I am sure that you, irresistible as you are, were able to extract all sorts of valuable information from the Marquess of Cranleigh."

Rosalind hesitated, unsure of how to read her interlocutor. The voice was pleasant enough, but those penetrating gray eyes under the straight black brows missed nothing. While there was warm admiration in his expression, there was also something else—a steely determination that brooked no denial. Lord, the man was handsome, she thought irrelevantly. Then, sighing gently, she replied slowly. "Very well. You are in the right of it. Harold did let on that more troops had been sent to the Peninsula."

"Which troops?"

"La, how should I—"

"Which troops?"

Rosalind hunched a defensive shoulder. "Well, the Thirteenth Light Dragoons, a battalion of the First Foot . . . er, a battalion of the Coldstreams, I think.

Something in her expression warned the earl that she had not divulged it all. "Come now, I already know enough to ruin you. If I am to help you, I must know everything."

The word *help* exerted a magical effect on the marchioness. For a moment the earl had looked so stern and uncompromising she had begun to wonder if she might wake up to find herself in the Tower. For all his wild propensities and his life of wine, women, and song, Lord Farringdon had a stern, almost uncomfortable moral streak. Rosalind knew that from experience. He had a very strict code of honor, which included a strong dislike for lying and deception of any sort.

"Well," she continued, "he also thought that a battalion each had been sent from the Third Foot, the Royal Scots, and the First Staffordshire, but he appeared less certain of that."

"Thank you," Alistair replied quietly. "Now I can do something to repair what damage may have been done." The dark eyes were fixed anxiously on him, and he could not help laying a reassuring hand on the marchioness's shoulder. "Never fear, I shall not involve you in the least. The lads at Whitehall are quite accustomed to my uncovering stray bits of useful information in the oddest of places."

This time the sigh that escaped Rosalind was one of pure relief. How strange and forbidding the earl looked with that firm jaw, the high cheekbones, and the determined set to the broad shoulders. Here was a man one could trust in and rely on. If only . . .

She gave herself a mental shake. There was no good repining over what might have been. That only led to regrets and did nothing to sort out one's future. And thinking about the future, she realized that in spite of her confiding them to the earl, her problems were still staring her in the face. "But what am I to do now?" she wailed. "Once he has discovered me to be a reliable source of information, he will never let me go."

Lord Farringdon nodded thoughtfully. There was no doubt that Rosalind was perceptive enough when her own welfare was at stake. "I am coming to that. We . . . er, I shall have to make up some false intelligence for you to pass along to the chevalier. After all, misinformation can be more damaging than no information at all. In a way, this could prove a fortunate circumstance now that you have established yourself as a credible source. You could be extremely useful to us."

"Oh, you are clever." Rosalind breathed.

The earl smiled, secretly acknowledging his debt to Sarah. As a man of honor, he felt compelled to admit that he was not the inspiration behind this particular idea, but as a man of the world, he knew it to be far more effective to have the marchioness think that such a suggestion had originated with him rather than with the sister-in-law she disdained. "Now you go and attend to your guests while I take care of the matter at hand." Alistair smiled encouragingly, and with a much lighter heart than she had felt in days, Rosalind headed toward the house.

Chapter Twenty

Having accomplished that particular part of the strategy that he and Sarah had concocted, Alistair felt inordinately pleased with himself. To be sure, he had completed far more complicated and dangerous missions in the past, but he had always done so on his own. Now he had a companion to share it all with him, and much to his surprise, he found that he rather liked the idea. His first impulse was to seek Sarah out immediately, but he thought better of it. It would not do her any good to be seen so frequently in his company. People were bound to talk and conjecture. Sarah would loathe that. It would also severely jeopardize his position with Rosalind if she were to think he had any interest in her sister-in-law. The marchioness did not take kindly to sharing any man with another woman, particularly as big a prize as the Earl of Burnleigh.

Lord, he did sound like the veriest coxcomb. It was not as though he rated his charms as high as the *ton* did, and he certainly did not set much store by the judgements of the *ton*. Why, a man could be a thief and a murderer and still be highly acceptable. Just as long as the man was of an exalted enough rank, possessed sufficient income, dressed well, carried himself with an air, and frequented the best society, he would find himself welcomed without hesitation into the fashionable world no matter what else he might have done.

Perhaps a man could not be a murderer, but Alistair had certainly known plenty of thieves—men who had married heiresses and spent their wealth, men who had won other men's estates and fortunes from them at the gaming table, men who had stolen someone else's reputation or position in the *ton* with a few well-chosen words. No, Alistair did not think the Earl of Burnleigh was such a prize, but the rest of the world did. He considered himself merely to be a person lucky enough to be born with a title, an easy competence, and a passable exterior. The remainder of his attraction lay in his utter boredom with the rest of the fashionable world. Women, especially, were intrigued by his aloofness and vied with each other to be the one who would capture the eligible bachelor and win him away from all the others. "The absurdity of it all," Alistair muttered scornfully to a large pink rose, before turning on his heel and making his way toward the library, where he hoped to snatch a few quiet moments in which to consider his next move. His wound was beginning to ache, and the idea of ensconcing himself in a comfortable chair in a room where he was certain no one but Sarah ever frequented was most appealing.

Meanwhile, Sarah, making the rounds of the village with Lady Edgecumbe and her daughters, would have liked nothing better than to be safely sequestered in the library. She had hoped that including the ladies in her visits to several aged and ailing retainers might take her mind off a subject that seemed to be occupying it almost exclusively for the past few days—the Earl of Burnleigh. However, she was not to be so lucky.

The moment the Edgecumbe girls had entered the carriage they began to discuss Lord Farringdon: his elegant air, his easy address, his prowess in athletic endeavors of any kind, and, of course, his reputation among the fair sex—not that either Lucinda or Cordelia had much firsthand knowledge of the last bit, but that did not stop them from repeating the latest *on-dits* as though they had been present at the very moment of occurrence.

"Yes, he has a most devastating effect on the unwary. Why, Lady Emily Saltash was quite convinced of his devotion when he suddenly, and without the least warning, began paying his addresses to Maria Melville," Lucinda pronounced in the most authoritative of tones.

"She had good reason to be sure of his interest." If possible, Cordelia spoke with even more assurance than her sister. "After all, he danced the first dance with her at the Duchess of Rothmere's ball and also at Lady Turnberry's rout, and all that quite apart from the attention he paid to her whenever they encountered one another. But of course, he is like that, carrying on a desperate flirtation with someone one minute and forgetting her name the next."

"But he can do that and no one minds. At least I should not." Lucinda smiled beautifically. "I could see that he wished very much to talk with me last evening, but the pianoforte was so loud, one could not be heard above it." She glanced significantly at Sarah and sniffed. "However, tonight I meant to wear the India muslin with the Persian silk sash. It is most becoming, and I have no doubt of its being vastly admired. This time I shall place myself somewhere quiet enough that Lord Farringdon is not afraid to interrupt."

Hearing the note of smug satisfaction in Lucinda's voice, Sarah found herself sympathizing mightily with Cordelia, who was looking daggers at her sister. She quickly changed the subject, hoping to find some topic that was less upsetting to all of them. "Do you have many villagers to attend to in Buckinghamshire, then?" she inquired of Lady Edgecumbe.

"Oh my, yes. Hatherleigh is a great deal more extensive than this and includes several villages." Lady Edgecumbe dismissed the charming high street and its rows of quaint half-timber houses with a scornful wave of her hand. "However, I do believe that as a rule, the cottagers in these parts of the world are a far simpler folk than in Buckinghamshire, and therefore I believe they must require a good deal more looking after."

She sounded for all the world as though Sarah's little section of Kent were darkest Africa. Sarah could not help wondering how such sturdily independent families as the Pottons and the Wittles would react to hearing themselves spoken of as though they were little more than primitives. Sarah had no doubt that they and the marshmen who made their homes not far from Ashworth required far less assistance than anyone in Lady Edgecumbe's vicinity. Surveying that redoubtable woman's formidable jaw and determined expression, Sarah had no trouble believing that a great many Hatherleigh tenants were forced to accept charity and advice from the lady of the manor whether they were in need of it or not.

By now they had reached the neat little cottage of Mrs. Walberswick, former housekeeper at Cranleigh. This sprightly little lady had been loath to relinquish her duties to Mrs. Dawlish, but at eighty, she had begun to find the multitude of stairs and the vastness of Cranleigh wearisome. Her rheumatism had worsened to such an extent that some mornings she was forced to stay in bed until noon, a state of affairs she found extraordinarily inconvenient.

Mrs. Walberswick really had no need of the beef tea that

Sarah brought her, being well cared for by her daughter, who was married to a local farmer, but she did relish the company and the gossip about Cranleigh. Besides, Sarah had always been a favorite of hers. However, it was obvious that her ladyship was not going to be able to stop long today, accompanied as she was by their three high-and-mightinesses. The sharp old eyes took in the situation at a glance, and the loyal old retainer thought to herself that once again Lady Sarah was being made to take on duties that the marchioness considered beneath her. The little lady had no doubt that these women who surveyed her so haughtily were guests at Cranleigh rather than Ashworth, for Lady Sarah would not have associated with such people of her own free will. Undoubtedly, Lady Melford had sent her sister-in-law off with these women so she would not be burdened by them and could spend more time on her own toilette or more interesting members of the party at Cranleigh.

Mrs. Walberswick revealed none of these uncharitable thoughts, however, receiving Lady Sarah and her companions with delighted gratitude and doing her best to make them feel comfortable in her snug quarters. "For I do so appreciate your stopping by, my lady." She beamed at the Edgecumbes. "You have no idea how kind Lady Sarah is, and how beloved she is hereabouts. Why, there is no finer lady to be had in all of Kent." Mrs. Walberswick was quick to detect the look of intense boredom that settled over Cordelia's hatchetlike features, and there was no mistaking her sister's yawn, which Lucinda did not even attempt to smother.

Thoroughly disgusted, Sarah patted the older woman on the shoulder. "I am afraid that we cannot stop now, Mrs. Walberswick, for we have several other errands, but I shall return tomorrow, and then we shall have a good coze." Smiling apologetically, Sarah hurried her guests out to the carriage, leaving the former housekeeper to reflect that lady Sarah was just as she had said, a true lady, not like some who had merely been born to a title.

Back in the carriage, Lady Edgecumbe, who had the grace to be ashamed of her daughters' ill breeding, began to demonstrate a livelier interest in the surrounding countryside than she had heretofore. Her questions were well informed and to the point, and Sarah was just beginning to feel more in charity with the woman when Cordelia sang out, "Oh, there is the chevalier!" and waved at him in such a way that even her mother, who was noted for her outrageously forthright manner, remonstrated with her. "Cordelia, you must not behave like such a hoyden. Really, I cannot think that you learned such manners in Buckinghamshire. If a Season in town is responsible for such behavior, it is obvious that we shall have to remain in the country after this."

Cordelia retreated into sulky silence, but the damage had been done, and the chevalier, who had been emerging from the taproom of the Red Lion, sauntered over to the carriage. He was the image of sartorial splendor, from the brim of his curly beaver set at a rakish angle on his glossy locks, to his bottle green jacket, dove colored breeches, and brilliantly polished Hessians.

Sarah thought he did not look best pleased when he first caught sight of them, but recovering quickly, he donned a brilliant smile and made as if to approach. Much to the girls' delight, Sarah requested John to pull up, and the chevalier hurried over, exclaiming at his good fortune in encountering so many charming ladies at one time. "There is something so invigorating about this fresh country air and the so beautiful surroundings"—he nodded toward Sarah—"that makes one wish to enjoy it all. In London I do not even rise until well after noon and never set foot out of my door until five o'clock at the earliest. But here"—he included the village in an expansive gesture—"one simply must be out enjoying the day."

Doing it rather much too brown, are you not, my fine sir, Sarah muttered to herself. Until this moment she had not paid much attention to the chevalier, but now she found his effusive enthusiasm a trifle overdone.

"Upon the recommendation of those who know, I have come down here to sample the local ale. It is said that the best to be had in all of Kent is made right here by the landlord." He gestured theatrically toward the Red Lion. "Of course, I allow for local prejudices, but, having imbibed mine host's home brewed, I can assure you it is excellent. We French have our wine, you know, but there is nothing quite so satisfying as a hearty tankard of ale." Then, noticing the slightly glazed expressions on their faces, he excused himself. "Please do forgive me for expounding on a subject that must be of the greatest indifference to you ladies, but I am filled with delight at this magnificent day and this charming spot."

Sarah had begun to ignore the chevalier's ridiculous prattle, but his mention of the ale caught her attention. She was not, naturally enough, unacquainted with the specialities of the local hostelries, but she had heard enough of their reputations to know that it was the George and Dragon, not the Red Lion that served the best ale—ale that was renowned far beyond the local village.

Richard, when he was at Tredington, often boasted of it to his guests, and Sarah had seen many a riotous party making its erratic way back to Tredington Park from the George and Dragon after several hours spent in the taproom. The chevalier was clearly up to something at the Red Lion, and it was not tasting the local brew. He must have been meeting someone there, but who? Was it one of the villagers or someone from London?

Having deduced this much, Sarah suddenly became most anxious to return to Cranleigh and the Earl of Burnleigh. She racked her brain for excuses to cut short their excursion, a move that was certain to please Lucinda and Cordelia, who were more animated in the presence of the chevalier than she had ever seen them. "It seems a great shame to waste such beautiful weather making calls to the villagers, and now that we have met the chevalier, it would be a pity to deprive ourselves of his presence. Will you not accompany us back to Cranleigh, sir? I believe there was some mention of a boating party on the lake. There is a most charming grotto on the island in the middle that is sure to delight anyone who visits it."

"Oh, yes." Cordelia clapped her hands. "That is an enchanting idea. I do so adore a boat ride. We have an elegant ornamental water at Hatherleigh, but Papa is never home so there is no one to row us about. However, I am sure that you are a most excellent oarsman, Chevalier." She fixed the Frenchman with a soulful gaze while her sister, furious at having missed her opportunity to win the chevalier's attention, scowled most dreadfully.

"It is set, then. John, please take us back to Cranleigh." Sarah glanced over at Lady Edgecumbe, who shrugged. Knowing the propensities of her flighty daughters, she appeared to be resigned to the change in plan. Meanwhile, Sarah settled back to plot an unobtrusive encounter with Lord Farringdon.

Chapter Twenty-one

Chance was in Sarah's favor as the little party that had gone into the village dispersed quickly upon their return to Cranleigh. Cordelia and Lucinda, each clutching an arm of the unfortunate chevalier, dragged him off toward the boathouse while their mother repaired to her chamber to write a long list of instructions to the housekeeper at Hatherleigh. They barely noticed Sarah as she bid them good day and slipped off to the library to sort out her thoughts and devise her plans.

The minute she entered the library, she grabbed a book off the shelf so as to appear occupied should anyone happen to find her there, but once seated, she stared off into space, the book unopened in her lap. How was she to discover the identity of the person the chevalier was meeting at the Red Lion, for meeting someone he was. It was highly out of character for the fastidious Frenchman to consort with the locals. She herself could not investigate this further, nor could the earl, who unless he was a master of disguise, was just as noticeable as she was and therefore unable to observe the Frenchman's movements without causing a stir. Truly, it was a sticky problem.

Sarah sat for some time considering it all when she was startled by a slight noise. She turned, listening intently. There it was again, as though someone had sighed heavily. She rose and crept softly toward the deep wing chair by the window. At first she perceived nothing, but then, as she drew closer, she saw a dark head leaning against one of the wings and long legs thrust under a low table in front of it. There was only one member of the house party of such a height as to possess legs of such length—Lord Farringdon. Closer inspection revealed him to be fast asleep, and the sound she had heard was the deep breathing of a man dead to the world.

Sarah remained transfixed, staring at him, enjoying the opportunity to observe Lord Farringdon without anyone's being the wiser. Somehow, he did not look nearly so forbidding this way. The thick, dark lashes lying against the high cheekbones softened the angular contours of his face, and sleep smoothed out the cynical lines around his mouth that gave him a perpetually sardonic expression. In fact, seeing his face in repose, Sarah found herself drawn to him in ways that she had not dreamt of before. Not put off by the defensive, mocking, knowing look she usually saw in his eyes, she could admit to herself that he really was most attractive.

The sleeper stirred, wincing as he did so. The regular heavy breathing faltered for a moment, and Sarah felt a twinge of remorse at having to interrupt his welcome moment of oblivion, but it was such a perfect opportunity to talk to him alone, and she had something of importance to tell him. There was nothing for it, but to give him a gentle shake.

The earl's gray eyes snapped open, instantly alert, and two purposeful fists half raised before he caught sight of Sarah and, recognizing her, grimaced ruefully. "A fine conspirator I am to awake in such a suspiciously hostile manner. It is a lucky thing that you and not someone else awoke me or there would be most uncomfortable questions asked as to what sort of person it is who wakes from a deep slumber prepared to come to blows."

Sarah was silent for a moment. What a shame it was that the earl led a life that made waking up such a tricky business. How lonely it must be to have to watch out for oneself constantly as he apparently did. For a fleeting moment she had the strangest urge to smooth back the dark hair that had fallen forward over his brow and assure him that she would stand guard while he slept. She banished such an absurd notion as quickly as it had come. The earl was a man of the world. What need had he of a green girl's assistance? "If you fall asleep in libraries, particularly this one, you need have no fear of interruption," she responded drily, revealing nothing of the treacherous thoughts in either her voice or expression. "I have come to tell you that we encountered the chevalier in the village, which is not in itself any way odd, but he was coming out of the Red Lion in what seemed to me to be a furtive manner. Furthermore, he claimed to have gone there to sample their excellent ale, and everyone knows the George and Dragon, not the Red Lion, has a reputation in at least two counties for its home brew."

"It does, does it? And how, pray tell, do you know?" Lord Farringdon quizzed her, smiling wickedly.

Sarah was not to be drawn. "Everyone knows. Why even you, being a friend of Richard's, must be well acquainted with it. At any rate, how I know is neither here nor there. The point is that *he* did not; therefore, he must have been there to meet someone."

"And how did you deduce that, fair lady?"

Sarah snorted in a most unladylike fashion. "Men such as the chevalier do not frequent common taprooms. You know that as well as I do. Consorting with greasy farmers and hearty squires is not quite in the chevalier's style."

The earl's eyes narrowed. "What a very observant person you are, to be sure, Lady Sarah. I believe that you are entirely correct in your suspicions. Now, the question is, what is to be done about it?" He gazed out over the gardens of Cranleigh, mulling over the various possibilities. "That must be where he meets the locals who help land his messengers from France, or perhaps he is sending word back to someone in London, though I doubt it, for it strikes me that our chevalier is not the sort to share anything with anybody, especially if it is power or information. I shall have to see what I can do to discover who this contact is."

"But you are wounded," Sarah objected. "You should not even be out of bed, much less chasing after someone, particularly a dangerous French agent. Besides, even if you do succeed in catching him meeting with someone, you will not know who that person is. If I send John Coachman, however, we shall know the identity of his contact and can then very likely figure out who else is involved because we will know his customary companions."

The logic was unanswerable, which did not necessarily do any more to recommend the suggestion to Alistair, who had begun to feel almost superfluous next to this fearsomely capable young lady. However, there was far more than his mere pride at stake. "You are in the right of it, Lady Sarah. What is this John Coachman like, and is he capable of such a task?"

"He is infinitely reliable and extremely loyal. He has been with the family for years and watched over me since he threw me on my first pony. If anything, he is overly protective of me."

Alistair could not imagine Sarah's allowing anyone watching out for her enough to be called overly protective, but he let it pass. "I would be exceedingly grateful for such information. In the main, most of the people who aid and abet someone like the chevalier do so purely for the money, and where money is concerned, one can usually enlist their assistance by offering them more money." Lord Farringdon nodded slowly. "We shall see who wins this round, Chevalier, we shall see."

The grim lines of his mouth and the determined set of his jaw boded no good for the Frenchman. What a change from his earlier peaceful expression, Sarah thought. At all times the earl appeared to be a force to be reckoned with; now he looked positively ferocious.

Alistair glanced up to see her regarding him with some concern. "Forgive me. I do not mean to trouble a lady with such things. However"—he cocked his head, eyeing her speculatively—"I do have my suspicions that you are enjoying this more than you are shocked by it." Detecting the sparkle of intrigue in her green eyes, he laughed. "I thought as much, and I must say, it is extraordinarily helpful to have an extra pair of eyes and ears as I cannot be constantly in sight of the chevalier." He twisted slightly in his chair and frowned as the stab of pain reminded him that his activities were also hampered to some extent by his injury.

Sarah was quick to notice his slight grimace. "Good heavens, your wound! We must attend to it. I shall return to Ashworth at once to procure fresh dressings and more salve. Miss Trimble has gone into the village to do some marketing, so I shall not be noticed. There is a large spinney on the road just before it turns into the drive to Ashworth. Can you contrive to meet me there in an hour's time?"

The earl nodded. He was loath to depend on anyone, especially a mere slip of a girl, for assistance of any sort, but he needed to remain as strong and healthy as possible, and lady Sarah's help would ensure that he did so.

"Good then. I shall bid you adieu and see you soon." Hastily gathering up her skirts, she hurried from the library, leaving Alistair to reflect on what an abundance of energy was contained in her slim figure and how much intelligence there was under the smooth gold tresses coiled so neatly at the nape of her neck.

Then he, too, arose and headed off to prepare for their meeting.

Lord Farringdon was as good as his word, and, entering the spinney precisely an hour later, Sarah found him seated on a fallen log, swinging one booted foot and watching the antics of a pair of squirrels chasing one another from limb to limb high above him. He was not so absorbed, however, that he did not look up the instant she entered the spinney. Dismounting and moving closer toward him, Sarah observed that his right hand, which appeared to be resting beside him on the log, was, in fact, gripping a most deadly looking pistol.

"Small wonder you have such a dangerous reputation among women of the *ton* if this is how you conduct your assignations." Sarah could not help chuckling as she pointed to his weapon.

"I carry this only because I am meeting with a most daunting female. In the main, I have no need of such precautions," he teased.

Not certain if this was meant as a compliment or an insult, Sarah turned to lift a satchel off her saddle and proceeded in a most businesslike manner to lay out a jug of water, fresh dressings, and more salve. "Now then, if you will let me help you with your jacket, I can examine the wound," she began briskly.

Suddenly serious, the earl turned quickly and captured one slim white hand. "Surely you must realize that I gave you a compliment of the highest order. Any other female I could be confident of winning over by flattering her with sweet nothings and all the admiring glances she hoped to attract, but not you. You are awake on every suit, and thus I treat you as an equal. But how do you know about my reputation? I thought you paid no heed to the gossip of the *ton*?"

Sarah blushed. "Ordinarily, I do not, but in the carriage today I could not help overhearing what Cordelia and Lucinda were saying."

"The Edgecumbe girls!" Alistair snorted in disgust. "They are typical of the worst sort of gossip. They select only the most scandalous *on-dits* to spread about because they have so little scandal in their own lives. They have so little real connection with the people involved that they have no way of knowing the truth, and care less just so long as it calls attention to them." He laughed cynically. "Furthermore, I have no doubt that it was all done for your benefit."

"For *my* benefit?" Sarah was mystified. "But why?"

"Because they are jealous of you."

"Jealous? Now you *are* offering me Spanish coin. Whyever would they be jealous of me?"

"Because you are beautiful and . . ." The patent expression of disbelief on Sarah's face at these words would have been ludicrous if it had not been so touching. Alistair felt oddly moved by it and the humble look of hope, or was it gratitude, in her eyes. Had no one ever admired her before, he wondered. How very sad. "Yes, you are beautiful, but I shall dwell on that later. Chiefly, they are jealous of you because they can see that I find you interesting and that I enjoy your company, that you are completely oblivious to this fact, and that you do not even care whether or not I do enjoy your company. It is bad enough to want something that someone else has, but when that someone else looks at the object of your envy with patent scorn, then that is even more humiliating." He smiled up at her. "You are a very clever woman, Lady Sarah, but you have a great deal to learn about the way of the world. If you care to learn about it, that is, which I suspect you do not. And now that is quite enough. I have been carrying on like a regular jaw-me-dead. I promise I shall be a good patient and take up no more of your time."

Sarah was grateful that she was so occupied with cleaning and examining the wound for the next quarter of an hour that Lord Farringdon could not see her face, nor did he appear to expect a response to his astounding revelations. That anyone could envy her anything, other than the fortune she had just inherited and which she set no store by, was an astounding idea to say the very least. What was worse, she could not help feeling just the tiniest bit gratified by it, though she despised herself for being so. Even more gratifying was the impression the earl seemed to have that she was so uninterested in him as to be—what had he called it?—oblivious to him. Would that she were oblivious to him! In Sarah's opinion she spent entirely too much of her time thinking about him, and she enjoyed his company far too much than was good for her.

Admiring the smoothness of his muscular chest as she deftly wound the bandage around him one last time, Sarah thought that she was definitely experiencing longings and urges that no proper young woman should even be aware of, much less relive, as she often did in the privacy of her bedchamber. Impossible though it was to believe, apparently none of these ridiculous impulses appeared to be noticeable, though she was uncomfortably conscious of them. Surely, it was a miracle that she had not betrayed herself, for it was not owing to any control or self-discipline on her part. Where the Earl of Burnleigh was concerned, she appeared to have none.

"There." Sarah tied one last knot and stood back, appearing to admire her handiwork when in truth all she could see was powerful square shoulders and a broad chest tapering to slim hips. Sitting there in the dappled sunlight, half dressed, the Earl of Burnleigh appeared to be some vigorous pagan creature of the forest, a Hercules rather than a man whose conquests were legendary in the ballrooms and drawing rooms of the metropolis. "It appears to be healing quite nicely. I do not think there is cause to worry about infection and, I daresay, in no short time you will be able to dress it yourself."

Sarah bent down quickly to gather up her supplies so that she was able to avoid looking at her patient, which was most fortunate. Alistair was regarding her intently, a curious arrested expression in his eyes. There was something in her manner, the speed with which she worked, the abruptness, almost curtness of her speech that was so in contrast with the gentleness of the first time she had ministered to him that he was at first nonplussed. Then observing her closely, he saw that the capable hands trembled ever so slightly when they touched him, and her breathing as she bent over her work was oddly ragged.

Lord Farringdon suppressed a smile. So Lady Sarah Melford was human after all. What an enormous relief it was. The earl rarely felt toward anyone what he was now feeling toward Sarah, and when he did, he never liked the vulnerability that came with it. He had never before been uncertain as to whether these feelings were returned. Now he was, and he liked that feeling even less. The pang of disappointment he had experienced when Sarah had told him that he could soon take care of himself had served only to show him just how much he enjoyed the enforced companionship. How pleasant it was to have her take care of him, to worry about him, and how heavenly it was to be touched by those gentle hands. The long, delicate fingers moving soothingly, her stroking the salve into his wound had been more comforting, more relaxing than anything he could ever remember. Surely, she could not be unaffected by it all? However, she had been so very businesslike that he had begun to doubt himself in a way he had not since childhood, until he had observed her more closely and then he guessed.

Instead of satisfaction or the heady sense of conquest that usually came with this recognition of attraction, there was now an astonishing sense of humility in the face of the powerful sensations she evoked, a sense of gratitude that a person such as Sarah, who was so much more than any other woman he had ever known, could be drawn to him as he was drawn to her.

These were the revelations of a minute and so unnerving that the earl thrust them hastily aside as he pulled on his shirt and turned his thoughts to the more obvious problems confronting them at the moment.

Chapter Twenty-two

"I have spoken to Ro . . . er, your sister-in-law," Alistair declared, thrusting one arm into his jacket, "and she admitted, though not without a great deal of prevarication, to having given information to the chevalier. I have no idea whether it is possible to undo the damage she has done, but I should at least pass that word along to Whitehall. As I know of no reliable messengers around here, it seems I must go to London myself to inform them of the latest developments."

Sarah, who had at last gotten herself well in hand, was thinking furiously while trying desperately to ignore the part of her that did not wish to say good-bye. Fortunately, there was another part of her that did, the rational part that longed for the peace of her former rather dull, but exceedingly comfortable routine. "I quite understand, but will not the chevalier suspect something if you leave so unexpectedly?"

"Suspect? Suspect what?"

"Well," she began reasonably, "he and his men are interrupted in the midst of clandestine activities one night, the observer eludes pursuit, but may possibly be hurt; then, practically the next day, you, who presumably had been planning to remain at Cranleigh for some time, suddenly depart for London."

For a minute the earl was silent, staring so fixedly at a tree trunk that Sarah was not sure he had heard her; then a singularly attractive smile dawned. "What ever did I do without you, Lady Sarah? It is a wonder I did not get myself killed long before this. You must think me very green indeed."

Feeling a rush of pleasure at these words, Sarah was thinking no such thing. Rather she was taking note of what a wonderful effect simple words of recognition and appreciation could have on a person. "Why, no. I had actually been wondering how you had been able to do it all on your own, but I expect if you have been conducting this sort of business mostly in the metropolis you would not have had to be so careful what with so many people about. Things are so much more confined at Cranleigh. It is rather like living in a zoo." The depth of feeling in her voice suggested that this was no idle remark meant to reassure him, and that she had often suffered from the stifling atmosphere of a small community where everyone's actions constituted much of the news of the day.

"It is true that one can disappear in a crowd much more easily in London than around here," Alistair admitted. He did not add that her presence was providing more distraction than he was accustomed to. While Lady Sarah had provided invaluable assistance both in helping him recover from his wound and acting as another pair of eyes, she was also beginning to intrude into his thoughts with dangerous frequency, and Alistair found himself devoting a good deal of time and energy observing her and thinking about her that he would otherwise have spent keeping one step ahead of the chevalier.

"I shall have to enlist the aid of someone to impersonate a messenger from my man of business in London. Do you know of anyone who is not well known in these parts?"

Sarah thought for a moment. "I believe that Thad . . . er, the vicar, has a brother who is also in the church. His parish is in Newington. He is a good deal younger than the Reverend Mr. Witson, and from what I hear from his brother, a rather lively young man. Perhaps he could be persuaded to help."

Sarah's use of the vicar's first name caught the attention of Lord Farringdon. He looked up, regarding her intently, but other than stammering, she did not act at all self-conscious. Still, Alistair could not help wondering. The vicar was an old family friend; that would explain it. Surely, she could not think of him in any other way, not Sarah. He was far too dull for her. Of course, the vicar was her intellectual peer, but beyond that, there was no comparison. She could run rings around him. She needed someone who was passionate and adventurous, not a man who was content to spend the rest of his days sitting cozily in front of the fire, reading scholarly treatises. Enough of such ridiculous speculation. Sarah was looking expectantly at him, waiting for a reply. "That is certainly a possibility." Inexplicably, the earl found himself loath to be indebted to Thaddeus Witson or his brother, however trustworthy they might be.

"I shall ask the vicar to speak to his brother if you like, and perhaps you could meet with him some day soon at the vicarage. That will give you some time to heal, which is all to the good because, strong as you are, it would do you no harm to be looked after for a little while longer."

Alistair grinned. "You are a very stern nurse, Lady Sarah. In this instance, though not in many others, you will find me a reasonable man. I need to be strong enough for whatever is to come."

Sarah did not particularly relish the sound of those words, but she gave no sign of it, moving on instead to other areas of concern. "I shall have to keep watch over the chevalier then while you are gone."

"What!" The earl sat bolt upright, too astonished even to notice the pain in his side. "You will do no such thing, my girl!"

"And whyever not?" Sarah's voice was ominously quiet.

Alistair could see the danger signals—the narrowed eyes, the firm little chin thrust forward, the mutinous line of the mouth—and knew it behooved him to tread most cautiously. "Do not fly up in the boughs. It is not that I doubt in the least your ability to carry out such a program. I have utmost faith that you would do excellently, certainly better than I have done thus far, but we are dealing with a very ugly customer here, and I should never forgive myself if anything were to happen to you." He held up his hand as she opened her mouth to protest. "No. I simply cannot allow you to risk life and limb when I am not around to protect and look after you."

Sarah was so struck with the idea of anyone's wishing to look after her and protect her that she could think of nothing to say in reply. For a good deal of her life, especially in her impressionable years, she had been nothing but a burden to people who tried to escape the responsibility of looking after her rather than welcoming it. Now someone was offering to do just that, and that he was one of the most intriguing people she had ever met only made it all the more incredible.

Alistair took advantage of this silence to press his point. "I shall send someone in my absence who will contrive to get in touch with you when he arrives. Naturally, any observations you have made of the chevalier's movements while you are in the company of the rest of the party at Cranleigh would be most invaluable. In the meantime, I shall confer with them at Whitehall and, with your permission of course, shall send you a letter instructing you what information to give Rosalind so that she may pass it along. It will necessarily be in code, so do not be surprised if I write to you of volumes of Spanish history instead of numbers of battalions. I suspect that we plan to send more troops to the Peninsula, and that it would thus be to our advantage to let the chevalier and his masters think that we are sending none, but I must confirm all this. It is a rather big favor to ask of someone who is an unwilling member of the party at Cranleigh in the first place, but I should be most grateful if you could do this."

There was no need for Sarah to answer. Alistair could read the response in her sparkling eyes and the eager look on her face. He chuckled. "I can see from your expression that I may count myself very fortunate that you have promised to give up all thoughts of following the chevalier, for you look more than ready to take on adventure of any sort." He reached out to tilt up her chin with one hand and look deep into her eyes. "You *have* promised, have you not?"

The gray eyes boring into hers were uncompromising and as hard as flint. There was no arguing with him. The earl was a man of infinite charm, but at the moment it was difficult to believe that this dangerous-looking stranger was the person whose disarming and captivating wit had attracted her to him much against her will. Sarah nodded. "I had not exactly promised, but I will now."

A gleam of humor lit his eyes. "It is a lucky thing I made you give your word, else, knowing you, you would have gone against my advice safe in the knowledge that you had led me to believe you had promised when, in fact, you had not."

Sarah opened her mouth to protest.

"No, do not bother to deny it. I know you are a woman of honor, a woman of your word, but you are also clever enough to equivocate when it is to your advantage, and you would do so in this case if I were not to ensure that you do not. I have seen how you court danger and excitement, given the least opportunity. I will not encourage you in this. Until now the excitement and adventure you have enjoyed have come from living your life differently from those around you and, yes, from thwarting the expectations of the hidebound and the respectable—your pompous brother in particular. This situation, however, is vastly different. It does not involve a threat merely to your reputation, but to your person as well, and that is something I cannot bear to contemplate."

"What makes you think all this?" Sarah demanded suspiciously. In truth, the man seemed capable of reading her mind, for she had intended to do precisely what he had just described—lull him into complacency by allowing him to believe that she was content to follow his orders when she planned to go ahead on her own keeping an eye on the chevalier. There was no denying it; unfortunately, the earl was awake on all suits and thus able to forestall her.

He was chuckling at her. "How do I know? Because I would have done the very same thing myself, gone ahead and conducted my own investigation unless I had given my word to someone, and then of course, I would not. We are not so unalike after all, you and I."

Sarah could not help being much struck by this observation. In the oddest way it was true. For all their differences—he was a rake and a libertine; she was more often categorized as being a prim bluestocking—they were similar in their independent turn of mind, their refusal to abide blindly by the dictates of society, their wish to discover things for themselves and live on their own terms.

Before encountering the Earl of Burnleigh, Sarah would have denied any taste for adventure. After all, she preferred the quiet of the country to the bustle of town, but having participated in something that was not only truly exciting, but also worthwhile, she was forced to admit to herself that she did enjoy this sort of intrigue and, if she was not mistaken, she had something of a talent for it.

The earl's words, besides forcing her to stop and reflect on these things, were also strongly reassuring. There had never been anyone else besides Lady Willoughby who had viewed life from a perspective even remotely similar to Sarah's, and Lady Willoughby was a blood relative. Here was a perfect stranger who seemed to understand things in much the same way she did. It was rather comforting not to be alone anymore. Sarah smiled and held out her hand. "Perhaps you are right, but we must continue to seem what we first appear, the very antithesis of one another. I must return to my duties at Ashworth and you to yours at Cranleigh."

Alistair clasped the hand that was held out to him, thinking what a difference a smile could make. It transformed Lady Sarah from a rather serious young lady into a beautiful woman. Now, why had he not noticed that before, or had he been afraid to?

Chapter Twenty-three

In the ensuing days Lord Farringdon and Lady Sarah were careful not to appear to spend any time in one another's company. During an excursion to Lympne where the party from Cranleigh spent a day viewing the medieval castle and the few remaining ruins of the third-century Roman fort that had supported Carausius in his bid for imperial power and had later become a defense against Saxon pirates, Sarah and the earl had no other contact than the briefest of greetings as the little cavalcade set forth on the journey.

This was not to say that each one was not intensely aware of the other's presence. To all intents and purposes Alistair paid far more attention to Sarah's discussion with Thaddeus Witson than he did to his own mindless exchange with the Edgecumbe girls.

A brief flirtatious interlude with Rosalind, who cared more that he was escorting her carriage and casting admiring glances in her direction with proper frequency than that he actually shared any worthwhile conversation, allowed him to position himself so as to keep Lady Sarah and the vicar in view for almost the entire journey. As he smiled mechanically at the Marchioness of Cranleigh and made sure to look deep into her eyes every ten minutes or so, the earl wondered endlessly what Sarah and her partner were talking about that could be so absorbing to both of them. What caused that half smile at the corner of her mouth? What inspired that vigorous nod of her head? And what had she said to amuse the ordinarily serious Thaddeus?

Had he known the topic of their conversation, Alistair would have been reassured, for it had to do with Sarah's enlisting the aid of Thaddeus's younger brother to deliver a message to the Earl of Burnleigh, urgently requesting his presence in London. The vicar readily agreed to this proposal with no more than a curious glance, but that was enough to elicit a stumbling explanation from Sarah.

"You see, Lord Farringdon is beginning to find it rather awkward here, what with the determined pursuit of the Edgecumbe girls and . . ." her voice trailed off as she directed a meaningful look toward the carriage where Rosalind was practically glowering at Lucinda and Cordelia, who were leaning forward so eagerly and chattering with such animation to the earl as to give abundant proof to Sarah's hastily concocted interpretation of his need for escape from Cranleigh.

"Ah." The vicar nodded thoughtfully. "Though it is rather unlike you, Lady Sarah, to concern yourself with the welfare of a fribble such as the Earl of Burnleigh, especially when his entire behavior positively invites such attentions."

"He is *not* a useless fribble." Sarah came hastily to the earl's defense. Then, appalled at the vehemence of her response, she carefully amended it. "Well, rather, there is more to his character than I had at first supposed. He is quite well informed on the current state of affairs both here and abroad. In fact, he is surprisingly knowledgeable about a number of things."

"I am gratified to hear that," her companion replied in a deceptively mild tone, glancing covertly at her. The vicar was no fool, and he had known Lady Sarah Melford for the better part of her life. Acting on his suspicions, Thaddeus had called Lord Farringdon a fribble with the precise intention of eliciting a response. And he had gotten one. So *that* is where the land lies, he congratulated himself. I had thought as much. Indeed, Providence did have a way of looking after things, and the vicar found that despite his best intentions, he could not entirely repress the smile of satisfaction that rose to his lips.

The Reverend Mr. Witson had been far quicker to see beneath Lord Farringdon's wild reputation and devil-may-care airs than anyone else. More at liberty to observe the earl, and less likely to compete with him than Sarah, he had recognized a clever, well-instructed mind under the irreverent exterior and had come to the conclusion that he was just what Sarah needed to encourage the lighter side of a character that tended toward gravity. Sarah deserved more of a life than the quiet round of charitable works and overseeing of affairs at Ashworth. She needed gaiety, though not necessarily the vapid frivolity of a London Season. The vicar had finally begun to believe that far-fetched as it might sound, the Earl of Burnleigh could just possibly introduce a more lively note into her otherwise rather dull existence.

In years gone by, both the vicar and Lady Willoughby had racked their brains trying to think of ways for Sarah to widen her circle of acquaintances so that she might encounter just such a person as Lord Farringdon. For his part, Thaddeus would have chosen a man a little less dashing than the earl, but the vicar was a man of faith, and he was not one to quibble with his Maker if He chose to provide Sarah with something slightly less than the vicar had requested.

To be sure, Thaddeus had encouraged Sarah to broaden her horizons as much as it was possible. It was he who had convinced her that she had as much right to be heard as the next person and enough wit to make her opinions worthy of consideration. To this end he had been tireless in his attempts to encourage her writing for such respected mediums of expression as *The Edinburgh Review*. Half believing that he was hoaxing her, or that his fondness for her was severely impairing his judgement, Sarah had nevertheless submitted an article under the name of William Redmond with most gratifying results. The correspondence it had engendered had led to lively debates conducted through the post, and Sarah, without being forced to attend a single assembly or endure a London Season, had gained several new acquaintances who could appreciate much more of what she had to offer than any partner of a quadrille could have.

The writing had been a start at enlivening her existence and making her feel valued as she deserved to be, but it was not enough, and now without the aid and influence of Lady Willoughby the vicar had despaired of anything occurring to improve the state of affairs. Certainly, he had never dreamed that help would come from the direction of Cranleigh, but the marchioness's craving for excitement and admiration had been responsible for the presence of Lord Farringdon. Of course, Sarah had grumbled to Thaddeus at the necessity of her participating in the activities planned by her sister-in-law, but, whether or not she scorned the company, it had certainly enlivened her existence.

The vicar sympathized entirely with Sarah's impatience at the pretense and emptiness that characterized so much of the life of Rosalind's coterie, but more than Sarah, he could see the benefits that could be derived from the time she was forced to spend at Cranleigh. The conversations, while they were not perhaps of such a high moral or intellectual tone as Sarah would choose, were conversations, nevertheless, and more than she usually enjoyed in her daily round of existence. Then there was the Earl of Burnleigh.

The moment Lord Farringdon had appeared, he had infused the gathering with energy and excitement. True, some of this arose naturally from the efforts of most of the women present to outdo each other in their bids for his attention, but it was more than that. The Earl of Burnleigh possessed a vitality and charm that lent itself to any situation, and no one could remain unaffected by it. Even Sarah, ordinarily oblivious to such things, had been unable to ignore him that first evening at dinner, and her preoccupied air had not been lost on her partner. Thaddeus had been amused at how she had bridled at Lord Farringdon's easy domination of his end of the table, and intrigued by her inability to keep her eyes from wandering occasionally toward that end of the table.

No less satisfying was the earl's interest in Lady Sarah. Thaddeus had felt the man's eyes upon them as he and Sarah had launched into their discussion of Sir Francis Burdett at the dinner table. The vicar had watched him make his way over to her when they rejoined the ladies in the drawing room. From then on he had kept track of the number of times the earl had sought out Sarah. When Lord Farringdon spoke to her, his customary expression of boredom vanished, and the languid air he cultivated dropped from him immediately. He became intent and animated in a way that he never was with anyone else, even the enchanting Marchioness of Cranleigh.

The Reverend Mr. Witson had ministered to the joys and sorrows of his parishioners for many years, and there was very little in human existence with which he was not conversant. He had been aware of the flirtation between Rosalind and Lord Farringdon and had hazarded a shrewd guess as to the motives of both of them. He was also well acquainted with the Earl of Burnleigh's reputation. At university Thaddeus had had ample opportunity to witness the machinations of youthful rakes, and he knew that the earl's attraction to Sarah was something more than his customary pursuit of females, though Thaddeus suspected that in the earl's case, much of the pursuing had been done by the females. No, Lord Farringdon did not appear to wish to add Sarah to his list of conquests as much as he wished to add her to his list of friends, a sign that gave the vicar hope for the relationship between the two of them.

Now, why was the earl departing in such a precipitate manner and what did Sarah's involvement in this departure mean? The vicar had begun to hope that more might come of their friendship, though he knew that it was expecting a great deal for a man of the world to forget the scores of sophisticated women in favor of a quiet country miss no matter how clever and unique she might be. Still, Thaddeus was a man who placed great faith in Providence.

"It is a pity that it has become so, er, *difficult* for his lordship. I was beginning to enjoy his company, were not you?" The vicar glanced curiously at Sarah and was delighted to observe just the faintest bit of color suffusing her cheeks.

"Yes," she replied as casually as possible. "Certainly, he is more interesting than Lord Edgecumbe, who speaks most eloquently on political matters, but knows very little else, or Lady Edgecumbe, who does not converse so much as she pronounces on her limited range of subjects with such authority that it would be foolhardy for one to differ with her, or even venture a reply. The Duke and Duchess of Coltishall are certainly unexceptionable enough, but they have very little to contribute beyond a civilized discussion of the weather at any given moment or the possibility of its changing in the near future."

Thaddeus could not help chuckling. "Faced with such a choice, you would be hard put not to enjoy the man's company, for from the little I have seen, he can speak to a great deal of purpose on a variety of subjects."

"Which is more than can be said for the rest," Sarah concluded with a darkling look at the Edgecumbe girls, who were laughing excessively while Lord Farringdon looked unmistakably bored.

The party had reached the ruins by now, and to Sarah's infinite relief all discussion of such a dangerous topic was dropped, as they dismounted and prepared to view the ruins. But Thaddeus was more than satisfied. He had seen enough to encourage him in his theory that Lady Sarah Melford and the Earl of Burnleigh enjoyed one another's company to the extent that Sarah at least did not relish anyone's observing it or remarking on it. "Just let me know how and when you wish Horace to proceed, and I shall send word to him at Newington," the vicar murmured as they joined the others where Rosalind was already claiming Lord Farringdon's arm as she floated down from the barouche.

"Ah, vicar," the marchioness greeted Thaddeus with eagerness. "I am glad you have come. Cordelia and Lucinda were just inquiring about the castle, and I knew you would be able to inform them about it as you are so well acquainted with the history of the area. I find that I am rather faint from the carriage ride and must walk a little in the sunshine to clear the dizziness in my head."

Cordelia and Lucinda, who had been inquiring about the object of their journey in only the most general way in order to capture the earl's complete attention, hesitated, unwilling to let the marchioness steal a march on them with the most eligible man they had come close to in quite some time, but they were no match for Rosalind, who smiled sweetly. "Do not concern yourself with my welfare; Lord Farringdon will look after me excellently, will you not, sir?" And, clasping the earl's arm more closely to her, she turned to lead him toward the other side of the hill and away from the Norman tower of the church.

However, the marchioness had reckoned without Lord Farringdon, who took great exception to having his choices made for him by anyone, especially the Marchioness of Cranleigh. Loath to be lured away and thus cast in a role of apparent intimacy, he surveyed the surrounding countryside, announcing, "Yes, it is just as I had thought, this is where the Roman road came from Canterbury, and, if I am not mistaken, we are also in the midst of *Porteus Lemanis*." He turned to Thaddeus. "Perhaps we had better explore this place in correct chronological order. Can you tell us anything further about the site? If I remember my history, it was the Roman general Carausius who was responsible for these fortifications."

"You are precisely correct, my lord." Thaddeus smiled appreciatively as he strolled over to join the earl and his fair companions. "Maximian gave Carausius the task of protecting Gaul from the attacks of Saxon raiders, and Carausius, anticipating that he might be accused of complicity with these same raiders, fled to Britain, where he protected himself by constructing such forts as these. He was entirely justified in his fears, for in 289 Maximian attacked him and was defeated."

"But eventually Carausius was murdered, was he not?" Alistair inquired, poking at a fallen slab with one booted foot.

By now the others had drifted over to listen to the discussion, and Sarah was able once again to admire the adroitness with which Lord Farringdon was able to turn a situation or a conversation to his advantage.

As if he could feel her thoughts, Alistair twisted his head slightly and winked at her before returning to the conversation, which had wandered from the Romans to the lords of the Cinque Ports and the former glories of the Kentish coast.

Chapter Twenty-four

The rest of the day passed without event, though Sarah, avoiding anything that might appear to be more than the most casual contact with the earl, had ample opportunity to observe him. He certainly did have the most enlivening effect on females. Cordelia and Lucinda vied constantly with one another for his attention, and Rosalind, though disdaining to indulge in such obvious ploys as tittering endlessly at every other word Lord Farringdon uttered, witty or not, was never far from him, darting provocative glances from under slyly lowered lashes. Even Lady Amelia's eyes followed him wherever he went, though she rarely left her parents' side.

At long last they returned to Cranleigh, and Sarah was able to break away with the excuse that she must return to Ashworth to dress for dinner and give Ajax some well-deserved rest. She made her escape with a sigh of relief. After a day spent in company, her senses attuned to each and every move of each and every person present, she found it extraordinarily soothing to ride along the country lanes, listening to nothing more taxing than the sweet song of the thrush and relishing the rich and varied greens of the hedgerows.

A sense of peace and tranquility descended upon her, though it was soon broken by the sound of pounding hooves that slowed as they approached her. Without having to turn in the saddle, Sarah knew it was Lord Farringdon; no one else would have ridden at quite that speed.

"Had enough idle chatter for one day, have you?" he inquired cheerfully. "So have I, though you got the best of the bargain, being able to spend most of your time with the Reverend Mr. Witson." Alistair shot a penetrating glance at her, but there was no reaction. Why he expected one or why he even cared that she enjoyed the vicar's company, he could not say, but he found himself feeling relieved that Sarah exhibited not the slightest bit of self-consciousness when she replied.

"Yes, I suppose I did; however, we were speaking mostly of you, so I leave it to you to decide how idle our chatter was." She smiled impishly and continued, "He volunteered his brother's services to you and awaits your instructions."

"Thank you for acting on my behalf. I would appreciate his delivering the *urgent message* as soon as possible, and if that could be arranged, I should be most grateful."

"Very well then, it shall be done. I shall send word to Thaddeus, and you shall have your summons. Until this evening then." Sarah gathered up Ajax's reins, dug her heels in, and was off before the earl could thank her.

Now why had she been in such a thundering hurry to leave him, and when had she begun calling the Reverend Mr. Witson *Thaddeus*? Alistair turned and made his way back to Cranleigh in a speculative mood. He was not accustomed to being dismissed so easily by a woman, especially a woman whose company he enjoyed as much as he enjoyed Lady Sarah Melford's, and he found the dismissal rather unpleasantly disconcerting.

After some moments he shrugged and urged Brutus to a gallop. It was no use conjecturing. He would be rid of them all and back in London soon, where he would be free to concentrate on the task he had set for himself—unmasking the Chevalier d'Evron. Somehow the prospect was not as exciting as it once would have been.

All went according to plan, and the very next day Horace Witson, breathless, his horse in a lather, appeared at Cranleigh, looking for all the world as though he were a junior clerk from a banking firm in the City. Claiming urgent business with the Earl of Burnleigh, he was led to the ornamental water where his lordship had at last been coerced by Cordelia and Lucinda into rowing them gently around the perimeter while they exclaimed continuously at the smoothness of his stroke, the breadth of his shoulders, and the strength in his arms.

For his part, Alistair had never known he could experience such relief as he did when he caught sight of Horace waiting expectantly by the water's edge, clutching a most important-looking document. Gratefully, he rowed toward the shore and allowed the more than willing messenger to hand out the boat's fair cargo, much to the dismay of Lucinda and Cordelia, who considered the earnest-looking young man a poor substitute for the dashing earl.

Hurriedly, Alistair scanned the note from his supposed man of affairs, and then, bestowing a dazzling smile on the two young ladies, he excused himself. "I must beg your forgiveness at having to cut short such a delightful interlude, but I am called to London on rather urgent business. Perhaps young Mr. . . ." he directed an inquiring glance at the vicar's younger brother, who was enjoying himself hugely.

"It is Horace, sir."

"Yes, er, perhaps Horace can escort you to the house in a more proper and leisurely fashion."

And without further ado Lord Farringdon made his escape, stopping only to ask Nettlebed to inform his mistress of the earl's imminent departure and to send word to the stables to ready his curricle. He then sought out Rogers to confer about the packing and preparations to be made for the return to London.

In no short order Rosalind appeared at the door of his bedchamber, her dark eyes wide with reproach. "What is this I hear about your leaving, Alistair?" In her dismay, the marchioness dispensed with formalities, addressing him in the most intimate of manners and clutching at his arm. "It is too bad of you. Whatever am I to do for amusement now? And"—she dropped her voice to a desperate whisper—"how shall I face the chevalier? What am I to do? You cannot desert me!"

Alistair laid a comforting hand on hers. "Relax, Rosalind. I have thought it all out, and directly I arrive in London I shall send word as to the next information you are to pass along to the chevalier." Seeing the words of protest hovering on her lips, he raised a hand to forestall her. "Never fear, I shall make sure you have something by the time your husband receives the next dispatch."

"But how am I . . . what am I . . . really, Alistair, it is too unkind in you. How am I to go on with no one to help me?"

"There is someone to help you." The earl spoke soothingly. "I shall send everything to Lady Sarah at Ashworth, and that way there is not the slightest chance of any suspicion falling on you."

"Sarah?" Rosalind's whisper rose to a muffled shriek. "Sarah? What has she to do to any purpose? She is no match for the chevalier. I need *you,* Alistair." The full red lips pouted prettily, and the beautifully rounded shoulders shook slightly under the lace that covered the neck of her gray scarcenet walking dress.

"You must not underestimate your sister-in-law," the earl replied not unsympathetically. "She understands a great deal more than you give her credit for. I should not be ashamed to accept her assistance. In fact, she has been a great help to me."

"Sarah?" There was no mistaking the surprise in the marchioness's voice, nor was she best pleased to discover the excellent terms on which Sarah and the earl appeared to be. The cunning jade! She had weaseled her way into Lord Farringdon's good graces without anyone's being the wiser. The deviousness of her behavior was appalling. Really, what right had she to steal the attention of one of Rosalind's most ardent admirers? If the idea of Sarah's attracting the notice of anyone, much less a gentleman of the earl's sophisticated tastes, were not so utterly absurd, Rosalind would have been furious; as it was, she was merely mildly annoyed.

Accurately assessing the emotions raging in her ladyship's lovely bosom, Alistair hastened to add, "She may not possess anything like your beauty and charm, Rosalind, but she does have a good head on her shoulders, and she does want to stop the chevalier from succeeding in his endeavors."

Rosalind was beaten, and she knew it. The earl would not be persuaded to change his mind. "Very well. If you say so . . ." Her voice trailed off. She might give up the struggle to keep him at her side, but she was not going to admit that she had any use for Sarah.

It was not fair. There was her sister-in-law inheriting an enormous fortune, which at best she would never use and at worst fritter away on charitable works, and now, to add insult to injury, she seemed to have cozened her way into Lord Farringdon's good graces. Why, she was not even passable-looking, being unfashionably blond with a nose that was straight instead of the currently popular retroussé. Her eyes were an uncomfortably intelligent green instead of celestial blue or melting brown, and her figure was so slim it lacked the enticing curves that drove men to distraction. Truly, it was too maddening that such a poor little thing was even noticed when the ravishing Marchioness of Cranleigh was present for everyone to admire.

"You will see." Alistair smiled encouragingly while inwardly he thanked his lucky stars that Sarah's presence allowed him to leave Cranleigh in good hands while he went to London. The marchioness was growing dangerously dependent upon his presence, and a re-establishment of their relationship, in any form, was something he most definitely hoped to avoid. "Now you must excuse me while I see to the packing." And after bowing low over her hand, he turned and entered his chamber, closing the door firmly behind him and leaving his hostess to seethe with frustration.

Men! Rosalind fumed. They were all the same, pretending to be entranced with a person until business or politics or both called, and then they completely ignored one. Lord Farringdon was the worst of the lot with his charming conversation and seductive ways. At least Harold never claimed to be interested in anything else besides his blessed affairs. It was enough to make one ill. Now she was left with a house full of people and no one to enliven it for her.

It was too selfish of Alistair to go off without a thought for her safety or happiness, but then why should he be any different from any of the rest of the men in her life? They had been leaving her for as long as she could remember to go off hunting or gaming, or heaven knows what. And if they didn't leave her, they forced her to leave them, packing her off to school in Bath as if she were no more than a parcel to be gotten rid of. However, Rosalind had had her revenge on all of them, for when she had returned from school, no man had been able to resist her, and all those who had deserted her in the past had come flocking around her begging for a word, a look. Even Richard and her father, realizing that she was a far greater draw for their cronies than anything else their hospitality could offer, had finally paid at least some attention to her.

But that was neither here nor there. Females could draw men by their beauty and their charm, but it behooved them to extract as much as they could when they could, for inevitably men lost interest and returned to their original pursuits. Rosalind sighed and headed back to join the rest of her guests in the garden. Catching sight of her sad, lovely face as she passed by the pier glass hung over a marquetry side table, she straightened her shoulders and chided herself. Feeling sorry for yourself never got you anything. Think, Rosalind, think. You can be more intoxicating than all the politics or state secrets that can possibly attract Lord Farringdon's interest. You will not be in mourning forever, and soon you will be able to wear costumes so daring and alluring that the earl will be able to concentrate on nothing else but you. A slow, sly smile crept over her face. We shall see, Alistair, she whispered to herself, we shall see.

Chapter Twenty-five

Few witnessed Alistair's departure sometime later. To be sure, the marchioness was there, making a graceful picture on the wide sweep of the stairs with the noble portico of Cranleigh behind her, the breeze gently waving the thin material of her gown, but Rosalind had made certain that Lucinda and Cordelia were safely off on a stroll around the garden with the chevalier when she saw that the earl was ready to leave. She had already rid herself of Sarah, who had ridden over that morning, by hinting that one of her maids had returned from the village with the news that Mrs. Walbeswick was feeling poorly.

Rosalind clung to Alistair as he climbed into his curricle, hoping against hope that a final glance into her pleading dark eyes might change his mind, but there was no stopping him. He took the reins from a groom, cracked his whip, and the curricle bowled down the drive at a slapping pace.

Once he had passed the lodge and the gates, he slowed down, scanning the fields in the hopes of catching a glimpse of Sarah, who, according to the lad in the stables, had left shortly before he had. There was no sign of her, and he tried not to notice the surprising pang of disappointment he experienced at the thought of missing a chance to say farewell. Alistair maneuvered around the stragglers from a herd of sheep that was quickly hurried out of the way by the lad tending to them, rounded a slight bend in the road, and caught sight of her ahead of him.

He urged his horses forward and soon was alongside of her, hailing her and pointing to a small lane that led off the main thoroughfare. Sarah quickly divined his purpose and turned off, riding toward a small grove of trees where she halted. The earl pulled up beside her, jumped down, tethered his team to a convenient tree, and strolled over to help Sarah dismount. "I am very glad to have caught up with you"—he reached up to grasp her waist as she slid off Ajax—"for I . . ." He paused as he looked into her eyes. How clear a green they were, sparkling with lively curiosity and intelligence. One had only to gaze into those eyes, fringed around with long, dark lashes to know that Lady Sarah was a very special woman. They were honest eyes, devoid of any coyness or flirtatiousness, that looked straight at you—eyes that understood a great deal about the world, eyes that were eager to see and learn more.

"You wished to tell me something?" Sarah's low voice broke into his fit of abstraction.

"Yes . . . er, well, no. I merely wished to see you before I left to . . ." What was it that he had wanted to do? Standing there with his hands still clasping the slim waist, Alistair was as tongue-tied as a schoolboy. He was going away. He wanted her to realize that. He wanted her to miss his companionship the way he would miss hers—an idea that had suddenly and unpleasantly dawned on him. It was a state of mind he had never experienced before. Many times affairs had broken off; a woman had become too demanding or had found someone willing to give more of his purse or his person to her, and Alistair had bid adieu, sometimes with more regret than others, but he had always been philosophical about it, had known he would soon find someone to replace her. Now he was not so sure. Previously, the women had been virtually interchangeable; Lady Georgiana de Villiers, though a ravishing blond, had been another Rosalind, and her successor, though not as well born, had been as dazzling as those before her. They had all been sophisticated, adept at lovemaking and dalliance, but Lord Farringdon had shared nothing of himself with them.

Lady Sarah was different. She knew him. With her perceptiveness she seemed to have sensed the loneliness under his carefully constructed facade. She appeared to understand the alienation he felt from the rest of the *ton,* even while he participated in it by establishing himself as something of a legend with his outrageous exploits, his refusal to tie himself to one woman, his constant search for something new and exciting. She recognized his underlying boredom with it all, his yearning for something that would engage his mind and his abundant energies. She had not revealed all this in so many words, but she did not need to. He could sense that she saw all this, understood all this, had suffered many of the same things he suffered—the ennui, the corroding sense that no one else shared the same perspective on the world. When she smiled at him, as she was smiling now, he knew he was no longer alone. He knew he did not even have to say what he was feeling, for she was feeling it, too.

"What I wanted to do was to say good-bye, properly, I mean." At last Alistair pulled himself together. "I wished to thank you for letting me impose on your hospitality, for taking care of me after my unfortunate encounter with the chevalier and his men. You have been a very good friend to me these last days; I cannot think for the life of me why, but I am most grateful for it."

Sarah laughed. Really, the earl was most unlike himself. It was almost as though he were ill at ease, and, absurd as it seemed, it appeared that she was the one who was making him feel that way. He had helped her off her horse and then fallen into something rather like a reverie. He stared down at her in the oddest way, forgetting that his hands were still clasped around her waist. In fact, they had been there so long she could feel their warmth through the heavy material of her riding habit.

"Why, whatever else would I have done, sent you off to bleed somewhere else? Besides, it is not often that excitement comes to our little corner of Kent. It is I who should be grateful to you for allowing me to join in." Sarah glanced up at him, suddenly serious. "And even when excitement does come, I am never allowed to be part of it; females are not supposed to know about that sort of thing. I cannot . . . I mean you cannot know what it meant to me to, to . . ." Now it was her turn to fall silent, grappling with a variety of thoughts and emotions she could not even identify, much less express. Sarah drew a deep breath. "Well, what I wish to say is that you are very kind to treat me as something other than a female."

Alistair threw back his head and laughed. "I had no idea that ignoring all the special claims of your sex was such an attractive proposition. You are unique among women, Lady Sarah. Usually females do their very best to point all the ways in which they deserve to be honored as creatures of excessively delicate sensibilities, sensibilities so exquisite as to be far above the vulgar understanding of the rest of us poor mortals."

"That may be, but as you ably demonstrated when explaining Rosalind's motives to me, what else do we poor females have but our sensibilities? It is you males who have all the fun, and I thank you for sharing it."

"I can hardly think that any other member of your sex would see it that way—a man stupid enough to be discovered and wounded blunders into your house, demanding succor—but if that sort of thing gratifies you, I am only too happy to oblige. And speaking of obligations, I fear I shall be trespassing on your good nature again by asking you to receive and relate my instructions to your sister-in-law. I dislike involving you further and possibly endangering you, but I do not know what else to do. Actually, that is what I most wished to speak to you about."

Alistair removed one of his hands from her waist to cup her chin, tilting it up so he could look deep into her eyes, his own dark with concern. "It is a most desperate business, Sarah, and the chevalier, for all his Gallic charm, is a most dangerous fellow who will stop at nothing to gain his purpose. I beg of you to be careful. No . . ." He frowned at her as she opened her mouth to protest. "Hear me out. You are a very clever woman, but you are a good person. You cannot conceive of the evil that men are capable of. I am accustomed to it, and believe me, I am not being frivolous in cautioning you."

The green eyes regarded him gravely, and the earl, without knowing what he was doing, swept her into his arms. He could not remember when a woman had gazed up at him without a calculating look in her eyes. "Oh Sarah, do take care of yourself," he whispered against her lips, and then he was kissing her—gently at first, and then more deeply, as though all his immediate care and concern could somehow protect her against all the possible harm he was leaving her to.

Alistair could not recall a kiss that had felt like this, not even in his salad days when he had fancied himself in love with the dairymaid. Now he was acutely conscious of Sarah's breath mingling with his, the trembling of her body, the slight hesitation of her lips before they yielded to his. He was experiencing her emotions as well as his own.

It was an overwhelming experience, to say the least, and even more so for a man who thought he had felt it all with every type of woman. As the full implications of it all washed over him, Alistair found himself as self-conscious and nervous as a schoolboy, instead of the rake whose expertise had overcome the resistance of the most unwilling young matrons or swept away even the most hardened of flirts on a tide of passion.

At last he released her, stammering slightly. "Forgive me, Lady Sarah. I had not the least intention of, of . . . I mean, I do not think of you as just . . ."

"Another flirt?" Sarah had at last caught her breath, and her composure began to return, increasing as she saw the earl's ebbing away. It was almost amusing to watch him floundering in this manner. His ineptitude gave her a heady sense of exhilaration and, yes, a certain sense of power. The thought that this was the way Rosalind must feel all the time flitted briefly through her head before the earl replied, "Not in the least," in such an injured tone that she stared at him. The man truly was serious!

During the entire astounding experience Sarah had kept telling herself a number of bracing home truths in order to keep herself from succumbing entirely—home truths such as this is what he does to every woman, you are just another weak female he is luring into doing what he wishes. She had been partially successful at keeping her knees from buckling under her and from casting herself with total abandon against the broad chest and winding her arms around his neck as she longed to do, but she had not quelled entirely the warm breathlessness that had threatened to overwhelm her nor the quivering in the pit of her stomach.

Her heart was pounding so loudly he must surely hear it. But she had retained her intellectual distance enough to appreciate that the earl was oddly ill at ease himself, and she had latched on to that fact as a shipwrecked man might have clasped a mast floating by. She had come up with a flippant answer to his apology in order not to reveal either to him or to herself how much his kiss had shaken her, for she was determined not to let the most notorious rake in all of London know that he had affected her in the least.

Apparently, she had been too glib, for Lord Farringdon was regarding her in a manner that could only be labeled reproachful as he reached for her again.

Oh, no. Sarah backed away. This was an exceedingly dangerous game they were playing. She had remained relatively self-possessed thus far, but she was not so foolish or so pigheaded as to think she could maintain her calm in the face of further assaults on her emotions.

"Sarah," Alistair began hoarsely, "you must believe me. I meant no harm. It is just that I am so concerned. You are so very, so very . . ." He grasped for words. The earl did not want to frighten her, yet he did wish her to understand that she meant something to him, that she was not just another woman, but something very different from that. As it was, she looked like nothing so much as a bird poised for flight, ready to escape the moment he tried to restrain her. "You are so very special to me. And I am forced into the position of taking advantage of your good nature, your intelligence, and so many other things. I would never forgive myself if anything, even the slightest thing, were to occur to upset you because of me."

She had paused to listen to him, and Alistair let out his breath slowly and carefully. Slowly and carefully he moved toward her. "Forgive me if I was carried away. I did not intend to cause you any distress"—he smiled ruefully at the guarded expression on her face—"in fact, quite the opposite."

Some of the wariness disappeared from her eyes, and he pressed his advantage. "Please do not let any excess of concern on my part get in the way of our friendship, for that is most precious to me. In truth, I have never encountered anyone like you, Lady Sarah, and I do find myself at a loss as to how to proceed. I do know one thing, however; you may trust me with your life as I trust you with mine."

That appeared to reassure her, and she relaxed enough for him to offer her his hand. "Are we still friends then?"

Sarah placed her hand in his. "Friends."

The twinkle was back in her eyes, and the moment of awkwardness was safely past. Alistair sighed in relief. "In that case, I hope you will allow me to help you up. We had best be on our separate ways. There is much to do."

The earl assisted her into the saddle, ignoring as best he could the slimness of her waist between his hands, the litheness of her movements. He slapped Ajax on the rump and watched as she took a nearby hedgerow in one glorious bound and galloped off over the fields. What a woman she was! Untying his own horse, he climbed into his curricle, backed his team carefully around, and headed on the road toward London, doing his best to put the immediate scene from his mind and concentrate on the task ahead.

Chapter Twenty-six

Sarah rode like a mad thing until she was certain she was out of the earl's sight. Then she slowed Ajax to a walk, a very leisurely walk. She had no desire to reach Ashworth until she had had ample time to think things through and to savor the past moments that were so precious to her, whether or not they had meant anything at all to Lord Farringdon.

So that was what it was like! Sarah had never thought to find herself in the picture she had carried so long in her mind of Rosalind crushed in the earl's embrace, but now that she examined it, she realized that she had in fact been imagining just that all along. The quivery sensation in the pit of her stomach that always accompanied the image had been one of longing, longing to feel the strength of those arms around her and the passion in his kiss. Now she knew what it was like. It had been more, so much more than she had dreamed of, so much more thrilling. Her body had responded in ways that had never occurred to her, and she had felt treacherously at the mercy of her senses. Fortunately, it had come about so suddenly that she had been too shocked to react at all, and the earl had come to his own senses before she had revealed too much.

The moment his lips had come down on hers she could hardly think of anything but the way he felt against her, from the mouth that caressed hers to the insistent warmth of his hands at her waist, pulling her hard against him. Sarah never wanted it to end, but at the same time she was desperate to escape the wanting that engulfed her. How she had managed to pull herself together when he released her, she still could not imagine, but thank heaven she had. This passion business was far more dangerous than she had ever expected.

It was a very good thing that the Earl of Burnleigh had gone from Kent. After all, if the picture of Rosalind and Lord Farringdon had remained so vivid for so long, how was she ever to forget this? In truth, she must throw herself into good works and political tracts with a vengeance if she was to regain anything of her sanity ever again.

Lady Sarah Melford was nothing if not a determined young woman, and by the time she reached Ashworth, she had herself well in hand. The only indications that anything at all out of the ordinary had occurred were her heightened color and a touch of breathlessness that could have been attributed to a brisk ride home from Cranleigh. Only Ajax, thoroughly put out by the snail's pace he had been forced to maintain since leaving the earl, knew that something more unusual than violent exercise was behind these telltale signs.

During the ensuing days Sarah refused to allow herself time to drift into any dangerous reveries. She was present at Cranleigh from morning to night, conversing with Lady Edgecumbe, listening to the endless inanities of her daughters, trying to coax conversation out of Lady Amelia, and in general making herself so useful that Rosalind could not help eyeing her suspiciously. It was not like Sarah to spend so much time in the company of others, especially those who confined themselves to the most trivial of topics.

More astounding yet, Sarah even smiled occasionally at the chevalier and allowed him more than once to accompany her and Lady Amelia on a stroll around the gardens. For this diversion Rosalind was so relieved that she did not even stop to consider the reasons behind it, simply remaining grateful for the moments she did not feel the chevalier's dark eyes boring into her, for the brief space of time when she did not feel like some poor rabbit mesmerized by the serpent's stare. The marchioness did her best to avoid the chevalier's company by flirting with Lord Edgecumbe and even the Duke of Coltishall—an old stick if ever there was one—but distract herself as she would she was constantly aware of the Frenchman's menacing presence.

For several days no dispatches arrived from London, a situation that kept the chevalier from seeking Rosalind out. However, she knew that it was only a matter of time before something arrived for Lord Edgecumbe, who would then consult with her husband, and the chevalier would be pressing her once again for the details. Oh, why had Alistair returned to London when she was so desperate for his aid? Whatever was she to do?

Rosalind had almost entirely forgotten that Lord Farringdon had promised help from Sarah and was thus taken completely by surprise when her sister-in-law sought her out several days later in the morning room. Rosalind had just finished conferring with Mrs. Dawlish and had given her instructions for the staff that day. She was in no mood to see anyone, but Sarah had just received a message from the earl that brooked no delay.

In a way Sarah had been relieved as much for Rosalind as for herself when the letter arrived, delivered by a mud-spattered courier who had insisted on handing it personally to the lady of the house, refused all offers of refreshment, and sped on his way without even descending from his horse.

"My dear Lady Sarah," the letter began, "I have done my utmost to execute your commissions in London, but to the best of my abilities I have been unable to locate the Spanish history you requested. There was reputedly an eight-volume set for sale, but on further inquiry it was discovered to be nonexistent. Not a single volume is to be had. As you can see, it is rather difficult to come by, and I have my doubts as to being able to discover one for quite some time in the future. Please accept my apologies in this matter. I find that I have been tolerably well amused here, having attended the Kembles' benefit performance of *The School for Scandal* and a concert in the New Rooms, performed by Master Pio Cianchenini. On the program was a most excellent quintet of Beethoven, which I make no doubt you would have enjoyed extremely. Surely, someone who plays Mozart as finely as you must also take pleasure in the works of Beethoven. I hope this finds you in good health and spirits. Again my apologies for failing to carry out your instructions. I shall continue in my endeavors to locate the books you wished. Believe me, I am yours to command, Farringdon."

Sarah had been unable to ignore the strange attack of breathlessness that swept over her when she saw the thick black strokes of ink on the rich cream-colored paper. Even the earl's writing was forceful and energetic, and it made her realize just how much she missed his vitality among the rather dull little group they now made at Cranleigh. Pushing such treacherous thoughts out of her mind, she had changed quickly into her riding habit, ordered Ajax to be saddled and brought around, and had ridden over to call on Rosalind.

"I beg your pardon for intruding upon you at such a busy time," Sarah apologized as Rosalind, ensconced in a comfortable chair in the morning room, looked up in annoyance from the stack of letters she was perusing, "but I have some news that is of interest to you." Giving her sister-in-law no time to reply, she closed the door behind her and sank into the chair closest to the marchioness.

Dropping her voice to a whisper, Sarah continued, "I have heard from the Earl of Burnleigh, who begs me to instruct you to report that no more troops are being dispatched at present, nor are they likely to be in the future." Of course there had not been the slightest reference to the Marchioness of Cranleigh in the letter, but Sarah, sensing her sister-in-law's antagonism, improvised, hoping to soften the unpleasant necessity of having Sarah as intermediary. "In addition, the earl begs me to assure you that he is most concerned for your welfare."

She had judged the situation to a nicety, and, hearing the message couched in such terms, Rosalind's hostility lessened somewhat. "That may be all very well and good for his lordship, but what I am to do with that information I have not the least notion," she replied pettishly.

This was not going to be easy. Sarah had no particular love for her sister-in-law, but she could understand how Rosalind would find it difficult to accept assistance of any sort from her. "I would think it most sensible," Sarah began tentatively, "to await the arrival of further dispatches from London and then pass this message to the chevalier when he demands to know the contents of the dispatches."

She spoke calmly, as if such matters were an everyday occurrence instead of something that was obviously troubling the marchioness. In truth, Rosalind looked as hagged as Sarah had ever seen her. The bluish circles under the dark eyes were testimony to sleepless nights. Her skin was quite pale with fatigue and had entirely lost its normal pearly glow. Sarah could not help feeling just the tiniest bit sorry for her. After all, Rosalind had not asked to be put in this uncomfortable position; someone was forcing her to do this. It must be something quite dreadful and extremely upsetting that was being held over her head in order to make her do such a thing.

"Yes, you are right." Rosalind sighed. "But that is only for this time. What shall I do the next, and the next one after that?" Her voice rose in desperation, and she twisted her hands in her lap.

"Well, I am sure that by then Lord Farringdon will have figured everything out and contrived to rid us all of the chevalier's, er, *charming* presence," Sarah replied reasonably. "I should not worry if I were you. He appears to be quite a resourceful person."

This suggestion seemed to find favor with the marchioness, who stopped wringing her hands at the mention of the earl's name. However, the idea of the chevalier continued to make her uneasy. "But you do not know the Chevalier d'Evron, Sarah. He will stop at nothing. He cares for no one. It does not make a jot of difference to him if he ruins me." Rosalind rubbed her temples, which were beginning to ache most dreadfully.

"Surely you are mistaken," Sarah contradicted her gently. Rosalind was vain and selfish, but Sarah could not conceive of her being anything worse than that. Surely, she could have no secrets that would ruin her if revealed. It could not be debts. True, she was extravagant and Harold was inclined to be clutch-fisted, but he was also far too proud to allow his wife to find herself in dun territory. Nor did she gamble as many women did. No, Rosalind was far too interested in masculine attention to waste time at the card table when she could have been listening to sweet nothings murmured in her ear by a besotted beau. Nor did Sarah think she was being blackmailed over a lover. Rosalind was not the sort to indulge in anything more serious than a light flirtation. So what was it that gave the chevalier such power over her?

"No"—the marchioness shook her head so vigorously the dark curls danced—"I am not. You do not know the *ton* as I do, Sarah. They will not forgive the slightest misstep from one of its members or even one of its member's family."

"Richard!" Sarah breathed. "I *knew* it was Richard." Rosalind's eyes widened in alarm, and Sarah hastened to reassure her. "Do not worry. I feel certain that Lord Farringdon can take care of any hold that the chevalier may have over your brother. But truly, Rosalind, everyone knows what sort of person Richard is. They would not look askance at you for . . ." A glance at her sister-in-law surprised a look on her face that Sarah had never seen there before. What was it? Was it sadness, fear? Then she realized that Rosalind actually did care what happened to that scapegrace brother of hers. Of all the queer starts, this was the one she had expected the least. All of a sudden Sarah felt very sorry for Rosalind, indeed. Raised in a household of weak, self-centered men, she had been forced to fend for herself, using the only thing she had—her startling beauty. And even that had not been enough to compensate for the failings of her relatives, for Harold had been her only means of escape, and Sarah knew how discouraging that prospect was.

Sarah rose briskly, remarking, "Richard has caused you enough heartache, Rosalind. It is high time he fended for himself. When we get ourselves out of this coil, I shall make sure that someone, probably Lord Farringdon, takes him in hand. Now if you will excuse me, I have some visits to make in the village." With these parting words Sarah rose, gathered her gloves and hat, and hurried out.

Chapter Twenty-seven

For a moment Rosalind was too astonished to think. What had Sarah said? "When *we* get ourselves out of this coil . . ." The marchioness could never remember that Sarah had ever been anything but eager to quit her company, yet here she was helping her in what was perhaps the most difficult situation Rosalind had yet faced in her life. Furthermore, Sarah was even offering to help her, knowing all about the wretched business with the chevalier. Rosalind could not recall anyone ever having offered her assistance or sympathy of any kind, and she could not help but be touched by it. To think that anyone cared what happened to her—for whatever reasons—was a most novel and surprisingly pleasant experience.

In addition, and much as she hated to admit it, the marchioness was impressed at how quickly her sister-in-law grasped the difficulties of her situation and how readily she offered up solutions. Rosalind had always known that Sarah was clever in a rather blue sort of way, but she had never expected anything practical from it or to have her demonstrate the quick energetic sort of intelligence that the marchioness generally associated with men of Lord Farringdon's stamp. Maybe Sarah was more than she had given her credit for. Maybe she was not such a mealymouthed prudish little miss as Rosalind had always assumed her to be.

The marchioness rose slowly and thoughtfully to make her way toward her bedchamber, where the long-suffering Framling was waiting to soothe her mistress's aching temples with lavender water, brush out her hair, and arrange it in a coiffure sure to dazzle the assembled company later on that afternoon. In the meantime there seemed to be nothing to do but wait with as much patience as she could muster, avoiding the chevalier as well as she could until more dispatches arrived from London. At least this time she knew the information she had to pass along and would not have to extract it from Harold. That was a good thing, for the less she had to speak to her husband the better.

At the thought of the stodgy Harold, Rosalind sighed. There was no doubt that it was a trial for a witty beautiful woman to have such a husband. If only Lord Farringdon had come up to scratch. However, there was no use repining; what was past was past, and an attractive lover was almost as useful, and certainly far more exciting than a husband. Rosalind had had her doubts about catching the Earl of Burnleigh in the parson's mousetrap, but she had none about adding him to her permanent court of admirers. She brightened at the thought. Mourning would be over, and she would be in London again where anything could happen.

In London at that very moment the subject of all this plotting was at his quarters in Mount Street, ensconced in a deep chair in front of the fire, idly scanning *The Morning Post* without really absorbing what he was reading, for his thoughts were on Sarah, wondering what she was doing, how she was managing to handle Rosalind, and whether she was putting herself at risk by trying to keep her eye on the chevalier.

On a sudden impulse the earl got up and walked to his desk, which was awash in papers, journals, and correspondence. Rummaging through it, he at last pulled out the issue of *The Edinburgh Review* with the review of Mr. Broadhurst's work *Advice to Young Ladies on the Improvement of the Mind.* He had been longing to peruse it ever since he had seen it in the library at Ashworth, along with letters addressed to the author of the review. Poring over it, he slowly made his way back to his chair. Yes, the phrasing and the energy were all Sarah's, and it was a topic sure to be dear to her heart. She must be the author. What other explanation was there for the letters he had seen on her desk that night at Ashworth? What a woman she was—the only woman he had ever known who improved upon acquaintance.

The more he learned about her, the more he admired her and wished he could do something for her, something to make her life more the sort of life she would like it to be. It seemed such a pity that a fine mind and spirit like hers were wasting away in the countryside when there was such a crying need for people just like Sarah to address the many problems besetting the country.

To be sure, she was contributing in a fashion through her writing, but it was so very little compared to what she could do. He knew that she scorned the empty world of the *ton,* but he would like to be able to introduce her to the few people whose acquaintance he did value—men of vision and ambition who were making valuable contributions to their world.

How much he wanted to give her all of that, and how little he could do for her, independent little thing that she was. Alistair finished the article and laid it aside, sighing as he did so. He missed her in a way that he had never missed anyone before. Ignored by his parents, he had spent a lonely boyhood with no one but his horses and dogs for companionship. At school and at university he had still felt set apart from the rest of his schoolmates, who all had brothers and sisters and who all seemed to know each other. Of course, he had covered up the loneliness by acting more daringly and more outrageously than all of them put together, thus winning their attention and respect, but never really their friendship. In truth, he had not been that eager to be friends with most of them, who wasted their time in aimless pursuit of amusement and were satisfied with trivialities. Alistair, too, had gone in search of pleasure, but he had done it in a slightly different manner, pitting his mind and body against ever increasing odds in curricle races, pugilistic matches, or any feat that required both skill and daring. However, the difference between him and the rest of the gay young blades was that he was ever striving to improve his wits and athletic prowess, always competing against himself to become better at everything. No one else he knew could even recognize this search for perfection in what seemed reckless abandon, much less understand or appreciate it, so he had done his best to cover up his rather disturbing intensity with an air of indifference and cynicism, a languid boredom that carefully hid these private parts of his character from all but a few people.

In Sarah he sensed that same sort of person—a person with restless energy, always seeking to learn, to grow, and to improve in whatever endeavor she threw herself into. He missed being around her, missed being with someone to whom he had to say very little to make himself understood, missed being with someone whose similarity of view only enhanced everything he experienced.

Thinking of Sarah brought Alistair back to the chevalier and the present. The earl had gone directly to Whitehall upon arriving in London, where his report was greeted with grudging interest by those there who had refused to believe that a man as gentlemanly and as widely accepted as the chevalier could stoop so low. "Those damned Frenchies have no honor whatsoever," Sir Thomas Belford had growled. "To send a man among us who does not even have the courage to wear a uniform is a low scoundrelly trick. This spying thing"—his beetling dark brows snapped together in a thunderous frown—"is a damned poor way to conduct a war. Shameful, I say, shameful." He snorted and looked accusingly at Alistair. "I say that no true soldier would stoop to such a thing."

The earl had kept his temper in check with difficulty, muttering darkly to himself instead, no true soldier would blindly follow the orders of a fool like you only to find himself slaughtered as your troops in Portugal were. Alistair had restrained himself with difficulty, but then such an attitude was nothing more than he was accustomed to. The very men who could most use the information he risked his neck to procure considered him and his efforts to be beneath contempt—so much so that they ignored it to their peril as Sir Thomas had. A bluff old gentleman with more bottom than sense, Sir Thomas had refused to employ any type of strategy in the Peninsula, throwing his men instead in wave after wave of useless assaults against a superior force of French. His troops hated him, and finally his superiors had been forced to admit his bullheaded stupidity was costing them good men and sent him out of harm's way to Whitehall, where he could harass people instead of kill them. That such a buffleheaded blowhard should treat Alistair in such a condescending way was infuriating beyond belief, but the earl knew that at least Wellington and his best generals had a healthy respect for all that he and others discovered, which was why Alistair was alone in London while most of the other members of the Depot of Military Knowledge—Sir George Murray, Colquhoun Grant, Andrew Leith Hay—were all in the Peninsula.

Thinking over his interview with Sir Thomas, Alistair sighed again. Now he was going to have to go back to Whitehall, hat in hand, to beg them to supply additional help to ensure Sarah's safety. If he could not be there to watch over her himself, then he needed someone there he could trust who could send him reports on a regular basis. He needed someone like Ferdie Summers, a likely looking lad who had helped him with the capture of several French agents the previous year. Lieutenant Summers was one of the few good men who had not been sent to the Peninsula, but was languishing on guard duty and bemoaning the lack of action in his life. In fact, just the day before Alistair had left for Cranleigh, he had shared a bottle of port with the lieutenant at Brooks's and listened to him complain about the stifling boredom of barracks life. "Can't I do anything with you, Farringdon?" the young man had begged. "I shall go mad here if they don't ship us out soon." Now Alistair had the perfect solution to the young man's dilemma.

Once again Lord Farringdon faced Sir Thomas, adopting as conciliatory an expression as he could summon up for the old goat. "You need *what*, sirrah?" the older man bellowed. "I was under the impression that you creatures skulked around in the shadows all by yourselves. And now you want to drag a perfectly respectable young officer into this dirty business. It don't bear thinking of."

With an effort Alistair bit off the retort that rose to his lips. A man who had enlisted to defend his country would surely find tracking down a dangerous enemy more honorable than mounting guard duty a few hours a day in the safety and security of the metropolis.

"And I suppose you will ask Lieutenant Summers to adopt some vulgar disguise instead of wearing his uniform like a man of honor and a true soldier." Sir Thomas was quickly working himself into apoplexy.

"I shall leave Lieutenant Summers's personal safety and the success of his mission up to his own discretion," Alistair snapped.

Sir Thomas was silent. He knew that he was obliged to give Lord Farringdon what he asked, but he did not have to give it willingly. The man was too valuable a resource to Wellington to be ignored. That had been made uncomfortably clear to Sir Thomas more often than he cared to remember. He loathed this man who was nothing but a wild and reckless rebel with none of the proper respect either for authority or for his elders. Let him stew a while. Sir Thomas stalled, frowning in a considering manner for some moments before replying, "Very well."

Without a word Alistair turned on his heel and strode from

the room. He was damned if he was going to give the pompous prig the satisfaction of being thanked or even of being addressed as *sir*. Lord Farringdon never called Sir Thomas anything, and he knew he irked the old man considerably. Good. The earl was not part of any regular command. He answered to no one except Wellington himself, and he was certainly not in the regular army, so he saw no need of treating a stupid, blindly authoritarian old man as a superior.

After his bout with Sir Thomas, Alistair was even more anxious to return to Kent and freedom from the petty politics of the capital. However, he consoled himself with strolling over to Brooks's where he was hailed with relief by young Summers himself. "Farringdon, share a bottle with me and tell me something more exciting than the name of the latest opera dancer who is all the rage."

The lieutenant was more than happy to be asked to spend time in the country, keeping an eye on a dangerous Frenchman and two lovely women. "But do not let Lady Sarah know you are there, else she is bound to try to help you," Alistair warned him with a gleam of humor in his eyes. "She is a little fire-eater, to be sure."

The lieutenant darted a curious glance at Lord Farringdon. As a rule, the man never mentioned his women, though his conquests were legion. Now he was not only speaking of Lady Sarah, but he was referring to her with a special warmth in his tone that the lieutenant had never heard before, and he knew the Earl of Burnleigh better than most. Their acquaintance was not of long standing, but they had shared danger together in a way that made men instantly close.

Ferdie was intrigued. What sort of woman was so special as to win the earl's attention this way? Certainly the Marchioness of Cranleigh, whom he was also instructed to protect, was a renowned beauty, who had commanded the admiration of the *ton* for several years, but Lord Farringdon had referred to her only in the briefest of manners. Lieutenant Summers brightened. His prospects had certainly improved since this morning. "I shall be delighted to keep my eye out on your behalf, Farringdon. It appears that once again you are awake on all suits. I do believe that no one else suspected the Frenchman of a thing."

Alistair's bark of laughter was cynical, to say the least. "You mean that no one else was willing to distrust a man who flirted so gracefully and lost so much so obligingly at the gaming tables." He rose, clapping Ferdie on the shoulder. "I trust you completely, Ferdie. You will keep in touch in the usual manner? And now, if you will excuse me, I have another, er, another appointment."

Ferdie winked, nodded, and called for another bottle of port as Alistair made his way to the door. Oh yes, Farringdon, he murmured to himself, I shall keep close watch, but it will not be on the Frenchman nearly as much as it will be on Lady Sarah Melford.

Chapter Twenty-eight

Alistair's other appointment was in the silken boudoir of the much neglected wife of a politician, Lady Violet Carstairs, whose exuberant animal spirits exhausted even Lord Farringdon. For years they had maintained a discreet relationship, even as he conducted more amorous affairs with other beauties. Violet had never asked for anything but passion and consummate skill in lovemaking, both of which the earl could provide in abundance. Besides that, the lady thought as she relieved Alistair of his jacket and shirt, no one could be a finer figure of a man than Lord Farringdon with broad shoulders, narrow waist and hips, and powerful legs, not to mention the piercing eyes and square jaw.

"But what is this, my lord, are you hurt?" Violet asked in some concern as she uncovered the bandage.

" 'Tis naught but a scratch," he murmured, pulling her into his arms and burying his face in the smooth white skin of her neck.

"A jealous husband, no doubt," Violet hazarded a guess.

"No doubt." His hands slid the thin muslin of her gown off her shoulders to reveal a voluptuously rounded bosom. "Ah," he sighed as his lips traveled slowly down her neck, dropping kisses so light and tantalizing that she shivered in anticipation.

Finally, Violet could stand it no more, and with a groan of satisfaction she fell back onto the soft pillows of the bed. Truly, she was a fortunate woman. No other female in all of London could have a more skillful lover she thought as her body came alive under his hands.

Unfortunately, her partner did not entirely share this rapture. Alistair found himself curiously detached from the entire scene, as though he were watching another man. Ordinarily, he enjoyed such activities a great deal, but somehow today it all seemed rather flat and mechanical, utterly lacking in mystery and desire. As he slid his hands along the generous curve of Violet's hips, he could not help thinking of Sarah's slim figure and wondering if he could spark the same sort of passion he now saw smoldering in the sapphire eyes that regarded his so hungrily. As he twined his fingers in Violet's copper curls, he could not wipe out the vision of how Sarah would look with her blond hair tumbled over bare shoulders.

Alistair sighed inwardly. What was wrong with him? Usually, he had no trouble keeping his women straight, never thinking for an instant of anyone but the woman he was with at the moment. Now it seemed that every woman reminded him of Sarah. All he could think about was those deep green eyes so full of understanding and sympathy, that finely sculpted face with its serene smile that always welcomed him and offered him a place of refuge and trust in a greedy and selfish world.

"Aaah." Violet's gasp of satisfaction brought Alistair quickly back to the present. Planting a deliberate kiss on the full red lips, he apologized, "I am afraid I must end this delightful interlude rather abruptly, my lady, but I am in the midst of most pressing business." Then, kissing her again, he released her, slid off the bed, and began to gather up his clothes, which were scattered all over the room.

"But my lord," the lady protested, pouting, "you have only stayed the briefest of moments. Surely you can linger a little longer."

Alistair summoned up a suitably desolated expression. "Alas, fair lady, my time is not my own. Believe me, I shall endeavor to return to the delight of your company as quickly as I can when I am again able to call myself my own master and am free to pursue my pleasures as I will." He let his eyes drift slowly over the ripe curves of her body before pulling on his breeches and grabbing his shirt.

Accepting that he was resolved on leaving her, Violet stretched languorously on the pillows and watched him as he dressed. His was such a magnificent body it seemed a pity to cover it with clothes. She sighed. Their encounters were far too infrequent to her way of thinking, but she was grateful for what little she did have, and very glad that he was back in London for the moment at least. Where the peripatetic Earl of Burnleigh was concerned, one could never rely on his presence anywhere for very long. Violet raised her head to accept his parting kiss and lay back again, enjoying the satisfaction lingering from his lovemaking.

Discreetly letting himself out, Alistair drew a sigh of relief the minute he gained the street. From the moment he had kissed Violet and the image of Sarah rose before his eyes, he had known his visit was a mistake. He had experienced the oddest sense of claustrophobia. It was almost as if he could not breathe, and he had wanted nothing more than to escape his lover's clinging arms and demanding lips.

Was this unpleasant experience going to be repeated with every woman? Alistair sincerely hoped not. Or would he just continue to feel dissatisfied until he had held Sarah in his arms once again. Why could he not forget the thrill of pulling her tightly to him and feeling her heart beat against his. He had never really experienced that closeness with any other woman, had always moved on to satisfy his desire, never stopping to relish his intimacy with another being. But with Sarah he had been instantly aware of the life, the vitality that was so nearly a part of him, yet separate. Seeing the pulse beating at the base of her neck and feeling her breath against his cheek had been almost magical, and something he had never sensed before, even in his most passionate liaisons.

Alistair shook his head. He must stop thinking this way. He had so many other things to do he did not have time to spend endless hours wondering about some chit of a girl who insisted on burying herself in the country with her books and journals. Besides, she was Ferdie's problem now and none of his concern. He did hope that Ferdie would keep a close watch over her. After all, Ferdie was young and occasionally careless, while Sarah was adventurous, headstrong to a fault, and bound and determined to help Alistair catch the chevalier. Damn! Would he never get her out of his mind?

Lord Farringdon would have been even less happy with the entire state of affairs if he had known what was transpiring in the library at Ashworth, where at that very moment John the coachman was standing before his mistress with his latest report on the comings and goings of the Chevalier d'Evron.

"You may be in the right of it, my lady. Yer chevally be meeting somebody at the Red Lion all right, and that somebody be Ned Wittle." Seeing his mistress's puzzled frown as she tried to identify Ned among the many Wittles that thronged the village and its environs, he added, "You know, he lives down in the marsh and does a spot of work once in a while as a grave digger.

Sarah nodded. "Yes. Now I recall. His youngest daughter used to be maid to Dr. Heatherton's wife, I believe. Thank you. I shall see what I can do about persuading him to describe the nature of his relationship to the Chevalier d'Evron."

"Now, my lady"—John began shaking his head in the manner of one long accustomed to useless remonstrances—"you'll not be visiting him alone."

"Thank you for your concern, John, but I must, you see. He will not take kindly to having any witnesses to our conversation. No, I must do this alone." Sarah had sounded confident enough at the time, though she did experience some misgiving later as she knocked at the door of the Wittles' tumbledown cottage at the end of a lonely track that extended deep into the marsh. It was an isolated spot with only the rustle of the breeze in the high grasses to break the pall of silence that hung over the place. The cottage itself was quiet and forbidding. There were no flowers, no chickens, no dogs or children, not even a puff of smoke to indicate any sign of life.

Sarah knocked again, louder this time. Eventually, she heard the sound of shuffling feet, and a hoarse voice growled, "What do you want?"

"I would like a few words with Ned Wittle." Sarah spoke decisively, hoping that none of the uneasiness she felt showed in her voice.

At last the door opened to reveal a grizzled old man whose wiry frame and weathered features spoke of a lifetime spent out of doors. If he was surprised at the identity of his unexpected visitor, he gave no sign of it, just stood there eyeing her fiercely.

Best take the bull by the horns, Sarah encouraged herself. "Now, Ned, I am sorry to be bothering you, but it has come to my attention that you have been doing business with the Chevalier d'Evron."

"It has, has it?" The marsh man sneered unpleasantly. "And what concern is it of yours, missy, I'd like to know. I am a free man, not one of your hoity-toity servants at the hall—slaves more like." He spat in the dust.

"I know you are, and that your independence is precious to you, which is why I have come to warn you." Sarah spoke calmly and firmly without the least sign of the anxiety she was feeling.

It was not the response Ned had expected, and he shot a suspicious glance at her.

"The chevalier is a Frenchman, Ned. We are at war with France, and people naturally look with distrust on such men. If you are caught having anything to do with him, you will, at best, be either imprisoned or transported. In either case, your precious freedom will be naught. The Frenchman has friends in high places to protect him should he be found guilty of any, er, *inappropriate* behavior. You do not, and I assure you, he will see you hang or dispose of you himself rather than lift a finger to help you.

The cottager shook his head angrily. "I don't see what business it is of yours," he responded sourly, but there was just the slightest hint of doubt in his voice. "A fine lady like you has no call to worry herself over a fellow like me."

"That may be," Sarah acknowledged, realizing that brutal frankness was more likely than anything else to win the man's trust. "But I have great call to dislike the chevalier. He is a very bad man and an enemy of England besides. Why, he would have Napoleon and his armies over here in a minute if he could. Ah, I see that you had not thought of that. What did you think he was doing? Napoleon has conquered all of Europe. He is not going to rest until he has conquered England as well, and believe me, the French do not prize freedom as we English do. The claims of a few yeoman farmers and marsh men are nothing to a man who is emperor of half the world."

Ned had fallen into a surly silence, jamming his hands into his pockets and kicking the dust with his foot. Sarah pressed her advantage. "Besides, the money will stop coming when he has used you to his purpose, whereas I need someone to help out in the stables for quite some time to come. John has more than he can handle at the moment, and he is not getting any younger. Of course, I could hire a lad from the village, but there is not enough work to keep one fully occupied. I just need someone every once in a while. Furthermore, I could probably pay you more to keep an eye on the chevalier than he is paying you to do whatever you do for him. Now what do you say?"

The cottager was still silent, but it was a less belligerent, more thoughtful silence. At last he spoke. "The wife was sick, you see. Ned Wittle don't have anything to do with foreigners usually, but I had to call the doctor and—"

"Yes, I understand," Sarah interrupted briskly, guessing how difficult it was for the old man to admit such weakness. "Why do you not come around to Ashworth tomorrow and speak to John. In the meantime, keep an eye on the chevalier for me." She gave Ajax a nudge and began to head back toward the lane, but at the last minute she turned around to add, "Be sure to continue taking his money, otherwise he will suspect something."

That won a reluctant grin from the marsh man. "You can be sure of that, my lady." And then as horse and rider disappeared down the lane, he muttered under his breath, "Thankee, my lady." Ned had heard tell that lady Sarah was a right one. Apparently, the reports were true, for she knew how to help a man without taking away his pride. Ned stepped back into the gloom of the cottage. "Rose, you are to have some more of that medicine, do you hear me?" he spoke to the figure that lay in the bed near the cottage's one window, breathing heavily. "We'll have you up and about in no time, my girl."

Chapter Twenty-nine

Ned had been working at Ashworth for no more than a few days when John the coachman came to Sarah to say that the new stable hand would like to speak with her. She thanked him. "And he is working out, is he, John? He is not too much in your way?"

The servant grinned. "No, my lady. Of course, I really do not need any help, but he does know how to make himself useful, and he doesn't talk a fellow's head off as some of the younger lads do."

When Ned was brought to her in the library, Sarah was pleased to note that the man looked a good deal less sullen than he had at their last encounter, and she was relieved to think that it was the expense of his wife's illness and nothing else that had led him to betray his countrymen. "Ned says that you wish to speak with me, but first I must ask if everything is working out satisfactorily."

"Yes, my lady. Thank you, my lady." Ned was considerably more subdued in the library at Ashworth than he was on his own land. Then, wasting no further time on pleasantries, he continued, "You'll be wanting to watch the Frenchy at the next full moon, for he is planning to meet some boat or other." Ned stopped, hesitating as he twisted his cap in his hands.

"Yes, what is it, Ned? You can tell me," Sarah prompted. Then comprehension dawned. "Aah, he's asked you to gather some men to help, is that it?"

Ned nodded reluctantly.

"Well, times are hard. Men do what they are forced to do. I am sure that those to whom I relay this information will pay not the slightest heed to anyone who is English. It is only the French they are after." The audible sigh of relief that greeted this brought a smile to her face. "I am very grateful to you, Ned. Just speak to Mr. Higgins as you leave, will you? He will show you just how grateful I am, and perhaps we shall arrange for a little something for the others, shall we?"

The faintest hint of a smile lightened Ned's weather-beaten countenance. "Very good, my lady." He touched his forelock and was gone before she could add anything more. Sarah rang for the butler to give him instructions as to the payment of Ned and his confederates and then settled down to write a note to the Earl of Burnleigh.

Deliberately ignoring the sense of happy expectation that kept intruding at the prospect of seeing him again, or, at the very least, hearing from him, she penned the briefest of missives, struggling to let him know what was transpiring without making it clear to anyone else who might happen to see her letter. She and Lord Farringdon had agreed upon all sorts of things before he had left, but not upon this particular case. At last she settled on, "My dear sir, thank you for all you have done to seek out the volumes of Spanish history for me; however, a local man I have charged with the same search has identified and located a set down here that he believes he can procure for me. He is an excellent fellow and, knowing your own interest in ancient and obscure volumes of history, I urge you to come make his acquaintance at your earliest possible convenience." There, Sarah nodded as she sealed it. That should do it. Even if it was not entirely clear to the earl what had occurred, it was sufficiently provocative to ensure his return to Kent. And what then? How was she to greet him after their last encounter? What was she to say to someone she had thought about entirely too much since she had last seen him?

Stop it, you ninnyhammer, Sarah scolded herself. He has forgotten it all completely, and you would do well to do the same. But oh, it was delicious to close her eyes and feel once again his lips on hers and sense the strength of the arms that held her. At least, she comforted herself, at least she had experienced what she had dreamed of so often—without realizing it of course—when she had pictured Rosalind and the earl together. At least once in her life her pulse had raced and she had felt entirely alive and completely at one with someone, however brief the moment. Be happy that you have had that which you never expected to have, my girl, she told herself severely. And do not wish for more; it is an impossibly silly dream. But she did wish for more all the same.

Contrary to her belief, the earl had forgotten nothing about their last meeting, nor did he wish to. The missives he received every other day from Ferdie, via a most circuitous route, only served to make him wish all the more that he was back at Cranleigh, enjoying Sarah's company and keeping an eye on her. Ferdie, by dint of his winning smile, a quick appreciation of the finer points of a prime bit of blood, and an uncanny ability to lose at whatever game of chance Lord Tredington chose, had turned a seemingly chance encounter with his lordship in the taproom at the George and Dragon into an invitation to Tredington Park. In fact, Richard had taken to him so much that he had invited Ferdie to stay as long as he liked or until he had lost all his blunt. Keeping in character with the role he had selected for himself of an aimless young man in pursuit of any sort of sport, Ferdie had accepted Lord Tredington's invitation with alacrity and had thus provided himself with ample opportunity to observe Lady Sarah Melford.

He liked what he saw. While it was true that he had been ordered to keep an eye on her solely in regard to her safety and particularly in regard to the machinations of the Chevalier d'Evron, he had also taken it upon himself to discover just what sort of a person this young lady was who had aroused such interest and concern on the part of a man accustomed to looking to women for amusement and gratification only and nothing more, never anything more.

What Ferdie discovered had surprised him. At first glance, Lady Sarah seemed a quiet, retiring thing, almost mousy in her appearance, but that impression changed upon closer observation. The more he looked, the more he was charmed by the alert expression and the depth of understanding in her eyes, the genuine interest with which she regarded everything. However, it was not until he had witnessed her on horseback that Ferdie had truly begun to understand the earl's interest in her.

One fine day when Ferdie and Richard had been on their way to sample some more of the George and Dragon's finest ale, he had happened to catch sight of her galloping at breakneck speed across the fields on the back of an animal that would have even challenged his skills as a horseman, and it had all fallen into place. On horseback she was a different person—wild almost and free—riding with a fluidity and grace that made her seem one with her mount.

After that, Ferdie, watching her more closely, was able to catch a glimpse of passion under the calm exterior, a passion that was greatly at variance with the serene smile and the quiet self-possessed air she adopted in company. No wonder Farringdon was intrigued. Ferdie was himself, especially when he compared her to the mindlessly flirtatious Edgecumbe girls or the deliberate seductiveness of the Marchioness of Cranleigh.

In fact, speculating about the earl's interest in Lady Sarah and the nature of his relationship with the fair Rosalind was more absorbing than keeping an eye on the chevalier. Lieutenant Summers was able to report that a dispatch had arrived for the marquess, that the chevalier had subsequently sought out the marchioness and had succeeded in luring her away to a tête-à-tête that appeared to have brought little satisfaction to the lady in question. Beyond that, all was calm.

This information both relieved and disturbed Lord Farringdon. On the one hand, he was glad to hear that Sarah was in no immediate danger and that she seemed to be behaving herself; on the other, there was no pressing reason for him to return to Kent, something he was becoming more anxious to do with each passing day. He loathed the restless limbo he found himself in, full of so many questions, not knowing any of the answers. Did Sarah think of him at all? Did she relive their kiss as often as he did, or was she doing her best to wipe it from her mind? Alistair had felt the response in her at the time—he was experienced enough to sense her attraction to him—but now he was beset by doubts. Was it only the reaction of a moment, unthinking and purely physical, or did he mean something more to her than that? And how was he to determine all this or convince her of his own feelings for her if he was forced to remain cooped up in London. It was a damnable state of affairs and one that went very much against the grain of a man accustomed to going after, and getting, what he wanted.

At the same time, however, he was rather glad of the necessity of his being elsewhere, because he was entirely unsure as to how to proceed or what the lady's reaction would be if he did. Even worse, he was not entirely sure of what he wanted precisely, except to be with her, to watch the green eyes light up with excitement at some new idea that caught her fancy, or to see the little frown that wrinkled her forehead when she was concentrating on some question.

Alistair liked the warmth of her smile when she recognized their mutual agreement upon some topic or their mutual appreciation of a certain situation. He liked it when he sensed her eyes upon him across the room and knew she was thinking of him and wondering what his reactions were. Mostly he liked it that she was there, that he knew she could be counted on for friendship, for advice, for assistance, for anything when he truly needed it. Alistair had never felt that with anyone ever in his life, and it was a wonderful, powerful feeling that drew him to her. Sarah was his escape and his refuge. She was his home. That was it! When he was with her, he felt as comfortable and at ease with himself and the world as if he were at home—not that he had ever truly had a home, but now he knew what it would have felt like if he had.

It was at this exact moment, as that realization dawned upon him, that Sarah's note arrived. Aha! He laughed exultantly before shouting for Rogers.

"Yes, sir?" His man was there in an instant, for it was quite unlike his lordship to express himself in such a vociferous manner. Why, he sounded positively exuberant.

"News, Rogers. Our presence is required again at Cranleigh. We must pack at once."

"Very good, sir." There was not a flicker of interest on Rogers's wooden countenance to suggest that this new state of affairs was almost as exciting to him as it was to his master. "Catched at last," the loyal servant muttered to himself. And it ain't the marchioness who has caught him. Rogers allowed himself a congratulatory tankard of ale before beginning preparations.

He had guessed how the land lay, and now he knew for certain he was right. Let all those high-flyers and marriage-mad young ladies chase his lordship though they would, he, Rogers, had known that they were nothing to the Earl of Burnleigh and never had been. But this lady Sarah was a very different situation altogether. She did not appear to try to attract much attention to herself, nor did she appear to be worth looking at, not at first anyway, but by the same token, once one had observed her, one kept being drawn back to her. She had a quiet beauty that was nonetheless real for its being less noticeable than the more flamboyant attractions of, say, a Marchioness of Cranleigh.

There was an indefinable, but distinctive air of quality about Lady Sarah that made all the other females gathered at Cranleigh seem vulgar by comparison. Rogers smiled to himself as he drained the last drop of ale. He had known, or at least he hoped he had known how it would be. He had never seen the master so happy. Now if only the lady were the same. Well, time and fate would tell, though if Rogers knew his master, the earl would have no small say in it. Rogers, for one, could not remember a woman who had not succumbed to the earl's charms. As far as the valet could see, both the lady and the gentleman in question deserved all the happiness it appeared they would have.

It was with a light heart that Rogers set about packing for the earl's removal to Cranleigh.

Chapter Thirty

And it was with an extremely light heart that the Marchioness of Cranleigh read the hastily scrawled note informing her of the Earl of Burnleigh's imminent return. I knew it, she exulted to herself. He could not stay away. With a vigorous pull of the bell she summoned Framling to confer with her mistress on her wardrobe for the ensuing days. Rosalind was to be nothing less than dazzling for the duration of the house party. From the bonnets that were to cover her carefully arranged coiffures to the slippers that encased her dainty feet, she was to be arrayed in a style designed to take the observer's breath away.

"Yes, my lady. Very good, my lady," Framling murmured as she mentally catalogued the contents of the marchioness's wardrobe. So his lordship was returning was he, and along with him her ladyship's good humor. Framling devoutly hoped so, for life since the Earl of Burnleigh's departure had been very difficult indeed for all those in service to her ladyship.

There remained one more task to be accomplished before Lord Farringdon arrived, and for that Rosalind needed the unwitting assistance of the Reverend Mr. Witson. The marchioness had decided that Sarah, despite her unprepossessing exterior, had attracted entirely too much attention from the Earl of Burnleigh. While she was grateful to her sister-in-law for her surprising offer of support and her understanding in such a difficult time, Rosalind was not about to allow her gratitude to extend to sharing his lordship's company.

To that end, Rosalind had hatched a plan, a plan that would free her of the worry and responsibility of being connected to a young woman who insisted on living her life in the most unbecomingly independent fashion, and it would ensure that any interest the earl had in Sarah's company would be effectively dampened. The plan was simple in its conception—to marry

Sarah to her old mentor and friend, the vicar—though delicate in its execution. Rosalind was forced to exert the greatest imagination and tax her considerable thespian skills to create a picture of charming sympathy as she delicately broached the subject to the vicar himself the next day.

Wearing a delightfully ruffled high-necked morning dress of black-and-white striped muslin, the marchioness was the image of sisterly concern when the vicar, responding to her request for an audience, was ushered into the morning room at Cranleigh. "I cannot thank you enough for coming so quickly." Rosalind smiled at him blindingly and indicated a chair with the graceful wave of one white hand. "It may seem all very sudden to you, but I assure you I have agonized over it for quite some time, and I can no longer contain my anxiety concerning Lady Sarah."

"Lady Sarah?" Thaddeus responded with some surprise. As far as he knew, the marchioness had never wasted so much as a passing thought on the welfare of her sister-in-law.

"Yes. I know that she has her books and her music to occupy her time, but she is dreadfully alone, now that her grandmother is gone. In fact, her spirits have been affected so powerfully, I fear one could almost say that she has gone into a decline." And with the greatest dramatic skill she could bring to bear, Rosalind proceeded to paint such a vivid picture of loneliness and despair that the vicar, no mean observer of human nature himself, had begun to question his own impressions.

Seeing that she was gaining ascendancy over his judgement, Rosalind clasped one hand to her bosom, laying the other imploringly on her visitor's arm, and begged him for his help.

Thaddeus was only a man after all, and as such, found himself to be no proof against such desperation. In a very short while he found himself agreeing to consider what only hours before he would have written off as the most ludicrous flight of fancy. But looking into the large brown eyes glistening with unshed tears, he could almost believe that offering to marry Lady Sarah Melford was the noblest thing he could do for a woman whom he had long admired. As he bid adieu to his hostess, he found himself promising to do just that in the very near future.

As the door closed behind the vicar, Rosalind could not conceal the smile of satisfaction that lighted her face. The chevalier was deceived about the true state of affairs in Portugal,

Alistair was on his way to her side, and her sister-in-law was about to contract a marriage that would keep her in the country away from the Earl of Burnleigh and force respectability on her all at the same time. Though it was true that Lady Willoughby's fortune was still lost to her, the marchioness could not help but feel that life was looking up indeed.

Life was looking up for the Earl of Burnleigh as well. Tooling his curricle along the country lanes among flowering hedgerows, he felt at peace with the world on this lovely sunny day. On the brink of exposing the chevalier once and for all—he trusted that Sarah would have summoned him for nothing less—he looked forward to vindicating himself in the eyes of the doubters at Whitehall. But more important, he looked forward to seeing Sarah herself. His joy and relief at being recalled to Cranleigh had ended all the doubts and confusion he had suffered over Lady Sarah Melford. The feelings that her note had evoked in him had proven as no amount of reflection could that he wanted to be with her for the rest of his days. All of a sudden so much about life that had eluded him for the longest time seemed perfectly clear, and so much of the perplexity, frustration, and lack of fulfillment was completely washed away by the prospect of sharing it all with her.

So full was he with all these promising thoughts that the earl was even able to face the idea of Rosalind with equanimity, though he knew very well what interpretation she would put on his return to Cranleigh. Lord Farringdon swept up the gravel drive in such a mood of eager anticipation that he barely noticed the man and the woman strolling along one of the paths among the trees that lined the drive. They were so deep in conversation that he did not pay much attention to them until he was well past them. Then he realized that it was Sarah and the vicar.

Trying not to appear as though he was doing so, he glanced back, only to discover that they were so engrossed in their conversation they had not even looked up. That was extremely unlike Sarah at least, for she was always supremely aware of what was going on around her. However, Alistair had no further opportunity to consider the question, for the stately portico of Cranleigh had come into view, and he could see from the flurry of activity in the direction of the stables that his arrival had been noted.

Lord Farringdon was forced to muster what patience he

could until a good deal later that evening when he at last seized the opportunity to speak with Sarah as she took her place at the pianoforte. She had seemed glad to see him, smiling at him with a warmth he felt sure she reserved only for him as they assembled for dinner. However, she had not gone to any special lengths to speak to him, allowing Rosalind to pair her up with the vicar and disappearing to the other end of the table without even so much as glancing up to watch her sister-in-law laughing and smiling coquettishly under her lashes at the earl. Afterward, when the gentlemen joined the ladies in the drawing room, she had spent so much time conversing with the Duchess of Coltishall and then Lady Edgecumbe that he almost began to suspect her of avoiding him. Had she put him out of her mind so easily then, once he was gone?

In fact, Sarah was doing her very best to stay away from the earl, certain that the breathlessness that came over her every time she so much as looked at him was highly visible to one and all. Surely, anyone could hear the pounding of her heart when he smiled at her. Why, it had been so deafening she had hardly been able to make out a word that Lady Edgecumbe had said to her.

Now, though, she was caught—trapped at the pianoforte with those gray eyes smiling down into hers in a way that made her stomach feel as though it were twirling around inside of her. Surely, it was not natural to be so affected by the mere presence of someone? Such agitation could not be good for one's health.

Sarah took a deep breath and forced her shaking hands to stumble through one gay country air after another until she had mastered herself enough to breathe regularly at least. Then, choosing an exercise she could have played in her sleep, she said, "I am glad you have come so promptly. I . . ." She made the mistake of looking up to find him smiling at her in such a way as to make her lose all thought of her next words. "I . . . yes, well, I was worried you might not quite understand that there is going to be another landing." There, now she had herself well in hand. "They were waiting for a full moon, you see, which should be tomorrow night. I was rather worried that you might not come, or that you might not come in time and . . ."

"Oh ye of little faith," the earl teased. "Do you think I have so little regard for your judgement that I would not come the instant I heard from you?"

"Well no. I mean yes. I mean . . ." That flustered her. Really, he was looking at her in the most disturbing manner—almost as though she were some delicious morsel that he was about to eat. The thought was both disconcerting and delightful.

"And what would you have done had I not appeared?" He probed gently.

Sarah was silent.

"Let me guess. You would have gone in my place."

She nodded, the bright color staining her cheeks.

"You are incorrigible! Fortunately, I suspected as much, which is why I appeared as quickly as I did and why I shall tie you up and lock you in the storeroom at Ashworth if you do not promise me you will let me take care of this now that I am here. I suppose that I should be grateful that you even bothered to summon me."

Sarah nodded again, but this time there was a distinctly impish twinkle in her eyes.

"You ought to be beaten, you know," Alistair remarked conversationally, "but I have my hands full at the moment."

"You would have done the same yourself," she countered.

"Very likely." The earl chuckled before continuing, "Now I presume you have your source who can explain in greater detail all that I need to know. Can you have him meet me at eleven tomorrow morning at the same place where I left you when I returned to London?" Alistair had chosen the location deliberately to see what sort of reaction he would arouse. It was not kind of him—he was fully aware of that—but he had to know what those last few minutes with him before he had gone away had meant to her, if they had meant anything at all.

There was a sharp intake of breath, her eyes widened, and her fingers stumbled over a chord before Sarah was able to regain control of herself. "Yes, I believe I can arrange for that." Her gaze returned to the keyboard, and she refused to look at him until the end of the piece, but Alistair could tell from the delicate flush on her cheeks and the dampness that made the tendrils of hair curl at the nape of her neck that she was thinking back to that day and remembering it all in the most vivid detail. Good! He smiled to himself. He wanted her to remember it, every moment of it as clearly and with as much longing for another such interlude as he did.

Chapter Thirty-one

True to her word, Sarah instructed Ned as to his meeting with the earl, and the next day the marsh man materialized as if from nowhere the moment the earl pulled his curricle into the grove of trees. He was clear and succinct as to the arrangements for that evening, but eyed the earl with a wariness that showed he remained uneasy about the London gentleman's abilities to ensure a favorable outcome to this adventure for him and his fellows.

Sensing this, Lord Farringdon hastened to reassure him. "I shall have someone else with me who is extremely experienced at this sort of thing, and it will be over in the wink of an eye. Lady Sarah has expressed the fullest confidence in you and your men, so I am sure that we shall, er, *take care* of the Frenchies and you will disappear before you can say King George, with no one the wiser." To be sure, Sarah had not said precisely those words, but the invocation of her name seemed to have done the trick.

The man relaxed enough to give the faintest hint of a smile—it was more of a grimace really—before replying, "Very good, sir." And then he vanished as quickly as he had appeared.

Apparently Lady Sarah commanded as much trust and respect from the marsh men as she did from Alistair himself, and with good reason, the earl thought as he turned the curricle around and headed back toward Cranleigh. There seemed to be nothing she was not capable of, no task too daunting or even too dangerous for her to attempt. In fact, the only time Lord Farringdon had seen her the least bit flustered was when it came to men and women and the more tender relations between them.

Alistair grinned. He was glad such things discomposed her, for it meant she was not so indifferent to them as she wished to be, and he was determined, once this business with the chevalier was settled satisfactorily, to discompose her a good deal more.

The evening was clear and cool, not a cloud in the sky to obscure the moon, and the earl, waiting in his bedchamber until the chevalier departed, was able to make the Frenchman out quite clearly as he headed across the fields. This time Lord Farringdon had made sure to have Brutus saddled and waiting and was thus able to keep much closer to his prey.

As Alistair neared the place where the track from the marsh joined the road, Ferdie emerged from the shadow of a hedgerow. He said nothing, but nodded and smiled, his teeth gleaming in the moonlight. They rode for some time, more quietly and cautiously than Alistair had the first time, for now that he was sure of his way and of what awaited them at the end of it, he had no need for speed.

At last they saw a flash of light, quickly dimmed, low in the grasses ahead of them. They dismounted, making their way on foot until they could make out the dark shapes gathered around the boat. Murmuring voices spoke rapid French, and the two men inched carefully forward until the could make out the speakers, who, luckily enough, stood with their backs to the stalkers. A few paces away stood Ned and another man, who had obviously manned the other set of oars in the boat. The marsh men, accustomed to every breath of the marsh, glanced quickly up and as quickly away again at the faint rustle of Ferdie and Alistair's approach.

Alistair pulled his pistol from his pocket and glanced over to see that Ferdie had done likewise before he nodded and sprang for the chevalier while Ferdie lunged for his companion. The Frenchmen were barely aware of the movement behind them before two wicked-looking pistols were clapped to their heads and the earl was tossing two lengths of rope to Ned, who threw one to his companion and hastened to tie the chevalier's hands behind him.

"*Diable!*" The Frenchman spat as the rough rope chafed against his wrists. "I shall kill you for this, Farringdon. This is no way to treat a gentleman."

Alistair smiled grimly. "As you are no gentleman, I find that not the slightest impediment. However, since I *am* a gentleman, I shall give you the choice of how you would like to die—with or without a blindfold."

"*Sacrebleu*," the chevalier muttered and was about to speak again when there was another rustle of grass and Lady Sarah appeared as calmly as though she were out for a morning ride, clutching her sketchbook and a pencil.

"Blast! Sarah, I should have known—" the earl began angrily.

"I beg your pardon, my lord. I would not for the world have inconvenienced you," Sarah interrupted him, "but I was afraid you might shoot him. That is of course what he deserves"—she swept the chevalier with a disdainful glance—"but it occurs to me that he might be far more useful to you alive. Send him back to France with misinformation. I am sure we have agents there who can keep an eye on him if need be. I propose that he purchase his life by writing here"—she held out the sketchbook—"the list of agents that he has here in this country. You can then verify the truth of this. If the names he gives you are false, why then you can arrange to have him killed or prove to the emperor that he has betrayed France. I also think he should be made to sign another paper releasing Richard from his debts. I am sure Rosalind would be much relieved."

The silence that greeted her remarks was deafening. Then Ferdie burst out laughing. "You hinted that she was something out of the ordinary, Alistair, and by God she is!" Still holding his pistol to the other Frenchman's head, Ferdie sketched a bow in Sarah's direction. "Lieutenant Summers at your service, Lady Sarah, and may I say that I am honored to make the acquaintance of so gallant and intelligent a lady."

Smiling ruefully and shaking his head, Alistair motioned to Ned to take his place guarding the chevalier, then sauntered over to take the paper from Sarah. "My little fire-eater," he whispered as he took the sketchbook and pencil from her. He returned to the Frenchman. "Now, sir, you will do as the lady directs." While Ned kept the pistol steady, the earl untied the chevalier's hands and bade him begin writing.

"But I have nowhere to write," the chevalier protested.

"Here is your desk." Alistair led the other prisoner over and pointed to his back. "Now write."

The chevalier did as he was bid, though not without a great deal of muttering under his breath. If the truth were told, he was extremely happy to be alive at this point. For a moment it had looked very much as though he would not live even this long. The chevalier was not a courageous man; he had become a spy because it was easy. The British with their stupid code of honor were so gullible and trusting that it had been child's play and most amusing to dupe them, besides which, it was extremely lucrative. As far as risking life or limb for some absurd devotion to a country or ideals, he was not inclined to do any such thing. If he could escape certain death at the price of handing over the names of a few agents, he was not bothered by it in the least.

The chevalier scrawled a few names on the piece of paper. "And their directions," the earl added, looking over his prisoner's shoulder.

"Very well."

"And now I believe that Lady Sarah will dictate to you what is to be written on the other piece of paper."

"But first," Sarah interrupted again, "he should add to the list of agents that he, as an agent of the French government, did order these men to spy on His Majesty's government and that he in turn passed these secrets along in order that the French might triumph over England in whatever field of battle they might be joined. Then he must sign it. Now he will know that you have an extremely damaging document to use against him, should he attempt any mischief in the future."

"You are in the right of it, Lady Sarah," Alistair agreed. "And while he is at it, he might as well write a confession to the French government that he gave up the names of his own agents freely. That should protect us against any eventuality and ensure his complete cooperation henceforth." He turned to the chevalier. "Now do it."

At last the papers were written and signed. The earl took them, perused them, and put them in his pocket. If any of the names on the list surprised him or were familiar to him, he gave no sign, turning instead to Ned. "I trust you know how to return this one"—he nodded toward the other French agent—"back to whence he came."

"Yes, sir, I do."

"Very well. Do you think that you and your companion here can take care of both him and the chevalier?"

The marsh men snorted in a fashion that left no illusions as to their opinions of their unhappy-looking prisoners.

"Excellent. We shall leave them in your hands. You are performing a valuable service to your country, Ned Wittle. If you will meet me at the George and Dragon tomorrow morning at ten o'clock, I shall prove to you that your country can reward you for such services and for your silence." He smiled at Ned in the most friendly way, but there was no mistaking the look in his eyes. The marsh man knew that his lordship was a gentleman who kept his word and expected others to do the same.

Alistair turned to Lieutenant Summers and Sarah. "And now I suggest that you and I escort the lady home, not that she needs it in the least, but we are going in the same direction, and we owe it to any other ruffians who might be abroad now to protect them from her. We have stopped enough villainy for one night." His tone was ironic, but as he bent over to help Sarah into her saddle, he breathed into her ear, "Thank you for all of this."

They rode silently back toward Ashworth, taking time to admire the desolate beauty of the marsh with its undulating surface bathed in the moonlight, the waving grasses appearing like a silvery ocean as the breezes stirred them. After the previous tense hours it was delightful to ride along enjoying the peace and silence of the vast expanse.

As the dark clump of trees surrounding Ashworth appeared in the distance, Sarah came to a halt, breaking the silence. "I shall bid you good night here. There is no need for you to go out of your way to escort me."

"What you mean is that you do not wish anyone to come along who might betray your presence or reveal your secret for escaping unseen," the earl corrected her.

Sarah laughed. "Now that is a most unkind accusation, my lord. You make it sound as though I regularly steal out like a thief in the night. Why, I hardly—"

Alistair raised a hand. "No. Whatever it is, I do not want to know, Lady Sarah. I find you a rare handful already. The less I know about your activities the better. However I do mean to see you to your door." They rode in silence to the French doors of the library. He guided Brutus close to Ajax and jumped off to lift Sarah down. Then raising one gloved hand he carried it to his lips. "Thank you, my lady. It was a brave though outrageous deed you did tonight. Your country, your sister-in-law, and I especially, owe you a great debt." Then, realizing that his thanks had flustered her, he released her, touched Brutus's flanks with his heels, and turned toward Cranleigh with the lieutenant close behind him.

The two men continued in silence until it came time for the

lieutenant to break off toward Tredington Park. "Good night, Alistair." He held out his hand to clasp the earl's. "It was a good night's work and a great success. You are to be congratulated. And she is a rare and wonderful woman."

With that he trotted on down the road, leaving Alistair smiling to himself in the moonlight. "That she is, Ferdie, that she is," he murmured before he too rode off in the direction of Cranleigh.

Chapter Thirty-two

Safely gaining his bedchamber without arousing any of the household, Alistair poured himself a glass of brandy and threw himself into a chair in front of the window. Gazing out over the moonlit gardens, he pictured the whole scene over again: Sarah emerging from the grasses, so cool, so calm, so self-possessed, taking up where he had left off; picking up and providing guidance at a moment when he could use it; taking his plans and refining them, improving upon them. What a team they made! What a wife she would be. Wife? Alistair sat bolt upright. Was that what he wanted? He had never truly articulated it before, even to himself, but that *was* what he wanted, and he wanted it so badly that he was ready to ride over to Ashworth immediately and tell her that.

He grinned. He probably could do that very thing, and she would think nothing of it. After all, she was used to having him crash in on her in the dead of night. But he would wait until morning so he could do it properly. Besides, he needed to see Rosalind to relate to her an abbreviated version of what had happened that night so she could concoct some story that would satisfy her guests. The earl tossed down the brandy and leaned back in his chair as thoughts of Sarah flickered through his mind, and he dozed gently off to sleep, a smile on his face.

Late the next morning after Alistair had met with Ned, he conducted as brief an interview as possible with Rosalind, whom he had arranged to encounter in the garden while Harold and Lord Edgecumbe were buried in the library and the others had not yet appeared for the day. That successfully completed, he rode over toward Ashworth, only to discover somewhat to his dismay the vicar's gig in the drive. He declined to let Wiggins interrupt his mistress's interview with the Reverend Mr. Witson, asking instead to be called from the garden when the gentleman had left.

Alistair had made up his mind to wait, for he did not wish to see Sarah with the vicar, nor did he wish to come back later. But he did not wait patiently. He was too eager to see the lady of the house. Instead, he strode back and forth on the terrace in full view of at least one of the occupants of the library.

In fact, Sarah only happened to glance up and see him by the purest coincidence as she found herself in the middle of the most astonishing conversation with Thaddeus. Too uncomfortable to meet the vicar's eyes, she had looked up only to catch sight of the earl pacing back and forth in a most impatient manner. Once having caught sight of him, she could not ignore him. Sarah wished desperately that he would go away. The more he remained, pacing back and forth, the more annoyed she became with him.

In the meantime, there was Thaddeus saying, "It would be the greatest happiness imaginable to me if you would do me the honor of becoming my wife."

Sarah could not believe her ears! Thaddeus had been the older brother she wished she had had, her teacher, her harshest critic, her sternest guide and inspiration. Now he was asking her to marry him? It did not make sense. At last she looked up at him. She saw a great deal of kindness in his eyes and, yes, even admiration, but nothing else—certainly not love.

"I know that you are convinced you enjoy your single state, Sarah, and you may very well do so at the moment when you are young, but what of the future? Will it not seem empty without a helpmeet to share it with you, to take care of you should you become ill or infirm? While it is true that I am a good deal older, we are fast friends, Sarah. I respect you and honor you above anyone I have ever known."

A curious smile played around the corners of Sarah's mouth. "I know, and I understand why you are doing this. I appreciate your gesture, believe me, but I could never marry without love, and I do not love you, any more than you love me. I, too, honor and respect you as you say you do me, and I treasure our friendship. Let us keep it at that—friendship."

Thaddeus smiled in return. So that was how it was. He had been correct in his first assumptions. It was the marchioness who was mistaken. Spurred on by her need to have Lord Farringdon as her own, Rosalind had deluded herself into thinking that whatever she wished to make happen would happen, including duping the vicar into believing, however briefly, that

Sarah needed to be rescued from herself. Sarah did not need rescuing, at least not by Thaddeus. If he was not much mistaken, the rescuer was waiting right outside, and most impatiently, too. "Yes, Sarah, we shall be friends always." The vicar took her hand in his, bowed over it, and left her alone to her own welter of confusing thoughts and emotions.

She was not to be alone for long, however. Wiggins appeared almost instantly with Alistair hard on his heels. "Lord Farringdon to see you, my lady."

"Yes, Wiggins. Thank you, Wiggins." Sarah nodded regally to the butler. She was not at all certain she liked the way the earl was practically bursting in on her without giving her the chance to collect her wits. She never liked to be told what to do, and at the moment she was under the distinct impression that this man was about to try to make her do something even though she was not quite sure what it was.

Sarah was correct. Already ill at ease as to how to broach the subject of marriage to an independent young woman who was terrifyingly capable of coping with any situation, Alistair had been entirely thrown off balance by the presence of the Reverend Mr. Witson.

"What was *he* doing here?" Alistair blurted out before he could think how blatantly interfering that sounded and of how such a remark would have infuriated him if he had been the recipient.

"How dare you!" Ill at ease herself, Sarah was goaded into a thoughtless retort. "He was asking me to marry him, not that it is any of your concern."

"What?" Alistair thundered.

"What do you mean, *what*? I do not suppose that it is such an absurd notion, my lord. I may not be as fashionable or as beautiful as Rosalind, but I am not repulsive, after all. It is not unthinkable that he might wish to make me his wife."

Ordinarily, Alistair, a past master at soothing feminine hysterics, would have stopped right there and done his best to calm her with reassuring words, but he was shaken to his very depths by the thought of her with another man—so shaken that he could only shout at her. "You are not going to marry that . . . that . . . prig!"

Sarah froze. No one, not since she had been eleven and Harold had tried to order her off his prize hunter, had addressed her in such a fashion. "And why, pray tell, am I not?" Her voice was dangerously quiet.

Too late, Alistair realized what he had done. There was nothing for it now but to continue on in the same reckless fashion in which he had begun. "Because you are going to marry me," he gasped, pulling her roughly into his arms.

Too astonished to do anything, Sarah stood there, her brain in a whirl, as he brought his lips down on hers. It was incredible. Lord Farringdon, libertine of libertines, the man who had not even succumbed to Rosalind's manifold charms, was asking her to marry him? No, he was not asking her, he was telling her, and that was something she was not going to stand for, no matter how heavenly it felt to be in his arms again. And it did feel heavenly. Her lips parted under his, and for a moment she longed to kiss him back, but with the greatest effort imaginable Sarah forced herself to pull away. "No!"

Alistair had himself well in hand now. The kiss had done it. He knew it was meant to be. He had felt it. It had been just the slightest of tremors, but the response had been there, buried deep below the surface, but it had been there. The fear that had been fueling his anger evaporated, and he finally stopped to consider what she must think of him. "I beg your pardon, Sarah, I truly do. I had not meant it to be this way, but I saw the vicar and I feared the worst. I know what you think of my reputation. I know how much you admire the Reverend Mr. Witson and, well, I was, er . . . jealous."

"Jealous?" Sarah was incredulous. "You?" She did not know what to think. She wished desperately to believe him. In fact, she realized that there was nothing she wanted more than to spend the rest of her life with Alistair, but she was afraid—afraid to become yet another one of the women who believed his flattering words and fell victim to his legendary charm.

Alistair saw the battle raging within her. "Please, Sarah. You know we belong together. No two people could have done what we have done and not be meant for one another." He reached out and drew her close to him again, tilting up her chin to look deep into her eyes.

"No. I can't, I mean I won't," she whispered.

"Won't what, sweetheart?"

"I won't be another one of your women, Alistair."

He laughed out loud. "I am not asking you to be another one

of my women, Sarah. I am asking you to be *the* woman in my life, just as you are the only woman I have ever said I loved."

That stopped her in her tracks, and she looked up at him in astonishment.

"I may be a rake, but I am not a deceiver, Sarah. I never promised any woman my love—only admiration for her beauty or her charm. I would never promise anything but love to you, and I do love you so very much. Please, Sarah."

He kissed her, gently at first, exploring her lips with his until they opened underneath his, and she kissed him back shyly and then with increasing passion. At last it was Alistair's turn to pull away. "Sarah, you have not answered me yet."

"I know. It's just, you see, that I am not sure. I have never been in love before and I do not know . . ."

He pulled her against him. "Neither have I, and I am as unaccustomed to this as you are. Please do not leave me to suffer this alone. I need you, Sarah. I want you and I won't stop trying to make you my wife no matter how long it takes me."

Recognizing that she was dealing with someone who knew his own mind as much as she did and who was equally determined, Sarah at last allowed herself to believe that what the earl was saying might actually be true. One look into his eyes convinced her of it. She had never seen such warmth and admiration—yes, it must be love—in anyone's eyes as she now did in his. "Yes, Alistair," she sighed as she allowed herself at last to relax in the magical strength and security of his embrace.